ALANNA KNIGHT has written more than sixty novels, three non-fiction titles on R.L. Stevenson, two true crime books, numerous short stories and several plays since the publication of her first book in 1969. Born and educated in Tyneside, she now lives in Edinburgh. She is a member of the Scottish chapter of the Crime Writers' Association, and a founder member and Honorary President of the Scottish Association of Writers and of the Edinburgh Writers' Club.

www.alannaknight.com

By Alanna Knight

a&b

Murders Most Foul

An Inspector Faro Mystery

ALANNA KNIGHT

Allison & Busby Limited
12 Fitzroy Mews
London W1T 6DW
www.allisonandbusby.com

First published in Great Britain by Allison & Busby in 2013.
This paperback edition published by Allison & Busby in 2013.

A CIP catalogue record for this book is available from
the British Library.

10 9 8 7 6 5 4 3 2 1

ISBN 978-0-7490-1318-9

Typeset in 10.5/14.5 pt Sabon by
Allison & Busby Ltd.

The paper used for this Allison & Busby publication
has been produced from trees that have been legally sourced
from well-managed and credibly certified forests.

Printed and bound by
CPI Group (UK) Ltd, Croydon, CR0 4YY

For Douglas Cullen,
who gave me the playing card

CHAPTER ONE

Edinburgh 1861

'Got what she deserved.'

Detective Constable Jeremy Faro bit back a shocked rejoinder at the sergeant's brutal words as the police surgeon's head shake confirmed that life was extinguished and signalled one of the waiting constables to summon the mortuary van.

Faro looked with compassion at the dead woman. Young, twenties perhaps, but she could have passed for thirty-five, despite the paint and scarlet satin gown, now muddied and torn, that advertised her trade. She had been strangled in this dark foetid close watched over by the lofty heights of Edinburgh Castle, dark and forbidding, wrapped in its own terrible secrets and a long and bloody history, no stranger to violence.

This area surrounding Fleshers Close had gained notoriety nearly forty years ago in the 1820s by association with Burke and Hare, serial killers with their den in nearby Tanner's Close. The stench of death and decay still lurked from the tanneries by which it got its name.

Faro hated this place, these vermin-infested tenements. Once they had been his own daily beat and he had never learnt how to establish communication with the inhabitants, who seemed part of an alien race. Occasionally he smiled to himself, for so was he; from the Orkney Islands, still regarded as a newcomer by the Edinburgh City Police – and that after ten years.

But the creatures who inhabited these foul closes seemed out with the general pattern of ordinary folk. Some lived out their short lives in indescribable poverty and neglect, never travelling more than a few streets away from the hovel where they were born. Some seemed hardly human, coated in filth, their speech never beyond a few words strung together, to read and write undreamt of, unattainable luxuries.

At Faro's side, the police surgeon was muttering to Sergeant Gosse. 'You in charge? Where the devil is Wade, then?'

Detective Inspector Wade should have been first on the scene of the crime. His non-arrival hinted at dereliction of duty. As Dr Grace departed with an angry shake of the head that threatened trouble at the Central Office, Faro said: 'A sorry business.'

Sergeant Gosse laughed. 'Who's sorry for her? I'm not! One less whore on the streets of Edinburgh, one less disease to spread.'

'The second murder in a week, Sergeant. Isn't that going it a bit?'

His sarcasm was lost on the sergeant, but the truth was that this would certainly put a strain on the Central Office's facilities.

The city was more or less peaceful during the long summer nights, apart from occasional eruptions with drunks, pickpockets and prostitutes, and a few easily suppressed riots – such were the general disorders they had to deal with. Except when Her Majesty or one of the Royals nipped up from London or down from Balmoral Castle to open a bridge or a hospital, or to graciously lend their presence to some other worthy cause, all of which necessitated a full muster of the police force. They might grumble but security had to be tight. Remember, 'the Hanoverian upstart', as some still called Victoria, had been the target of assassins several times. Occasions only known to the Central Office records and kept with difficulty out of the news-sheets.

Two constables clattered down the stone stairs behind them, sent to talk to the occupants in the six-storeyed tenement.

'Well, get anything?' Gosse demanded sharply, but even as he asked the question and before heads were shaken, he knew the answer and shrugged. 'No surprises there,' he grumbled.

It was always the same. Where they were willing, by persuasion or implied threat, to open the door a couple of inches, still no one ever knew anything, had heard nothing. The sight of a uniformed peeler was enough to turn any of them mute. They would give away no information, bound together by a strange loyalty – anything to avoid being hauled into the dreaded 'polis' interview room at the station – especially those, and there were many, whose occupations would not bear even the feeblest scrutiny while further enquiries were made.

This could be a leisurely procedure and Faro knew that the suspect might be detained for some considerable time, left to rot in a prison cell, the cause of their incarceration overlooked entirely, the reason for his or her detention conveniently forgotten while more important matters of criminal justice were being pursued.

From their earliest days of comprehension, even the youngest inhabitants of Fleshers Close had dinned into them that one golden rule: 'Have nothing to do with the polis; whether ye've done anything or no, once they have yer name on their books they'll never be off sniffing about yer doorstep.'

Gosse looked thoughtful. 'We've got our killer for the first one. Pity that, we could have nailed him for this one. Two for the price of one.'

The only similarity, Faro realised, was that the victims had been strangled, the first woman a victim of domestic murder in the Pleasance ten minutes' walk away from where they stood. She had been strangled by her jealous husband who, contrite, had confessed all and was awaiting the gallows in due course. This was obviously a bitter disappointment to the sergeant's eager expectations. Gosse enjoyed executions and had been known to bribe the hangman for a substantial piece of the rope used, to be sold on at so much per inch, a macabre but popular souvenir of the day . . .

Faro was aware of a small face in the gloom. A child's face, watching them, white and scared. No tears or cries, already well trained in suppressing feelings of fear, knowing that in her short life, far from gaining any sympathy for pain or affliction

– a struggle for survival did not include such luxuries as sympathy – all that cries of pain would incur was another brutal blow.

'The bairn over there must have seen it all,' he whispered to the sergeant, who after a quick glance, shrugged.

'Too young to give us any help. Pity.'

'Poor wee mite,' muttered Faro, wishing he could approach and thrust a coin into that tiny hand, but well aware that such actions were forbidden and any approach would have her fleeing in terror. 'What will become of her?'

The sergeant shrugged. 'The workhouse – the usual – and the best place for the poor little bastard. Till it's old enough to go out and work.'

'It' indeed. Neither male nor female as far as the sergeant cared. 'She's a wee lass,' Faro protested indignantly.

The sergeant sniggered. 'Aye, and chances are she'll turn out like the one over there and get herself strangled too,' he said, pointing his foot towards the body on the stretcher now being carried out to the mortuary van. Seeing Faro's expression, he grinned sardonically. 'You've either too much imagination or you're too sensitive, Faro. Surprised you got your promotion when you're so soft on the job.'

Faro knew that his promotion was a sore point

at the Central Office. God knows he had earned it and almost lost his life down in England on his first case. Shot, barely escaping death, he had been sent to Orkney – home – to recover, and had promptly got himself involved in another violent death.

'Don't take it to heart, lad,' said his one friend, the elderly now retired detective superintendent Brandon Macfie. 'Envy and jealousy, they'll get over it. You've proved yourself.'

And the superintendent's regard for the young constable who reminded him so much of his only son, dead from consumption these five years, was, although the old man did not realise it, another thorn in Faro's popularity with his colleagues, especially with beat constables older than himself, grinding away for years on dull and boring incidents hardly worthy of the word crime. Many were content – they didn't want to put their lives in danger – but it gave them a good talking point, something to grumble about, that they had been overlooked by the authorities. Favouritism, aye, that's what it was.

Dawn had turned into what passed for daylight, a dull twilight from which any luxury such as pure fresh air was forever excluded in closes like this one, so narrow that, separated by only a few feet, the occupants of the tall tenements could shake hands – or fists – at neighbours opposite.

'We're done here,' said Gosse, their bullseye

lanterns extinguished – necessary accessories for patrolling areas like this one where gas-lit streets were still a distant and not very welcome dream.

'She might not be from these parts,' Faro offered helpfully.

There had been nothing on the body to identify the woman and Gosse said: 'Right enough. As you well ken, this wasn't one of your whores with fancy clothes who offer beds for the hour like in yon Leith Walk brothels; this kind do their business against the walls here. "Gi' ye a quick one for a penny, mister."' His laugh was a grating humourless sound. '"Next customer, please."'

Faro had been woken up that morning by Gosse, summoned by the beat policeman who had discovered the body, and with enough examination by lantern light, had ascertained death by manual strangulation, the bruise marks clear about her neck. He had also noticed that her gaudy and provocative dress didn't belong to the local variety of street women but signalled one used to patronising a better clientele.

Faro's glance took in the immediate area. 'She had no reticule, Sergeant.'

Gosse shrugged. 'Probably stolen,' he said, apparently unaware of the significance of its absence.

Now, as a new day struggled through heavy

clouds frowning down over Salisbury Crags, the dark closes were coming sluggishly alive. Smoke poured from chimneys in residential areas where Edinburgh was opening its eyes and its newspapers to the second killing in a week.

Murder was news, although deaths were commonplace in a city where a vast number were carried to the local cemeteries each day – stillborn babies, blue as tiny monkeys, laid to rest beside the young mothers who had given their lives in vain.

For the very young and the very old – fifty was an average age – and those in between, the dreaded consumption was relentless, carrying off increasing numbers, many from the cream of society, whose young people were unable, by any means of wealth, position or medical care, to escape its deadly hold.

A rattle of wheels and the large frame of Inspector Wade emerged from a hired cab, looking flustered, angry and even somewhat sheepish.

'Where's Dr Grace?'

Gosse and Faro were aware that the body should not have been moved until his arrival. An explanation was called for and rapidly supplied. The inspector had not been at home.

'I was away visiting friends for the night,' he said shortly.

Friends, eh. Gosse gave Faro a wink. The

inspector was well known as a womaniser. If he ever hoped to achieve chief inspector, he had better either reform or be very careful indeed at covering his tracks. Involvement in a divorce case would be the end of his career.

'Anything to report, Gosse?'

As the inspector nodded vigorously to Gosse's negative information, Faro noticed a piece of paper – no, a playing card – jammed in the cobbles where the woman's body had lain. Crumpled and dirty, it had remained invisible until what passed for daylight entered the close.

'Sir,' he interrupted the two men. 'This might be evidence.'

Silencing Faro with a look, Gosse sniggered. 'Go on, so she played cards.'

Ignoring Gosse, Faro handed the card to the inspector. 'Sir, I remember that at the first killing, that other woman in the Pleasance, there were cards. I picked up one like this.'

A sigh and a dagger-like glance from Gosse at this interruption. The inspector's smile was thin and dismissive as Gosse said: 'A coincidence, sir.'

'I agree. The other woman's husband was a notorious gambler.'

'Whores all play cards, sir,' Gosse put in eagerly. 'Probably told fortunes too.'

'Like enough,' said the inspector, but Faro

wasn't convinced. He vividly recalled the domestic murder. A pack of cards scattered on the table. The nine of diamonds, the same card he now held in his hand. A coincidence or—

'They're always gambling, this lot, making a bit off the side,' said Gosse.

'Exactly,' said the inspector, anxious to get into the fresh air again.

'This one might be of significance, sir, to the killer's identity,' Faro insisted.

Wade gave him a withering glance and Gosse chortled: 'Get away, you daftie.'

Faro looked round, suddenly aware of the child's presence. She had been brushed aside or fled at the arrival of Wade, but there she was again, standing, watching them. Had the dead woman been her mother? He needed to know, overcome by reluctance to just abandon her to this tragic vigil.

'Well, what are you waiting for?' demanded Wade.

'The child, sir.'

'What?'

Faro nodded in her direction. Gosse had clearly forgotten all about her, a possible witness to that terrible act of violence.

'Oh that! Someone will take care of her – none of our business.'

Faro stared at Gosse and at the small girl. He

couldn't leave a terrified child here. Should he take her to his landlady, Mrs Biggs?

The police van with its burden had left, accompanied by Wade. A woman, Faro presumed a neighbour who had prudently kept out of sight, appeared and scooped up the child who now gave way to sobbing long suppressed.

'Whesht, now!' And to Faro, 'I'll take her. She can bide wi' me. I have six o' my own, another wilna' mak much difference.'

Faro said. 'You know her?'

The woman regarded him through narrowed eyes. 'Aye,' was the cautious answer.

Faro halted her imminent departure with: 'A moment! Her mother?'

It was a question and the woman's expression tightened. She shrugged. 'Seen her around.'

'What was her name?'

'I dinna' ken that. Just like I said, she came here. Dinna' ken where she bided.'

'Last night—' Faro began hopefully.

'I saw naethin', naethin',' was the sharp and not unexpected answer. 'I was asleep in ma bed till yon noisy polis wi' his rattle wakened us up, alarming folks.'

'How did you know the wee girl was with her mother?'

The woman thought about that for a moment.

'Saw her walking in the street yonder wi' her one day.'

That was feeble enough, and conscious that the woman knew a great deal more than she was prepared to admit, Faro asked: 'She must have lived somewhere nearby, then.'

The woman shrugged, closed her lips tightly. 'She wasna' from around here.'

And that was the end of the conversation as, without another word, the child now silent and safe, pressed close to her bosom, the woman hurried towards the stone stair.

'A moment,' Faro called. 'What number are you?'

The retreating footsteps were his only answer. She either didn't hear or more likely didn't want to.

As he caught up with Gosse, heading up the Lawnmarket towards the Central Office, all around them footsteps skittered over damp cobbles, as if the city stretched itself on awakening from sleep. The sound of heavy boots, belonging to those who were rich enough to possess such luxuries, as working men headed towards the city's areas of employment: fleshers and bakers and candle makers – respectable jobs in a world away from the lawless closes of the High Street areas, that last resort dreaded even by beat policemen as some kind of penance or punishment.

He knew from experience that he must be wary. Faro was ever conscious of Gosse's hostility; the sergeant would enjoy any excuse of putting him back on the beat here again. He was aware that his remarks concerning the playing card had been the subject of whispered apology to the inspector.

Gosse was wary of this newly appointed detective constable assigned to him. Bad enough having an ex-detective superintendent's protégé, but a foreigner from some godforsaken barbaric island in the far north tenaciously owing allegiance to Scotland! Faro, he was convinced, would never have the guts needed in the Edinburgh City Police.

But Gosse had another, darker reason for being wary of Faro.

CHAPTER TWO

Sergeant Gosse was a law unto himself and he didn't mind twisting the evidence a little, or even a lot on occasions, to enhance his growing reputation as a renowned criminal-catcher. His efficiency was a byword at the Central Office and he claimed to have an intuition about criminals. The fact was that he was not above adding to or rearranging the clues in order to catch a malefactor and allow the course of justice to run smoother with the swift and gratifying conclusion of hanging.

Once he had been caught in the act by Faro. A trivial matter, perhaps, but having observed Gosse planting evidence in a suspected thief's pocket as they grabbed him, Faro actually had the nerve to question him. Furious, mumbling an excuse, Gosse had to recover the offending piece and, for lack of all but circumstantial evidence, he was denied the satisfaction of seeing the man he had decided was guilty receiving the sentence of being transported.

After all his efforts to keep a clean record he could not forgive Faro and resolved to keep a sharper eye on him in future.

There might be something in Faro's private life that would be useful. The fact that he kept himself to himself and wasn't exactly popular with the other lads out for a pie and a pint and a bit of skirt on an evening off suggested that digging a little deeper might reveal secrets worth investigating.

A wife was a vital ingredient in the climb for promotion, assuring the public of the respectability expected of a God-fearing, churchgoing police officer. Gosse, a very plain lumpish figure with a face scarred by smallpox and a somewhat disagreeable personality, had an eye for the ladies, albeit he was notably unsuccessful, his excuse a long, loveless and childless marriage to a shrew of a woman who had recently gone south to take care of a dying sister.

At least that was her excuse; Gosse was fairly sure that her return was neither imminent nor intended. He thanked God for that, pleased to be rid of her, his sole consolation that his abysmal marriage to a woman belonging to the class above him, this local baker's only daughter, included the prospect of inheriting a thriving business. Mrs Gosse was also distantly related on the distaff side to a local important and affluent family, a fact he never missed an opportunity of mentioning. In his wife's absence, Gosse considered himself as something of a Casanova, much to the amusement and astonishment of his drinking colleagues. His lack of success was further cause for resenting his tall, well-set-up detective constable who had netted an exceptionally attractive young lady with whom he seemed to be on excellent terms.

How had he achieved this? A puzzle, especially as Faro hadn't much – except in the way of good looks – to offer.

'Nice looking young widow lady I see you've got yourself,' he said, having met the couple walking in Princes Street Gardens. Pausing, hoping for an introduction, he received a mere salute from Faro as they swept onward.

He was furious and next morning decided to tackle Faro again and was gratified by the younger man's look of surprise – but no embarrassment – at his question.

'A widow – what makes you think that, sir?'

Gosse tapped the side of his nose. True, it was not a recent bereavement since she wasn't in widow's weeds, but as she was walking in public with Faro on a Sunday afternoon, it was unlikely that they were having an affair. Gosse was sharp, and did some quick calculations, especially as the young lad she was dragging along, sullen and rebellious, was protesting: 'Let go, Ma.'

'Is that her bairn? She doesn't look old enough.' Gosse decided on an approach by friendly observation. 'Her man – a soldier, was he?'

Faro had the story ready. 'Killed in India.'

Gosse nodded. 'Lucky to find another man, especially with a bairn. Not every man wants second-hand goods. You know what I mean,' he added slyly.

Faro knew exactly what Gosse meant but there was much more to it, had Gosse known the truth. Lizzie was no widow, there had never been a husband and Vince was the child of rape when she was a fifteen-year-old maid in a big house in the Highlands, the victim of an aristocratic guest there for the shooting. In desperation she might well, like so many others, have taken to the streets to support the baby she refused to abandon. But Lizzie was made of stronger stuff; she invented a soldier husband and fought her way up the ladder of domestic service. Her dream, her one ambition, was to rise to the role of housekeeper in some great establishment and she was stepping up the ladder, recently appointed lady's maid to the mistress of Lumbleigh Green in Newington, Edinburgh's new and elegant south-side suburb.

Faro lodged with several other unmarried constables in a boarding house in the Lawnmarket. His room was up a spiral and dirty stair to the third floor, but at least for an extra shilling a week it was his alone – unlike some of the constables, who for the sake of economy shared a room and slept three or four to a bed. Faro was horrified, as he liked his space and looked forward to being alone at the end of the day and staring out of his narrow window. Across Princes Street Gardens with its line of shops and beyond the New Town Villas and over the distant waters of the Firth of Forth to the Kingdom of Fife.

The care Mrs Biggs bestowed on her lodgers was minimal. A strait-laced, heavily corseted lady, formidable, respectable, God-fearing and churchgoing – as she was never tired of pointing out to them – she would put up with no nonsense and that included female callers. The constables rolled their eyes at that – who would wish to take a lady up to a bedroom shared with three other blokes? Had she no imagination? There were plenty of rude and lewd rejoinders to that.

On the plus side, she was a reasonable cook; she prided herself on good, solid food, and they certainly did not starve – porridge for breakfast, meat for supper and an occasional suet pudding.

On the minus side, a widow of uncertain age, she had taken a fancy to the handsome newcomer, tall and fair, so polite and reserved, and with such good manners.

'Treats me like a real lady from the New Town, he does. Not like some,' she said darkly to her friends, and whispered, 'From the Orkneys, he is,' with not the least idea where they were but they did sound so romantic. This air of reverence was not lost on Faro's fellow boarders, nor was that extra helping of this or that sliding his way across the table, matters that did nothing for his reputation or their goodwill.

'Orkneys, eh. Have they put doors on your caves yet?'

Faro merely smiled and refused to be provoked, which annoyed them even more. Goading him, they would have enjoyed an angry reaction and particularly the chance of some fisticuffs, which would have seen him ousted from their lodging.

'Man, he dinna' even get drunk on a Saturday.

What sort of a bobby is he going to make?'

Heads were shaken. One thing's certain, he'd never get any promotion. Hardly human. They grumbled, always ready to knock a captured thief about on the way to the station. Not so Faro – he was calm and restrained.

And what about the lasses? Always on the lookout for a night's entertainment, some stolen kisses as a prelude and a promise of better things to come, off duty and out of uniform they haunted the howffs on the Leith Road, but Faro, invited along, shook his head.

'Well provided elsewhere, are you?' they sneered. It was either that or he was that dreaded word, a 'pansy' – a pansy policeman. Wait till Mrs Biggs got wind of that for her fancy lad. Aye, that would put her off, right enough, and see him booted out.

Aware of all these whispers in the house, Faro was delighted to meet the lads one Sunday afternoon when they were wandering through the Gardens, on the lookout for 'skirts', as they called them.

He had Lizzie on his arm and the trio were taken aback. Small wonder, since Lizzie was an exceptionally attractive young woman, and from her attire, her gentility was never in question. She had a little lad with her. As Gosse had discovered on a previous occasion, there was no denying that she was a widow and 'a damned handsome one at that', the lads agreed with backward glances of envy.

Small and slender, she was undeniably pretty, her outstanding features the abundant yellow curls and bright hazel eyes. There was only one problem for Faro, a secret he nursed: the woman he longed for with all his heart was Inga St Ola, tall with long black hair and blue eyes, and she lived in faraway Orkney.

Faro sighed. Inga had been his first love, older and more worldly-wise, his initiation into manhood on a moonlit beach one summer night. Seventeen years old, he had wanted to marry her but she had firmly rejected him. Declaring herself a free spirit, she had scorned the idea of being a policeman's wife living in a great grimy city full of people; her entire life was centred on an island with its wild seas among folk like herself whom she had known all her life.

The business of being in love was a mystery to Faro. He knew he had loved Inga, but would he ever experience the ecstasy of being in love, a love that one died for, like the great romances of history, the kind Shakespeare wrote about? He shook his head solemnly. The prospect, alluring as it was, also scared him. He doubted if he even wanted to have his foundations being shaken by such an overwhelming destructive emotion for another human being.

And certainly he was safe enough with gentle, unassuming Lizzie Laurie, who offered no such threats to his existence. He respected her, was fond of her and wanted to protect her. Stretching a point you could call that love, he thought, and he was certain she loved him. But even after a wild party and far too much to drink, ending with a return to her tenement lodging and a night spent in her arms, he hadn't woken up to feel anything but faint regret that he had perhaps let himself in for a future he wasn't quite prepared for yet: marriage, making her an honest woman, which she would doubtless now expect as her right.

Inga would have laughed at such sentiments. She had advised him at their meeting in Stromness last year to go back and marry his Lizzie. She would make the perfect wife, Inga had said, attending to all his needs, ready with slippers before the fire after a long day, with food on the table, loving arms in a warm bed.

He sighed. Doubtless he would settle for that in the end. He did love Lizzie in a way and could maybe convince himself that was all he was ever to know, this mixture of tenderness and sympathy for all she had suffered in the past – but was that enough?

For there was another fly in the ointment, so to speak. The petulant eleven-year-old Vince who made no secret of his dislike and scorn for his mother's suitor. The dislike was mutual, the idea of living under the same roof with Vince as his stepson intolerable.

Faro shuddered, thinking of what such years ahead would involve before the lad reached adulthood and left home. He didn't doubt that Vince was clever; Lizzie was delighted with his school reports, proudly showing Faro homework books with their neat writing and bright stars and teachers' 'excellent work' comments.

The signs were there already that Vince would do well enough to make something of his life, have a future beyond that expected of a domestic servant's offspring, and an illegitimate one at that. And certain that she had a brilliant son, Lizzie had always spent what little she earned only on the necessities of life, and she told Faro that since his birth when she had decided to keep him, she had been saving up, her dream to have enough money to send him to the university here with its grand reputation.

Faro said nothing but thought plenty. She was wasting her time. He saw the sad reality that, clever as Vince was, by the end of his schooldays in a few years, Lizzie's tiny income would never have reached the money necessary to send her boy to Edinburgh University. And what of his future when he got there? She had no idea of the snobbery of the rich men's sons from Edinburgh's middle class, and his brilliance as a student would not save Vince from their scorn.

Faro did not care to disillusion Lizzie, but from his own experience, he had and was still suffering from being a policeman's son. Only a miracle could answer Lizzie's dream and miracles of that nature were in very short supply.

CHAPTER THREE

At the Central Office, Chief Inspector McIvor was lying in wait.

'Anything to report?' he snapped, his voice curiously reminiscent of the bark of a very impatient small terrier. Before his promotion, he had earned the reputation of shaking criminals like a dog shaking a rat. With sharp-looking protruding teeth, a bush of gingery hair, heavy moustache and small eyes under bushy eyebrows, his resemblance to an angry terrier was unmistakable.

McIvor's boast was that he did not suffer fools gladly and into that category he slotted all the constables and detectives under his command.

Sergeant Gosse narrowly escaped this definition; he certainly produced results, and the overworked chief inspector was apt to close the book of evidence rather swiftly, without looking too closely at how such evidence had been obtained. He had a job to do. He was a busy man. McIvor expected results, results that a more moderate officer might have thought could only be rendered as miracles produced with the assistance of a visiting band of angels.

Gosse, who hated to admit defeat, straightened his shoulders. 'Nothing, sir.'

At that Faro came forward and held out the playing card. 'There was this lying beneath the woman's body, sir. Perhaps it might help.'

McIvor shifted his withering gaze to this new detective constable.

'A playing card, eh,' he yelped. 'And what kind of evidence do you call that?'

'All these women play cards one way or another – gambling and telling fortunes, sir,' Gosse put in hastily, rewarding Faro's interruption with a scowl that said, clearer than words, that the book containing the rules of conduct before senior officers had been disobeyed: 'Know your place. Show respect for your superiors and speak only when you are spoken to.'

Ignoring him, Faro addressed McIvor: 'Not

just any playing card, sir. This is the nine of diamonds, sir, known throughout history as the curse of Scotland. With respect, sir, as you will recall—'

'You're not engaged here to teach me my history, Faro,' McIvor barked. 'It's the present we're interested in, not what happened a hundred years ago—'

'With respect, sir,' Faro interrupted again, 'we found the same card in the room where the last woman was killed—'

It was Gosse's turn to cut in. 'As I have explained to the constable here, sir, the woman's killer, her husband, was a known gambler, the room littered with cards.'

McIvor chewed on his moustache, regarded Faro from under lowered brows and in the manner of a terrier putting his front paws together murmured, 'So you are hinting that we have a killer who marks his territory by using a playing card as warning? A bit far-fetched, Faro. I can only suggest that this is a flight of imagination and a too-close adherence to coincidence which does not become a newly promoted constable to this force, whose wits should be heavily engaged on present crimes rather than reminders of Scotland's past history.'

His words heavy with sarcasm, his head bent

over the notes like a dog sniffing a ripe odour, indicated a gesture of dismissal. 'Have to do better than that, Faro. Keep in step with your senior officer here and you won't go far wrong.'

As Gosse and Faro backed smartly out of his presence with a respectful salute worthy of a royal presence, Faro mentally digested McIvor's parting shot of 'not far wrong' as 'not far right, either'.

Gosse did not intend to let the matter rest. 'Watch your step, Faro. The boss is not a patient man and a few more fanciful ideas like that, instead of attending to detail, and you'll find yourself demoted – back on the beat again, I shouldn't wonder.' And feeling that he had also been made an example of by implication, he added: 'And don't expect any recommendation from me, either.'

Faro's thoughts were as gloomy as the weather that evening as he prepared to meet Lizzie at the servants' entrance of Lumbleigh Green. En route, he paused in the Pleasance, staring up at the windows of the house where Andy Davy murdered his wife, claiming manslaughter rather than murder. His excuse, his violent temper and jealousy – he had never meant to kill her. But the scene of violence, and pity for Davy, too, remained indelibly printed on Faro's mind. The circumstances that would pass in France as a *crime passionnel* were not recognised on this side of the English Channel and Andy Davy would pay with his life.

The playing cards at the scene of Mrs Davy's murder had misled him. Were they a coincidence, since the only connection with the more recent murder was distance, their apartment a mere ten minutes' walk away from Fleshers Close? Beyond the Pleasance and St Leonard's, the 'Seton side' of the city was striving to escape any connection with the nearby Old Town with its closes and teeming population housed in towering tenements on both sides of the High Street.

On summer days fine weather offered Faro and Lizzie walks on Arthur's Seat, Salisbury Crags and the Queen's Park or a stroll in the Princes Street Gardens where a couple might indulge in the gambit of normal courtship, gently getting to know one another, exchanging a few kisses – maybe. But when autumn came with darker evenings – and the signs were already present, with unpredictable heavy rainstorms and icy east winds across the Forth replacing calm autumnal sunshine, heralding snow soon to come – what then? Where would they go?

A notice in the hallway at his lodgings with Mrs Biggs announced the forbidden: No smoking in the bedrooms. Baths once a week – the latter a modern innovation to be arranged with the landlady (of which she was especially proud), the sequence sternly kept to. He had been warned by his fellow boarders: 'If you miss your night, then you'll have to wait until it comes round again next week.' The warning notice also sternly included 'No followers', sex unclassified but undoubtedly alluding, in that all-male boardership, to the presence of females.

Leaving the Pleasance, Faro was out of Edinburgh city, the open country lying ahead. Here there was little habitation beyond a few secluded mansions with wooded gardens and exclusive villas like Blacket Place.

Locked gates sheltered these precincts from the coach road that for many centuries had served the city, the carriage route still linking Edinburgh to the Border towns and across the Cheviots to England and then to the world beyond, always watched over by the glowering extinct volcano that was Arthur's Seat, on whose slopes were still to be seen the runrigg lines of a bygone farming community. At the base of this prehistoric settlement, whose origins were lost in time, a modern innovation dear to the hearts of travellers – Waverley Railway Station.

Faro loved the fresh air of the road before him,

a steep hill with glimpses far across of the Pentland Hills and, on a fine day, the heights of Sutra Hill. Trees, farming and a few mansions. Venturesome merchants having made their fortunes had, for various reasons, felt that while a town house in the New Town would be fine enough, it would be rather splendid to have one's own estate on the city outskirts where land was cheap, and to build a handsome turreted mansion on the lines of a medieval castle in imitation of the Queen and Prince Albert's new Highland home at Balmoral, the ambition for every man with a few thousand pounds in hand.

And so it was that Lumbleigh Green came into existence on the edge of the Dalkeith Road, far from the less impressive home of William Lumbleigh, owner of a small coal mine near Leuchars, in Fife – not a fashionable place to live, William's grandson Archie decided, while Edinburgh fairly zoomed in prosperity for the newly rich.

Approaching the gates, Faro was acutely aware that for his social life with Lizzie there was a limit to what he could afford in the way of entertainment, apart from the variety theatres and a few dance halls, which had such a low reputation that respectable young women avoided them. Besides, he couldn't dance, so it seemed that their future in a fast-approaching season of inclement weather would be reduced to cups of tea in a High Street café.

And, as always, there was the problem, persistent as an angry wasp at their meetings, of the presence of Vince Laurie.

Earlier that week, however, Faro had discovered a welcome change in Lizzie's life. She had run to the gate to meet him, smiling eagerly, full of excitement. Matters had been moving apace at Lumbleigh Green and Lizzie's promotion to lady's maid meant that she was now expected to live in.

'Of course I want to live in, madam,' she had said. 'It's an honour.'

In her efforts to save every penny, Lizzie had long occupied one room in a grim tenement in the Pleasance, in fact quite uncomfortably close to what was now being called 'the murder house', scene of the recent domestic killing of Mrs Daly by her husband. However, Lizzie's lodging had one advantage: it was a ten-minute walk from Lumbleigh Green.

She was in a quandary. She did not know if she could afford to keep that one room, nor did she want to, if she was honest, apart from providing a home for Vince. The attic room in Lumbleigh Green was magnificent by comparison, even in its spartan state, overlooking gardens far below and with a distant glimpse of the Pentland Hills.

The second Mrs Lumbleigh was young and quite lovely. Infatuated, Archie had married her for her looks in the same manner as he normally acquired beautiful possessions at auction houses.

Clara was aware that her own origins would not bear too close a scrutiny. She liked Lizzie, who was so different from the friends she met in their social circle, women with whom she always felt she had little in common. She would look at Lizzie and wish she could be her best friend, longing to share with her the often scaring details of her early life. But she thought better of it, ashamed to confess such emotion even to herself, or to Archie, of whose disapproval she was a little afraid, and who made it his business to educate her, impress upon her their role in this new society. Had she even hinted about liking her lady's maid he would tell her sternly that one didn't express such feelings where a servant, a mere employee, was concerned.

She had no such problems with the other servants, had no desire to unburden herself to the formidable Mrs Brown or the two maids, the giggling, rather bold Ida, or Betty, painfully shy and inarticulate, a condition she shared with the coachman.

As for her lady's maid, Clara felt more

comfortable with her than anyone else in the house, even Archie himself. Laurie was a skilful hairdresser and seamstress; Clara needed to have her on hand. Lately, however, she had sensed some preoccupation and agonised with fears that Laurie might be after another situation. Unable to bear the suspense any longer, she sat her down and asked: 'What's wrong? Is something bothering you, Laurie?'

Archie insisted on the use of surnames for servants. Clara thought this was silly, it made her uncomfortable, but Archie believed this was not only fashionable but proper in the upper echelons of Edinburgh's New Town society. Questioned by his wife he wasn't quite sure why, but believed it was to prevent servants getting on too familiar terms with their betters.

Lizzie had sat up straight and said: 'I am happy to serve you, madam. I cannot turn this down but what am I to do about my little son, Vince? He's at school at St Leonard's, just a step from where I've been living in the Pleasance for the past few years.'

True, it wasn't much, but it was her home, after all.

And so, the whole story rolled out as she dressed her mistress's hair preparatory to an evening concert at the Assembly Rooms.

And Clara Lumbleigh, studying her reflection in the mirror, had the divine inspiration of a solution. At the far end of the extensive gardens were the remains of the small farm cottage that had once occupied the site of Lumbleigh Green. Dilapidated, almost a ruin, to Archie it presented possibilities. With a barn that would serve as a stable, he had decided to keep it as accommodation for the coachman Brown who had come to Archie with excellent references from long-term employers in Glasgow and Aberdeen. Brown was prepared to also do duty as gardener/handyman, which pleased his tight-fisted master exceedingly, especially as Brown's wife was an accomplished and experienced domestic servant, ready and willing to take on the role of housekeeper and cook.

Archie had rubbed his hands with glee at this splendid piece of economy. What a find! As for Clara, she remembered there was a tiny attic with a skylight window accessible by ladder where Vince could sleep, having his meals either with the Browns or in the servants' kitchen.

'What do you think of that, Laurie?'

Lizzie was dazed, almost speechless with gratitude.

'Oh, madam, would you?'

'Of course. The master may wish to make a reduction in your wages, but I will do my best.'

'Oh, thank you, this is wonderful, wonderful.'

And this was what Lizzie had been waiting to tell Faro when they met that evening earlier in the week. It still did not solve the problem of future meetings in chilly winds and darkness with frozen hands and feet. Not much place for a lingering kiss either, because that and more, Faro suspected, was certainly what Lizzie now expected. Perhaps as Ida and Betty, the table and kitchen maids, didn't live in, there might be possibilities of secret meetings over a cup of tea.

Lizzie would love to show him her attic, she said, but there were dangers. Such visits could be subject to misinterpretation, and she shuddered – if the master found out, it might well cost her her situation as well as her reputation.

Now, this evening, Faro had news of his own – for a special treat he intended taking Lizzie to the theatre.

As Faro stood by the iron gates framing a drive and a large and very ornate front door, Lizzie, always so punctual, failed to appear. Wondering anxiously what was wrong, he was considering whether he should ignore the forbidden entrance and the even more forbidding presence of two large black dogs patrolling the grounds. Lizzie assured him they were friendly but past experience had taught Faro to view dogs as the beat policeman's enemies.

At last a patter of footsteps announced the approach of Lizzie from the direction of the discreetly unseen tradesman's entrance.

She ran to greet him. He sensed immediately that all was not well. An anxious frown replaced her usual delighted greeting.

'Sorry to keep you waiting, Jeremy. I've had an awful day, fearfully busy. I wondered if I was going to get away at all, having to serve supper. Had to take over from Ida. She's so unreliable.' And she proceeded at some length to talk about the trial that Ida the table maid was these days, disappearing, supposedly sick and not for the first time, either. 'Madam had been very indulgent—'

Faro only half-listened as he had very little interest in the goings-on inside the 'big house' which were of such compelling interest and daily excitement to Lizzie. She spared him no detail of how difficult Madam had been about that new hairstyle, and her gown with its torn hem, how lace was almost impossible to mend. As for Mrs Brown, the housekeeper and cook, she was always complaining about everything. And so on and on as Lizzie took his arm and they walked towards Clerk Street and the small café newly opened where they might have refreshments, cups of tea and cream cakes.

Faro was eager to forget for a while the trials of

a long exhausting day; he never discussed any of his cases with Lizzie, particularly where a murder was involved. This was one occasion when he would have preferred something stronger than tea but he could hardly invite Lizzie to accompany him to one of the public houses.

When at last the waitress took their order and Lizzie had hopefully come to the end of her domestic saga, he said: 'I've a nice surprise for us this evening. Tickets for the concert, good seats for the second performance.'

'Oh, Jeremy, I can't – not tonight,' Lizzie wailed. 'I told you. I only have an hour off tonight – I'll have to go back soon. Haven't you been listening, Jeremy?' she demanded.

Faro hadn't been listening. 'But it's at the New Royal Alhambra,' he protested, 'the one that's replaced Dibdin Hall we all liked so much.'

Lizzie nodded absently, remembering the old theatre that had been so popular before it literally fell to pieces, as Faro went on: 'Just been open a couple of months, Lizzie, and I've been waiting for an opportunity, something we would both enjoy . . .'

She held up a hand, looked tearful and said: 'Jeremy, I'm disappointed too. I've been looking forward to that as well. But some other time, not tonight. I have to wait on table, you see. And I can't let Sir and Madam down.'

'Why have you to wait on table?' he said shortly. 'I thought you were the lady's maid.'

'So I am, Jeremy – have you not been listening to a word I've been saying?' she repeated shortly.

He felt suddenly guilty as she continued: 'I told you about Ida. Madam says the master's had enough and she's not to come back this time—'

'Yes, but isn't there another maid—'

'Betty, the kitchen maid? Heavens! Never her,' was the shocked reply. 'She wouldn't do at all. She couldn't possibly – it would be . . . well, awful. She might make mistakes about cutlery and serving courses in the right order – you see, I do know all the procedure,' she said proudly. 'I did that sort of thing once before I became lady's maid to Madam . . .'

Poor Lizzie felt very let down when instead of repeating how delighted he was about her promotion, how proud he was of her, Faro, who was feeling exasperated, merely shrugged and asked: 'Could they not manage, just for one evening?'

'They could if it had just been themselves and Master Paul. But it's a proper dinner party, six guests—'

'What about the housekeeper? Could she not serve as well as do the cooking for once?'

Lizzie's laugh was a trifle bitter. 'You don't

know what you're asking, Jeremy. It would be a disaster. Mrs Brown would be all hot and flustered – sweating, her feet hurting. No, she wouldn't even consider demeaning herself for that sort of thing. Serving at table – that's far beneath her.'

It was no fault of Lizzie's, Faro understood that, but he felt angry, especially as he had bought tickets for the concert.

'What were we going to see?' she asked.

'A concert of operatic music.'

'Oh, how nice. I am disappointed.' But Faro thought he also detected relief. Lizzie's taste in entertainment was what could be termed 'broad', mostly of the burlesque variety. He was trying to educate her to something a little more subtle, music and plays, particularly Shakespeare, his own particular favourite.

'Perhaps you can return the tickets, get an exchange,' she said, 'or take your nice friend Mr Macfie. He likes that sort of thing.'

He did indeed, but Faro was out of luck.

CHAPTER FOUR

Macfie was not at home and Faro, standing outside his closed door in Nicholson Square, remembered that this was the weekend he was going to Glasgow for a reunion with old colleagues.

So he went alone. It was a beautiful evening; a glowing moon flooded the quiet streets with light that begged for romantic dalliance. Inside the theatre, surrounded by cheerful, excited faces and happy chatter, waiting for the curtain to rise, he took his seat in the circle, painfully conscious of the empty one that should have been occupied by Lizzie.

His thoughts turned to the moment he had

left her, feeling guilty that he had somehow not concealed properly his anger and disappointment that she could not come to the concert. Did he detect feelings of relief in her refusal? He should have known that opera was not her kind of entertainment, he thought, as the curtain rose on the two singers with their heart-rending last scene of *Tristram and Isolde*.

Alone in the interval with his gloomy thoughts while those around him adjourned for refreshments, he told himself Lizzie had no option of refusing to help out her mistress at a time of emergency, especially for the privileges she had been given. She had every reason to be grateful for promotion to lady's maid, especially when a comfortable secure home for Vince had been thoughtfully included by Mrs Lumbleigh.

As the curtain rose again and he joined in the applause for a solo pianist and a Beethoven sonata, he thought bitterly about the maid Ida, who had no such feelings of loyalty and could take leave on the flimsiest of excuses. He frowned, remembering Lizzie as she talked about Ida. Perhaps it was his imagination but he had a feeling she wasn't telling him everything.

Lying awake that night with the moonlight streaming through the window, the music from the opera excerpts throbbed through his head, refusing to be banished as memory presented the scene of reality he had witnessed – a murdered woman, and the tragedies in her life that had ended in such violence still unknown.

Would they ever learn her identity or find her killer? And what would become of that small pathetic child? Had she witnessed the violent death of the woman who was her mother? Would she remember, and what sort of a future lay in store for her?

If the police failed to discover the woman's identity, or that of her killer, she would be taken to Surgeons' Hall and become the object of study for the students eagerly awaiting fresh corpses to dismember, lessons in surgery to be learnt for the benefit of medical science and future mankind.

The murder scene at Fleshers Close continued to haunt him and he decided that he would carry on a further investigation, talk to the woman who had rescued the child.

He wondered if Gosse was also lying sleepless and doubted it. The sergeant, if he was awake at all, would be considering wider issues of criminal-catching or, if that failed, tying the murder neatly to a likely suspect. There was worse in store, as Faro discovered when he was awakened not by the peaceful church bells on a Sunday morning but by Mrs Biggs, saying crossly that there was a policeman to see him. He dressed hurriedly and found Gosse waiting downstairs for him.

'There's been another murder – at least, attempted this time.'

'Another woman, sir?'

'No.' A shake of the head indicated disappointment. 'An elderly man this time. Attacked in St Leonard's and left for dead; attempted strangulation, though, just like the women.'

'What was it this time? Robbery?'

Gosse shook his head again, and said gravely, 'I think we are dealing with something more serious than we first thought. Not a man killing whores but a madman – attacking anyone who comes his way.' Gosse paused, yawned deeply. 'And it was a full moon last night,' he ended ominously.

Faro remembered that the insane asylum had to put on extra guards each month when the moon was full; even the quieter docile inmates showed signs of aggression and some even turned wild and uncontrollable.

'Victim is in the Infirmary and if he's conscious there are some questions. Hopefully he will have answers leading not only to this incident but to the women's murders as well.'

* * *

At the Infirmary an elderly man, white-haired and dishevelled, sat up in bed, his head bandaged, a dazed and frightened look in his eyes at the sight of two uniformed policemen standing at his bedside.

'What am I doing here?' he quavered. 'I've done nothing wrong. Why have they brought me to this place? I want my own home.'

Gosse said: 'You are lucky to be alive. You were attacked last night at St Leonard's.'

'Was I? What was I doing there?' The man seemed utterly bewildered, his senses lost. Gosse looked at Faro, tapped his head significantly, his helpless shrug indicating they weren't going to get very far with this one.

The man shut his eyes, his fingers pulling at the bedclothes, then swallowing he touched his neck, winced. 'Throat's sore. Can you tell me why I'm here?' he wailed. 'What happened?' And before Gosse could explain, he sat up and shouted: 'Oh, now I remember; I was walking home when a man came from behind, put his arm round my neck' – he tried to demonstrate – 'tried to strangle me – like this. We staggered a bit, but I used to be a prizefighter and I've still got a bit of strength – aye, and I remembered the dirty fights, the tender bits to aim for.' A hoarse chuckle. 'I kicked out, he yelled and let me go, I fell and I must have hit my head, 'cos I woke up here.'

Gosse asked: 'Can you describe him?'

The old man frowned. 'Tall as me, I think. But I can't be sure, he was behind me.' He shook his head. 'When you find him, hope you'll let me have a go at him first.' And suddenly alert, his senses restored by indignation, clenching huge knuckles, he stuck out his chin, nodded vigorously. 'Aye, I'll soon show him what's what.'

Gosse said coldly that punishment was police business, not his, but the old man shook his head firmly. 'Any man who hits me – that is my business. And now can I go home?'

'Where's home?' Faro was taking notes while Gosse did all the questioning.

'Liberton Brae. I was on my way home to see my daughter when it happened.'

A nurse approached with a bundle of clothes. 'You're free to go home now, Mr Webb.'

'Anything missing?' the old man demanded. 'I had two shillings in my pocket.'

'There they are.' And she shook out a handkerchief, two coins and a playing card.

Faro picked it up. The nine of diamonds.

Gosse seized it from him. 'Where did you get this?'

The man shrugged. 'Never seen it before in my life.'

'Are you sure?' Gosse demanded suspiciously.

'Course I'm sure,' was the indignant reply. 'I'm a temperance man since my wife died years ago. Never play cards, don't approve of gambling, either. Wife was God-fearing. Always—' he began.

Gosse interrupted shortly: 'If you remember anything about the man who attacked you—'

'I'll let you know, officer. I want to catch him too, you know.' Aware that the two policemen were edging away from the bed, and anxious not to lose his audience, he said: 'Wait till I tell you about the time I was fighting in the ring, when I won cups, belts and things – it was in the newspapers—'

Gosse wasn't prepared to listen. Motioning to Faro, he shouted over his shoulder: 'Let us know if you remember anything else about last night, will you?'

Hurrying along the corridor they were overtaken by a young doctor. 'Excuse me, officer,' he said. 'The old man who was attacked, Jock Webb – I'm afraid he's been in here before.' He paused to tap his forehead significantly. 'Found wandering a couple of times, fell and hurt himself. Don't take too much notice of what he's been telling you about being attacked. He thinks he's still in the boxing ring.'

'You mean he's imagined the whole thing,

made it all up, getting us over here, wasting our time?' said Gosse angrily.

The doctor frowned. 'Well, it could be true, sir. We just weren't sure. When we examined him, he definitely had marks on his throat this time. Might be quite genuine, but I thought I should warn you. He doesn't always know where he is. Likes the opportunity to remind folk of his days as a prizefighter—'

Gosse snapped an abrupt thanks, and at the exit, he handed Faro the report the nurse had given him, complete with the man's home address. 'Look into it. Talk to the daughter.'

Faro glanced at the notes, guessing that there would be little information forthcoming at Liberton Brae about an old man already having problems with his memory.

Only the nine of diamonds in Webb's pocket had a sinister ring of truth about it. Perhaps Gosse was right and its presence at the Pleasance murder, one card among a whole pack, was sheer coincidence. But Faro was now convinced, with the appearance of this one particular card, that the attack on Jock Webb must be linked to the woman in Fleshers Close.

Faro said: 'That playing card, sir. Like the others. What do you think?'

At his side, Gosse growled: 'I'm already

thinking, Faro. And do you know what – I think he could be lying. Has it not occurred to you that we have maybe solved the crime of the murdered whore? He might well be our killer,' he added in tones of excitement.

Faro said: 'Hardly likely, sir.'

'You're not seeing the obvious once again, are you?' was the contemptuous response. 'He could have attacked this man, who unexpectedly fought back, and he became the victim himself.'

It did not seem even remotely feasible to Faro that an old man who, according to the young doctor, was showing all the symptoms of dementia, wandering about and already known to the Infirmary, could be the killer. When he said so, Gosse looked angry and said sharply: 'That's just it – an elaborate pretence. You don't see into the minds of murderers as I do, Faro. Wait until you've had years of chasing criminals like I have before you lay down hard-and-fast rules of behaviour. They are up to doing anything to conceal their vile purposes – no character is too difficult for them to assume.'

Faro listened, knowing further comment was useless. All this fitted so neatly into Gosse's anxiety and determination to pin down the woman's murderer as quickly as possible, stretching a point here and there if necessary, to put it mildly.

At the Central Office, McIvor was waiting for them.

Another death had been reported: a woman's body was waiting in the mortuary.

Gosse sighed as he and Faro parted company. 'Just a suicide this time, thank God. Off the North Bridge.'

The bridge above the railway station was a favourite place for desperate, unhappy people, particularly young females, betrayed by lovers and more than often pregnant, eager to leap into oblivion and put an end to their disgrace.

CHAPTER FIVE

Faro set off for Liberton Brae armed with the old man's address. A long line of smart villas facing each other across the steep street, owned or rented by Edinburgh's lower middle class: artisans, shopkeepers or office workers. All houses alike, even to the lace curtains, the carefully kept gardens and well-painted doors and windows, an indication of the respectable, decent lives that a passer-by might expect of the inhabitants within.

As a measure against arousing alarm, despondency or guilty consciences and an outbreak of furious neighbourhood gossip, Faro had decided to abandon his uniform in favour of plain clothes.

Even for the innocent, the sight of a policeman's helmet hinted at bad news. There was something formidable, even discreditable, about the sight of a constable walking up the garden path, and Faro had discovered that he gained a great deal more information by posing as an ordinary citizen. His gentle manner and quiet voice made the folk being interviewed feel less vulnerable, more trusting.

And there was the house he was looking for. Number 124. The door was opened promptly by a young woman. By her expression, smiling then swiftly overtaken by a frown, he was not the visitor she expected and he sighed with relief. Her appearance and age suggested that this was Mr Webb's daughter or even his granddaughter.

Raising his tall hat, he asked if Mr Webb was at home. The woman frowned, asked him to repeat the name and shook her head. 'Never heard of him. You've come to the wrong house, I'm afraid.'

This was a setback. 'You don't know anyone of that name?'

'Never in our time and we've been here for five years. There was an old woman before that, took in lodgers.' And asking him to repeat the name, again she shook her head firmly. 'No, Webb definitely wasn't her name.'

Apologising and thanking her, he walked down

the path, closed the gate and wondered what on earth to do next. He looked again at the address. The writing was shaky but it was definitely 124. Then he looked up and down both sides of the brae.

He could hardly go from door to door. No, there must be some mistake. Mistake or no, when Gosse heard of this he would pounce upon it as a deliberate attempt to put the police off the scent.

Maybe Gosse was right, but Faro still couldn't believe from what he had seen physically of the old man, and having observed his confusion in that brief infirmary visit, that he was capable of going out on the rampage and killing anyone. And yet . . . and yet Webb had been a very strong man once and knew all about strangleholds from his boxing days. He had almost certainly left the Infirmary last night, so Faro looked up and down the steep hill.

Webb must be in one of these houses. He crossed over and decided to try one or two numbers, on the off chance that there had been an error in writing down 124.

He was out of luck, soon made to realise that he was facing a hopeless task. Doors when they were opened at all were drawn back just a couple of inches wide, with a suspicious voice, usually female, demanding what was he selling and stating she didn't want any. The men were less polite.

After a dozen doors, humiliated, he decided the most likely person to have information about the sporting community, even a non-drinking former boxer, might be the local public house he had noticed earlier. It was also a much needed excuse. The stiff wind that had travelled with him from Arthur's Seat had turned into heavy mist and fine drizzle. He was cold, wet, thirsty and his feet were sore.

Presumably he was also the first and only customer at opening time. He felt less than hopeful as he ordered a pint of ale. The fact that the barman was young suggested that he might not have useful information either.

'Jock Webb. Aye, everyone's heard of him. Local hero. A great fighter.'

'I believe he used to live here on Liberton Brae.'

The barman shook his head. 'You've got me there, sir.' It was the reply Faro expected. 'Came here from Glasgow a couple of years ago. Can't help you much.' A pause. 'Wait a bit though, my granddad may know.'

An ancient man, stooped and leaning on a stick, was summoned from the back premises. Faro almost immediately got a feeling he was delighted to talk to anyone, especially about the famous Jock Webb.

'Aye, must be over eighty. Younger than me. Died, has he?' There was a certain relish of one old man outliving a contemporary.

'He was very much alive when I saw him last night – asked me to call on him when I was in the area,' Faro lied. 'But the address – number 124 – was wrong. I didn't remember it correctly.'

The old man was watching him intently, looking him up and down, assessing him. 'You from the newspapers, young sir?'

Faro laughed. 'No, just an acquaintance. Interested in his boxing career.'

What followed needed time and patience as the old man, proud to state that he had been Jock Webb's close friend, embarked on a full biographical story. Finally, he paused to draw breath and have another half-pint of ale, donated by Faro, who much regretted this impulse now because it seemed that as a captive audience he was unlikely to make his escape before closing time.

While maintaining an attitude of polite listening he was frantically inventing excuses to interrupt the flow when Tom, for that was his name, announced: 'Aye, this was his first home. Liberton Brae. I was best man at their wedding. Jock hadn't made his name in the ring at that time and couldna' afford a fine house like the one he has now. Boarded with a Miss Ginny, old lady who had a boarding house.'

A pause for thought, and Faro asked: 'Do you happen to know the number?'

'Aye, I do that. Top of the hill, 124.'

So that was the explanation. Jock had simply given the wrong address, because he had complete recall of his first home as a married man and doubtless imagined he still lived there.

Faro had one more question. 'Where is he now – this fine house you mentioned?'

'Och, I dinna' ken that.' Tom shook his head. 'We kind of lost touch when he got famous. Sort of thing that happens – he didna' have the time for old friends,' he added bitterly.

'Any family in Edinburgh? He mentioned a daughter.'

'Is that so?' Tom shook his head. 'While we were still friends they had two bairns. I well remember . . .'

Unwilling for the onslaught of another wave of philosophical reminiscences, Faro stemmed the flow by saying: 'I presume Jock is still in Edinburgh, though.'

'Last I heard, he had one of those grand new houses in Newington.'

When Faro announced that he must leave,

Tom seemed reluctant to let him go, saying how much he had enjoyed their conversation and what a treat it was to meet a real gentleman with a taste for boxing.

Faro's eyes widened a little at this, since the conversation had been entirely one-sided, apart from a couple of questions he'd edged in, and to be truthful his leisure hours had never included any visits to the boxing ring.

The possible whereabouts of 'a grand house in Newington' suggested another futile investigation but Faro left with a feeling of relief that Jock Webb was unlikely to fit Gosse's role of prime suspect. There seemed little point in searching any further when Tom had revealed of his own accord that Jock's family connections had been in Aberdeen, Fife and over the Borders. It only confirmed that mention of visiting his daughter in Liberton Brae had been a figment of the old man's confusion.

As he walked back towards the city, the glowering shadow of Arthur's Seat emerged from the mist that so often turned it into a sleeping giant. There were patches of sunlight on its many crags. Such a secret place to have on the edge of a city. A million or more years ago and the very place where they all lived and worked, Macfie had told him, had once been inside the volcano from which the whole city, with its fine castle, owed its being.

Faro found such information difficult to imagine – an erupting volcano where, on grassy, heathery slopes, sheep grazed and the occasional deer might be glimpsed, and where Edinburgh folk exercised horses and walked dogs and children played. He thought of what lay beneath the surface in those dark and secret caves.

A group of boys had once found ten miniature coffins, wee dressed dolls inside each one, a weird discovery that had no doubt thrown a cloud over laughter and childish games. To this day no one had ever discovered the identity of the coffins, or for what strange and sinister ritual they had been buried there. A mystery worthy of any lad deciding to become a policeman.

His road lay direct ahead, but at the Pleasance on impulse he returned to the murder scene at Fleshers Close. Even on a day that threatened sunshine and fresh air, he shuddered away from the filth and decay that marked the area, wondering whether he might see the woman who had taken charge of the little girl.

And then he had a stroke of luck; she was walking towards him, a basket over her arm, a trail of small children at her heel, the wee girl he remembered holding tightly to her hand.

He had to stand aside to let them pass and raised his hat. She nodded, looked him over, seeing him as a toff, a stranger to this area of the city. Without uniform and the forbidding helmet that had concealed the upper part of his face, she obviously did not recognise him again as one of the policemen and he had to think of an excuse to delay her, ask her some questions.

He stammered out that they had met before. She frowned, shook her head, but there was a gleam of hope in her glance. Was there perhaps a coin or two in this meeting? He explained that he had called the other day, that he was concerned about the woman who was killed.

'Was she a friend of yours?' he asked.

A cautious glance. 'Who wants to know?'

'Friends,' he said non-committally. She nodded and held out a grubby hand. An unmistakable gesture indicating information available but to be paid for.

He handed her a coin. 'Tell me about her, if you please?' He smiled down at the little girl and said: 'Hello!' In return she gave him a terrified glance, hiding her face in the woman's skirts. 'Is that her daughter?'

'Saw them once or twice together – down here, looking for business. Not from these parts. Had a word, gave her a bite to eat one day, the bairn was weary of walking. Came from over yonder.' She pointed in the vague direction of Leith. Her voice was getting slower, thoughtful. 'Came to meet someone who hadn't turned up.'

Here was hope indeed, but before he could ask any further questions he was aware of her candid glance, looking him over carefully, and she said sharply, 'Is it the bairn you're after? It'll cost you more than a few coins, mister – she's only six years old.'

Faro stepped back, shocked as the enormity of her proposition dawned upon him. Had she assumed he was one of the dealers in child prostitution? He tried to keep his voice calm as he replied: 'You are mistaken. I am only interested in what happened to the child's mother. When they found her, had you heard anything, any disturbance, any commotion during the night?'

The woman frowned. 'A carriage nearby in the early hours, night. Like drunks – young toffs larking. It was dark. Next thing I heard was them polis rattles.' She stopped and shook her head, remembering. 'Polis crawling all over the place, up and down the stairs, knocking on doors. asking questions. Came down to see what it was about.' She paused, sighed. 'And there she was lying there dead, before they took her away.'

She looked at the little girl still clinging to her.

'Didna' want them putting her in the workhouse, fine strong, healthy wee bairn like that. So I took her in.' A hopeful glance at him. 'D'ye ken anyone who might want a wee lass? She's very clean and a good worker.'

Six years old, Faro thought, maybe too young for a year or two for the child dealers to be interested. As for the workhouse, factory owners were known to seek out youngsters for cheap labour. He said: 'Can you keep her? She's better off with you.'

The woman thought about that. A moment's indecision, then she shrugged. 'Ah well, she'll be a help with the washings meantime,' she added, clearly disappointed at the breakdown of what had seemed a promising financial negotiation. 'Till something else turns up.'

'Thank you.' Faro handed her another coin. He realised he could go no further. All he had learnt was the possibility that the dead woman had been strangled first and then thrown out of a carriage at Fleshers Close.

As for the little girl, sadly he could do nothing for her facing years of slavery to the woman with six children, who made a living as a washerwoman. When she was older, with luck, she would find work as a servant.

And that made him think of Lizzie. Had he

come in by the direct south-side route he would have walked past the gates of Lumbleigh Green. He wasn't due to see her tonight and, in a way, he was relieved. There was too much tension between them just now. Questions asked and unanswered hovered in their relationship, and guiltily he was aware of his own reluctance to make the move that would solve all Lizzie's problems.

Marriage . . .

CHAPTER SIX

At that moment Lizzie was dealing with some of those problems and would have welcomed his advice. Ida Watt's mother had arrived at the tradesman's entrance of Lumbleigh Green in a frightful state.

By chance, the door was answered by Lizzie who was in the kitchen alone. She had never met the girl's mother and was taken aback by the angry demand:

'Where is our Ida? I want to see her – right now.'

Concerned by the tearful woman obviously in great distress, and as Mrs Brown was busy in another part of the house, Lizzie asked her in and seated her down at the table where she looked around as if hoping to see her daughter walk in.

'Where's Lizzie? I want to talk to her.'

Lizzie smiled. 'That's me.'

Mrs Watts sighed and took her hand. 'Thank God. I came looking for you, 'cos you're her friend and you'll be able to tell me' – her voice trembled – 'where's she gone.'

Lizzie was uncomfortably aware of Ida's secret, confided in her. She shook her head. What could she say, by way of evading the truth, with some sort of comfort and reassurance?

'Don't pretend you don't know. Thick as thieves she said you are. Well, it was her birthday – you knew that, of course.'

Lizzie didn't. Mrs Watts sat there wringing her hands. 'I made a cake and everything. She never came. Let me down and her cousins and everyone. It's not like her, she's never caused any of us a minute's worry before. Maybe it's different now, doesn't care about us any more if she's away off with this rich lad she's so daft about.' Sighing, she went on pathetically: 'Ashamed of her family, us being poor farming folk. But poor or no, her da will take a stick to her backside, that's for sure.'

Lizzie, bewildered, shook her head. She could think of no reply. Obviously the story Ida had told her mother was a somewhat idealised version of the fact that they were far from 'thick as thieves'. In truth, they were nothing more than working colleagues and now, for the first time, Lizzie was infected with Mrs Watts' feelings of panic.

All she could say was, 'I'll tell Ida you came and you're worried about her.'

'And you'll let us know. Here's where we live.' She scribbled down an address in Bonnyrigg.

Lizzie promised to do so and watched the girl's mother depart, feeling she had offered little in the way of reassurance as she went upstairs with Clara's morning chocolate and had to apologise for the delay.

Where was Ida? Had something happened to her? She had to tell her mistress, who wasn't particularly upset, worried or even interested in the table maid's fate. She could think only of Ida's continued absence as merely an inconvenience.

Pursing her lips, Clara said sternly: 'Please don't worry yourself, Laurie. Doubtless she will turn up, and when she does decide to put in an appearance again, I'm afraid it will only be to be dismissed by the master. He has already decided she was unreliable on many accounts and this, I fear, will be the final tax on his patience.'

Lizzie did not sleep much that night, troubled by scaring dreams about the missing girl and how Ida had sworn her to secrecy about this wealthy, handsome young fellow she said was going to marry her.

'We're going to elope, we've got to, now I'm pregnant,' she had crowed. So if she had gone off with this lad she was so daft about, as her mother described him, who was he, anyway? And Lizzie kept wondering where she had found the opportunity to meet him, seeing that she had little leisure life away from work and her visits home to her parents. It was all very mysterious, and not sending them a note saying she had eloped, well, that was a bit scary and sinister too.

Surely, as such a devoted daughter she would have tried not to let them worry, especially as it was her birthday, a family celebration – something else she had never told Lizzie.

When dawn broke next morning she had made up her mind. If Ida was missing, perhaps some accident had befallen her on her way to meet her secret lover. Well, there was only one person who could help find her. And that was Detective Constable Jeremy Faro.

And telling him couldn't wait until their next meeting. How to get an urgent message to him? Leave a note at his lodgings? But she wasn't absolutely sure about that, afraid of facing Mrs Biggs, the formidable landlady she had heard about. With a despairing sigh, she realised the only correct thing to do in the present circumstances was to go to the police, so she decided to venture through the sacred portals of the Central Office and report a missing person. Hopefully she might even see Jeremy when she was there.

Only it didn't work out like that. She lost her nerve, surrounded by the imposing and intimidating atmosphere. The constable at the desk studied her with interest. A look she was used to men giving her these days, which she failed to interpret as a man's natural interest aroused by the appearance of an exceptionally attractive young woman.

He smiled. 'Well, miss, and what can I do for you?'

She explained about Ida, and producing a notebook and pencil, the constable asked if she was her next of kin.

'No, we are friends. We work together.' As the constable frowned, Lizzie said: 'Her mother would have come but she was too poorly to make the journey from Bonnyrigg.' That was a lie, but she decided it was a forgivable one in such anxious circumstances.

The young constable considered her thoughtfully. Was this a case for serious investigation? A couple of days. Sounded as if it might be a panic and she'd walk in tomorrow.

But mothers were like that, always harping on about nothing. So the lass had run away – lots of them did and very few left notes saying where they had gone. If it wasn't a fellow the parents didn't approve of, it was likely to find another situation, because maids soon got fed up with the present one and were eager to better themselves with the lure of a bit of extra money. Often they headed for factories where the hours were long and references weren't demanded.

While the constable hesitated, Lizzie said, 'I thought the police should be told.'

At the sound of footsteps approaching, she looked around hopefully, but this was a strange policeman, not the one she wanted to see.

The constable saluted the newcomer gravely and indicated Lizzie. 'Missing persons enquiry, sir.'

McIvor looked at Lizzie and shrugged. He was in a hurry. 'Get her to sign an official statement, then.'

Watching her write, a neat hand too, the constable wondered why her appearance seemed oddly familiar. Thanking her, he smiled at her anxious expression, and promised to hand it to the proper authorities immediately. As she walked away he remembered where he had seen that pretty face, the bright eyes and yellow curls before. Out walking with DC Faro in Princes Street Gardens. A stunner, he whistled, even if she was a widow with a young lad in tow.

Lizzie had missed Jeremy by a mere ten minutes. When he approached the desk, Constable Ryan whispered slyly: 'Your young lady has just called.'

'What did she want?' And the constable made a mental note that Faro looked startled and embarrassed. What on earth could have made Lizzie come to the Central Office? Only some dire emergency would have led her to try to contact him at work, he thought nervously.

Ryan shrugged. 'Worried about one of her friends who has gone missing. Apparently the lass's ma is demented about it, but wasn't well enough to come herself . . .'

Faro was only half-listening, looking towards the door. Gosse would be arriving any moment and he had no desire for the sergeant to know that his detective constable's 'young lady', as he called her, had been tracking him down at work in the Central Office.

Ryan said: 'I had her sign an official statement . . .'

Faro held out a hand, and the constable grinned and shook his head, looking wary, as

Faro said impatiently, 'I will see it gets to the right department.'

He took it into the office he shared with Gosse and began reading Lizzie's neat handwriting. All this fuss about an unreliable maid, he thought. He hadn't realised that Ida was such a friend either. Perhaps that was just to help the girl's frantic mother, typical of Lizzie too, always willing to carry other folks' burdens as if her own weren't enough.

The bit about the birthday party did seem strange. Such a devoted daughter, according to her mother – surely she would have let her parents know, spared their anxiety.

Gosse had come in. 'Any progress on Liberton Brae?'

Faro told him about the visit, the search for Jock Webb. Gosse sighed, clearly disappointed, reluctant to have to admit that it now seemed unlikely that the ex-boxer was the killer they were looking for.

'There is still the business of that playing card in his pocket, like the one under the woman's body in Fleshers Close, sir,' Faro reminded him.

Gosse gave a snort of disbelief. 'You're making too much of that, Faro. Letting it throw you off the scent. A coincidence, that's all – disregard it . . .'

Faro's silence indicated acceptance. However, he would continue to keep it well in mind until some explanations of how the cards came to be there were forthcoming.

Gosse was saying: 'From the evidence so far, Webb is still our main suspect. After all, remember what that doctor said and that false address. All a pack of lies,' he added firmly.

'Not deliberately, sir,' said Faro desperately. 'His memory seemed to be a bit confused.'

Gosse tapped his nose in that familiar gesture. 'Cunning, Faro, cunning, that's what it is.' And he repeated once more his favourite warning. 'Wait until you've been on the force as long as I have. You'll soon learn there's no trick they won't get up to. Have to be sharp and on your guard, all the time – never miss a trick.'

Faro knew there was no point in arguing and said: 'On my way back I looked in at Fleshers Close, met the woman who appeared when we were leaving. She took the wee girl,' he reminded him. 'I asked her if she had heard anything that night before the body was discovered. She mentioned a carriage, some commotion outside in the early hours.'

'Sounds as if the woman was murdered and dumped there afterwards. You did well, Faro,' he added with unaccustomed praise. 'Ryan tells me you have an official report of a missing person for me.'

Faro pointed to the desk. 'Went missing at the weekend. Family are worried.'

'Just a couple of days ago, no cause for concern.' Gosse sighed wearily. 'She'll turn up. If we tackled every case like this we'd get nothing else done, like tracking down murderers.' And pointing to papers on the desk, he added: 'We've had plenty overnight to keep us busy. Look at those. Three burglaries in the New Town, reports of poachers busy on the south side, domestic fights in Leith – that's not news – except that the wife is in the Infirmary.' Pausing he shook his head. 'Four pickpockets arrested. Must be the full moon got to them.'

'Maybe they are just taking advantage of the extra moonlight nature has obligingly provided, sir.'

'Apart from your fanciful interpretations, Faro, the main thing that concerns us is that there has been another woman murdered. See for yourself.' Ushering him in the direction of the mortuary, Gosse said grimly, 'Lass that jumped off the North Bridge. She was killed first and her body thrown off the bridge, no doubt about that.' Gosse shook his head. 'According to Dr Grace, no evidence of pregnancy this time.'

Faro thought with compassion how frequently that was the cause of suicides with young unmarried girls, betrayed by lovers who were mostly married men. Many unfortunate women, too poor to afford more than a few coins, died under the backstreet abortionist's crude knife; others took their own lives, unable or unwilling to face a future with the burden of an illegitimate child. Lizzie had been one of the brave ones, an exception.

Gosse said: 'This was no suicide. She was strangled. Nothing on the body to identify her, clothes suggested working class, servant maybe.'

Faro felt a chill of dread as he followed Gosse. Sheeted, on a trestle, a young girl who might well be the missing Ida.

'Any identification?'

Gosse shook his head. 'Not as yet, I gather.'

Dr Grace, the police surgeon, had heard them. He came over.

'We have some information. Your colleagues always search the spot for possessions after removing the body. In the fall they can be scattered in a wide surrounding area. Well, they found in a clump of bushes, a reticule. It contained a note to her parents, letting them know she would be in Gretna Green getting married.'

With sinking heart, Faro asked: 'Was the name Watts?'

Gosse's eyes widened. 'How the devil do you know that?' In answer, Faro pointed to the missing persons report. 'I don't think you need to read this, Sergeant. We know who she was, poor lass.'

Gosse took the paper to the light, read it, and picked up the list the police surgeon had brought in.

He swore under his breath. 'There's something else, Faro, for your interest,' he added grudgingly. 'Among other things in that damned reticule, a playing card. We could say she had been a gambler and lost—'

'Was it the nine of diamonds, sir?'

'Yes,' said Gosse shortly and glanced towards the sheeted figure. 'Our killer's third victim. And as there was no evidence of pregnancy, maybe he killed her for the wrong reason.'

Laying the report aside he turned to the official missing persons statement, and reading the signature he said: 'This Lizzie Laurie, describes herself as a servant. At Lumbleigh Green.'

He had no reason to connect her with his detective constable's 'young lady' but Faro's heart sank, expecting trouble as the sergeant's eyes brightened with sudden hope.

'We'd better head there right away. I suspect that's where we'll find our answers – and our killer too.'

And Faro's scalp crawled, a familiar instinct of foreboding, as he followed Gosse out of the Central Office and headed down the High Street on their way to yet another murder investigation.

CHAPTER SEVEN

As they made towards the handsome mansions bordering Dalkeith Road, Faro and Gosse were glumly silent. Both guessed what lay in store, that their presence would be ill received by the owner, indignant because a maid in his employ, who he didn't even know and wouldn't recognise, had been murdered.

Lumbleigh Green presented a scene of perfect tranquility and affluence behind its closed gates. The sun shone down benignly on Arthur's Seat, touching impressive gardens with well-tended flowerbeds and immaculate lawns bordered by respectfully disciplined shrubs. Splendid trees provided shady corners, many already ancient in the woodland that predated the mansion's building; they had watched as their less fortunate neighbours were cut down to make way for landscaped gardens. Those favoured enough to remain had regained their composure and even a certain dignity of age, their leafy tops moving gently in the breeze, their branches home to sweet-singing thrushes and a variety of chirruping garden birds.

The shadows of two uniformed policemen crossing the lawn viewed from the windows also cast shadows over the occupants of this pleasant suburban tower, raising doubts and a certain amount of dread, since everyone under the handsome roof with its turrets and crow-stepped gables had reason for disquiet at the approach of these guardians of the law.

In his study, Archie Lumbleigh sat at his wide mahogany desk, where the sight of helmeted policemen aroused unpleasant memories of a long-past interview with their Glasgow equivalents and a very unsavoury court case to be settled before he sought refuge and a new life in Edinburgh.

An unfortunate and murky interlude in his career, his business partner had shot himself after making it public that Lumbleigh had robbed him, leaving him and his family penniless. He had lost everything, including his shares in the company, through Archie, a notorious gambler, cheating at a game of cards. His only son had had to quit university, where he had a promising future, and go to work on the canal in order to look after his widowed ailing mother, who died a year later – some said of a broken heart.

Archie meanwhile soared into a fortune. A few successful shrewd and lucky ventures and his future was made. The tragic fact that his partner's money brought him these ill-gotten riches, he firmly put out of his mind. But that now distant court case, the police enquiries, and even the rumour that his partner's death was not a straightforward suicide, that Archie had been present and even helped to support the gun at his head, occasionally revived memories that brought him out in a cold sweat at the sight of two grim-faced policemen walking purposefully towards him.

He had another reason for disquiet. The business of his first wife, his stepson Paul's mother, Alice, refused to lie quietly buried in the past. She had been a widow and he had treated her badly, marrying her for her money which was considerable. Since she already had a son, he hoped she would provide him with heirs. But it was not to be.

The years passed and as there were to be no

children, disappointment led to bitterness and blame. He despised this plain woman and sought pleasure in high-class brothels the length and breadth of Edinburgh. Mavis Rayne, the madam in York Square, had become a particular friend over the years, almost a confidante.

Alice had known about Mavis and, loving him more than he deserved, was so unhappy that she tried to take her own life, providing her faithless, heartless husband with just such an opportunity he had never dreamt would come his way: to get rid of a wife he no longer wanted. What a piece of luck, especially as wealth had bought him a young and beautiful mistress he was eager to install in his handsome home as the second Mrs Lumbleigh. He presumed that his efforts to conceal Mavis's existence – not out of any shame but to avoid possible disruptions in the smooth running of his personal life – had succeeded.

Attempted suicide was a crime that played into Archie's greedy hands. He had doctors called, Alice certified as insane and she was locked away in a private asylum. Mercifully, on all accounts, she did not long survive and he had done his best to raise her son Paul as his own. But the lad showed no gratitude for his fine education, and now grown up he solidly blamed Archie for his beloved mother's death. Sometimes looking across the length of the dining-room table, Archie caught the boy's eye and saw anger and hatred there which included his new and lovely young stepmother.

Paul was unimpressed by Clara's eagerness to have him love her and to take the place of his mother. There was only ten years between them, and he treated her with a cold politeness that verged on insolence.

Looking out of the window, Archie sighed. At least his lovely Clara had no reason for concern as, frowning, she turned and asked him: 'I wonder what they want; perhaps a donation to one of their charities.'

If only it had been that simple. Had Archie been permitted to see beyond that lovely face framed in dark curls, and into the brain with its thoughts that surged like dark waters beneath, he would have seen another version. A strange, terrified woman he had never met and would hardly have recognised.

That other Clara, born Ethel Wyner, was the child of a millworker and an office clerk whose goal in life was to gain the lower rungs of the local social ladder. He worked himself into heart failure trying to make a fortune. Her mother had kept her good looks (Clara's sole inheritance) and took as her second husband a man who was the exact opposite of her first. Jabez Bodvale was a great strong brute of a man, manager of the site labourers on the new railway line.

The marriage was very soon a disaster for both Clara and her mother. Bodvale had no intentions of being faithful, marrying Honor believing that her late husband was a toff and she might have come into a bit of money he was eager to lay hands on. Sentimental only when drunk, he tried to win sympathy for the misfortunes of his early life, but she wasn't interested, never listened. He soon realised she was a disappointment and he sought other women of his own kind.

But the main target of his lewd desires was her little twelve-year-old daughter, Clara. Her mother never knew, nor would have believed, much less understood, what was going on in that bedroom when he went to kiss his 'wee girl', as he called her, goodnight and tell her a story. And Clara had no means of finding the right words to confide in her mother any detail of his secret midnight visits. Sometimes she was too disgusted to think about them in the bright light of day. But mostly she was too terrified, for he had sworn that if she ever breathed a word, he would kill not only her but her mother too.

'Both of you, don't forget that!'

But as she matured into womanhood and

showed signs of becoming a great beauty, Jabez was obsessed by her. When her mother Honor died of cancer, Clara was fourteen, trapped in the house with him, living a nightmare with this great brute whose only sign of tenderness was to swear that she must never leave him. Every bit of her was his alone and he swore that he loved her above all living things on God's earth. There wasn't anything he wouldn't do to keep her at his side for ever.

There was no escape. She ran away several times but he followed her, dragged her back to her prison and locked her in. Then one day the police arrived, two uniformed constables, like the ones crossing the lawn beyond the windows of Lumbleigh Green at that moment. Bodvale was one of a notorious gang of robbers, long sought by the police. One of them had been taken and promptly turned Queen's evidence.

He was going to jail. It was a miracle for Clara. Her prayers answered, her wildest dreams come true. The policemen come to take Bodvale prisoner were transformed into angels of mercy.

She was free at last. Oh, how her heart rejoiced, she could have danced for joy! She even laughed at his last words as, handcuffed, he struggled and swore and tried to get back to her.

'You're not free of me, lass. You're mine,

always have been and always will be. Never forget that. I'll find you. As long as we both live, I'll track you down. No one else will have you. I'll kill you first.'

Clara didn't mind, didn't believe for a moment that could happen. She was safe at last. He was going to be transported away to the colonies. Vast oceans, continents between them. And then one day she read that during a fire in the prison, cells had been opened and he had escaped. Her dream of freedom was over; her nightmares and his last words haunting her, she lived in dread from that day forward.

She had left Inverness and headed south to Glasgow. Taking a new name and always with a good singing voice combined with outstanding good looks, it had taken little effort to get a job entertaining gentlemen in dubious clubs.

One day her fortune smiled on her. In a Glasgow vaudeville theatre, Archie saw her on stage singing and flashing her lovely legs, and all Archie knew was that he was a wealthy man who could afford beautiful things – lovely possessions made him feel protected, his money building a barrier between him and his unfortunate past.

And Clara was a beautiful possession, like that precious Chinese vase bought at auction, to add to the collection he was surrounding himself with. And he wanted her there among them, to admire every day. Perhaps slightly flawed inside, but no one would ever notice, he least of all. Infatuated, he didn't really want to know about the life she had reinvented for herself and passed on to him. He never knew about Bodvale. Clara hoped that he was dead long ago, but she could not be certain. She still expected him to appear like he did sometimes in occasional but terrifying nightmares.

Archie she believed provided security; she would be safe married to him, a rock to lean on. Although she did not love him, trembling she remembered the huge gross beast, strong and mighty, and sex with any man after Bodvale was bearable. Bodvale could have crushed her husband between his two hands.

But there was one flaw in this domestic bliss, so perfect on the surface: Paul Lumbleigh, for Archie had insisted that in the lack of an heir, his stepson should have his name. Now everyone, it seemed, loved Clara, except Paul who had so far resisted all her attempts to win him over. All she ever received was a look of cold hostility. Hatred, actually, if she had allowed herself to consider such emotion.

She knew his hatred ran deep, and although Archie tried to pretend otherwise, her shrewd guess was Paul hated both of them. And with good reason, when she had become Archie's latest mistress while his own mother lay dying in the insane asylum. He had reason for bitterness, when they had been counting the days to Alice's demise and as far as he was concerned, had murdered her.

Clara told herself that everyone had secrets. Even Archie, she knew, had quite a few – boredom had led her to indulge her insatiable curiosity and find out about his past business negotiations, his foes and friends and his long-term mistress Mavis, who had a nice house in the New Town, which, Clara concluded, was also a high-class brothel. Although there was no possibility Archie could find out about her safely buried past, knowing about Mavis gave her a sense of power, a trump card to play if her security was threatened and the rock on which she leant threatened to crumble . . .

She cradled her secret. Nobody ever told it all, but she sometimes yearned for a friend to confide in. A girl like her lady's maid, gently smiling Lizzie Laurie from her own class, who did her hair so well, who would understand and not condemn.

And in the kitchen, too, there was disquiet and anxiety. For Betty the kitchen maid, who no one ever noticed except Mrs Brown to slap her and issue orders, always nervous and expecting the worst from life, the sight of two policemen advancing so purposefully towards the house made her feel all trembly and faint.

Her voice a frightened whisper, she asked Mrs Brown: 'What do they want?'

The grim reply: 'You'll soon find out,' had her reeling away from the window sick with terror. She had been found out.

For Betty was a thief; in the sight of God she had broken the commandment 'Thou shalt not steal'. Maybe it was too elaborate a term for helping herself to a bit of leftover salmon, or some nice food from the pantry after Mrs Brown went home. After all, it was for her ailing mother to help out their meagre diet, and she told herself it would never be missed – it was going off and would be thrown out next day. But the housekeeper had an eagle eye. Her last foray, a nice piece of lamb and a few sausages, had been only last week. Had Mrs Brown told on her and were the police here to arrest her?

What was the punishment for stealing food – was it transportation? Betty leant against the kitchen sink for support. She was going to be sick. However, she was surprised and so relieved when, a little later, the two policemen showed little interest in her beyond asking her name and how long she had been at Lumbleigh Green.

It was Ida they were interested in.

Was she a friend of hers?

No.

Had she any reason to believe Ida would take her own life?

Definitely no, was the answer. She didn't add that Ida, only interested in men, never exchanged a word with her if it could be avoided. To Ida, as to everyone else under this roof, she was invisible.

Later, interviewed by Gosse, he dismissed her, saying that he might need to have a look at her room later. That threw her into a flutter of panic, destroying the brief consolation that she wasn't the one he was looking for, because Betty sometimes kept a secret hoard of stolen food in her room.

CHAPTER EIGHT

Murder investigations were normally in the charge of detective inspectors, but Stan Wade, at a wedding in Inverness, had the misfortune to fall and break a leg.

Drunk as usual, was the cynical observation among the constables. McIvor had informed Gosse that he was to take over Wade's duties until other arrangements could be made, depending on how long Wade was expected to be absent. And Gosse was aware that for an inspector this was likely to be for some time, since a broken leg was an impossible impediment to all the footwork needed.

Expressing the usual comments of concern about his senior officer, Gosse was, in truth, delighted at this unexpected temporary promotion. He and DC Faro headed through the ornate gates of Lumbleigh Green and across the bordered lawns where steps guarded by two stone lions led up to the handsome front door, opened after a short interval by Mrs Brown.

They showed their cards, which the housekeeper eyed narrowly, then, in the manner expected of her, told them to wait in the hall while she would enquire if the master was at home to receive them.

This was Faro's first occasion to set foot inside the mansion, its splendours related in awed whispers from Lizzie. Expecting a kind of Ali Baba's cave of wondrous luxuries, he was a little disappointed in the reality. He had not been in many big Edinburgh mansions and found this one quite extraordinary. A lot of large rather ugly china vases and ornaments, chosen for size to fill empty spaces, rather than for quality, were overlooked by walls of gloomy pictures. In the absence of ancestral portraits, they were of horses, dogs and dark, forbidding Highland landscapes.

At his side, Gosse scowled. He did not care to be kept waiting and signalling to Faro he marched boldly in the direction of the door in which he had seen a maid disappear.

'Might as well save time and start with the

kitchen, see what the servants have to say. You can interview Lumbleigh.'

Faro was somewhat taken aback by this move but Gosse was well aware that, in the class they were dealing with, Lumbleigh would be unable to recall having exchanged more than half a dozen words with this Ida, who had had the audacity to commit suicide. That was bad enough, but to be murdered and thereby involve a grand house in an exclusive area of Edinburgh and a highly respected family in sordid police enquiries was beyond the pale.

Lumbleigh made these objections, addressed from behind the mahogany desk, clear from the outset. The tiger skin rug on the floor eyed Faro more kindly than its owner.

Faro took out his notebook. 'I have to ask you, sir, if you were at home on Friday evening.'

'Am I hearing you correctly, Constable? Are you having the temerity to ask me for an alibi for a maid's disappearance?'

'This is a purely routine matter, sir,' Faro said politely. Himself a mere constable, it was up to DS Gosse to further enlighten Lumbleigh that this was not merely suicide but murder, as he continued:

'This is outrageous, Constable, an intrusion into my private affairs.' And shaking a fist in the direction of Faro's face, he added: 'Let me tell you, I have some influence in this city and I shall complain to my Member of Parliament . . .'

Archie Lumbleigh continued to express his anger in no uncertain terms at the idea that all the occupants under his roof were to be interviewed, their movements over the weekend queried and pried into. His face grew redder and redder, his grievances accompanied by the thumping of his fists on the table. At last, realising that the young constable standing there, notebook in hand, was quite unmoved by this tirade, with a snort of exasperation he sat back in the armchair.

'I was at home all evening and my wife will confirm that,' he said coldly. Breathing a sigh of relief that his visit to Mavis had been during the afternoon, he added: 'I won't waste your time and mine by mincing words with you, Constable. The unfortunate girl was a servant here. Of course I did not know her. We are not on intimate terms with employees, they are expected to serve and not be seen.'

Archie had heard approvingly of servants in Balmoral Castle ducking out of sight as Her Majesty approached. An excellent idea and one he was keen to imitate.

The door opened to admit Gosse, who, bearing

a fragrance of tobacco smoke, introduced himself rather grandly to Archie.

'Detective sergeant, did you say?' Was Lumbleigh Green not worthy of the attentions of a chief inspector? And Archie looked him over, a glance that suggested Gosse might have been something he picked up on his boot while walking in the garden.

Gosse explained the circumstances of Detective Inspector Wade's non-appearance, that he was at present in hospital with a broken leg.

'Indeed, I am sorry to hear that.' But Archie's expression told a different story. 'I will have to take this matter up with my friend who is the chief constable, and I am also on excellent terms with the Lord Lieutenant.' He paused: 'Well, man, get on with it.'

Gosse's face was a study. Not only had he received a mere shrug on arrival instead of an expected handshake, but neither was the offer of a chair forthcoming. Seething inwardly he took his place at Faro's side and said:

'It's about this young woman who went missing, sir.'

The presence of uniformed policemen in his study still made Archie uneasy but at least the interview promised to be brief if boring. And all the fault of that damned lady's maid of Clara's, having instigated a missing persons enquiry the police had been forced to follow up.

'Well, get on with it,' he repeated shortly.

'This young woman, Ida Watts, was believed to have committed suicide, but we now have reason to suspect foul play.'

'Foul play . . . you mean . . . murder?' Archie gulped.

'Yes, sir, that's about it.'

Archie sat back in his comfortable chair. Suicide was bad enough, a shadow on his house's reputation. But murder! His groan, mistaken by sensitive folk for sympathy and shock, was altogether different. In his mind's eye he was already seeing the news-sheet's large black letters 'Murder at Lumbleigh Green'.

'This is intolerable, intolerable.'

Clara Lumbleigh, curiosity aroused, had entered the room during her husband's outburst of indignation, and her presence briefly acknowledged, now lingered by the window with her back to them, intently studying the garden. She gasped.

'How dreadful – dreadful!' And she exchanged a tearful look with her husband. 'She came with good references. That was all we knew about her—'

'And was all that was required to know

about her,' Archie interrupted impatiently. 'Servants are here to obey orders and wait upon us; further communication or details of their personal backgrounds are of no possible interest to us.' Servant girls were normally recruited from the workhouse – always eager to get rid of another orphan, they were apt to exaggerate when a reference was demanded. Ida Watts, he was to learn with regret, had been taken on by Mrs Brown in an emergency and had stayed.

Archie was furious at the kind of publicity he could expect when this sordid story hit the newspapers' readers, always eager to throw aspersions on their betters, those they envied – the decent well-off members of Edinburgh society who had earned the right to elegant homes. Lumbleigh Green, so cherished, would be for ever tarnished. Suicide was bad enough, but to have been brutally murdered meant problems employing local girls, cautioned by gloomy parents against setting foot in that 'murder house'.

Later, moaning to Clara, Archie was hurt by her reaction. He thought that as his wife she should support his views, appreciate their predicament, and all her sympathy should lie with the disturbance to her husband's comfortable existence rather than with a maid whose unfortunate end had caused everyone such inconvenience.

As for that damned Lizzie Laurie. Only Clara's tears stopped Archie dismissing her on the spot as he said angrily:

'I cannot help you. What do I know of this girl? I do not talk to the maids but I expect she wore a white cap and apron, a dark dress.' His shrug was an expansive gesture. 'All maids look alike to me.'

Gosse hoped for more success with Mrs Lumbleigh. He addressed her politely, and turning reluctantly from her intense study of the garden, she said wearily: 'I gave her instructions as we have no butler, but that was the limit of our communications.' As she spoke she looked at her husband and as if for his approval she added: 'I'm afraid I would never recognise her either, without her uniform.'

At least, Faro noted, she wore an expression of concern.

Gosse was bidding good day to Archie with a civility he was far from feeling. He nodded to Faro and headed to the kitchen, their entrance to be greeted by an outraged housekeeper. How had he dared to interrupt the master? But Gosse cut her off by saying that time was short and as the enquiry concerned servants, he had every right to do so.

Answering his questions, Matilda Brown looked him straight in the eye, answered him firmly and had no information to add to his enquiries regarding Ida Watts, her manner indicating that this unwholesome business was a sheer waste of her own, as well as the master's, precious time.

Faro decided the housekeeper was so ordinary that without the routine identity particulars, it would have been difficult even to guess her age – she could have been anything from thirty to fifty.

'You are not from this area?'

She thought about that for a moment before replying: 'I left my folks' farm in Angus when I met my husband.'

As he so often did, Faro found his thoughts wandering on a number of lines: how cautious even the innocent were when replying to police questioning, the impossibility of imagining Mrs Brown as a radiant bride and the equal inability to picture what had she been like as a child.

'Lizzie Laurie?' Gosse was asking her.

'Mrs Lumbleigh's maid. You will find her upstairs in the mistress's room.'

Faro did not relish the embarrassment of having to interview Lizzie, and hoping that task would fall to Gosse, was considerably relieved when the sergeant sent him out to seek the remaining servant, the coachman Brown, muttering, 'I doubt you'll get anything useful there. It's just a matter of course.'

As Faro approached the Browns' cottage Vince was standing at the window. He sighed. This was their first meeting since Lizzie had moved into the big house. Greeting him, Faro made an effort to sound friendly, despite Vince's stony expression. Asked how he liked his new lodging, the boy merely shrugged.

'It must be a very pleasant change living away from the city, almost in the country, like this. Lots of interesting places to explore on the hill out there,' Faro continued enthusiastically, determined to be agreeable and ignoring another indifferent shrug. In the face of such hostility, he had to give up and asked: 'Mr Brown?'

'He's not here. Probably in the garden somewhere.'

There was nothing more to say. An awkward moment's silence, then Faro walked away wishing for Lizzie's sake that he could get through to Vince. She little knew that Jeremy Faro saw her young son as the main impediment to the possibility of marrying her.

Vince watched the detective constable walk away. Everyone asked him how he liked living here. It was no big deal. Asked the same question constantly by his mother, who was anxious to know if he was comfortable in the Browns' little cottage and if they were kind to him, his attitude had been identical to his reply to Faro: a shrug of indifference.

'It's as if I didn't exist, Ma, like I was invisible. They never notice me, or even speak to me, except to nod towards the table that food is ready, when they have to feed me.'

'Do they give you enough to eat?' Lizzie asked anxiously, her first concern for a young growing lad.

He laughed. 'Oh yes, there's always plenty of food on the table. Don't worry, Mrs Brown sees to that! But a dozen words is what I could count since they took me in.' He shook his head. 'I feel like an intruder. They had to take me because the mistress's said so. They're not used to children, expect it's not having any of their own.'

'Perhaps they're grown up and away.'

'I don't think so, Ma.' Vince shook his head solemnly. 'There are no family photographs.'

The fashion instigated by the Queen had been eagerly adopted, taking over from daguerreotypes or painted miniatures for the rich, the explanation Lizzie gave to Vince when he asked what his father had looked like: poor folk knew no such luxuries.

* * *

105

But the coachman had been a soldier, a veteran of Indian wars. 'Guess what this is, Ma,' and Vince showed her a medal in a silver frame, proudly displayed on the kitchen sideboard. 'It's for bravery. But he never talks about it.'

Lizzie found that version of the inarticulate coachman, always muffled up to the ears against the cold, unsmiling and mumbling his way through life, hard to imagine, but Faro could have told them both that many veterans of the Indian wars were like that. Brown should have confirmed that a soldier's bitter experiences and cruel memories had perhaps brought about that unsociable state of mind. Had they enquired further they would have discovered that it was, in fact, his brave record as well as good references that had made Archie take him on. Never having been on active service fighting for his Queen and country himself, having better things to do at home, it gave Archie a feeling of patriotism, that he would be regarded in a good light by his business associates as well as his well-to-do friends for having helped an old soldier to a settled future.

As for Gosse, he had had enough of Lumbleigh Green. He withdrew and absented himself on pretence of a sharp look outside, an excuse for smoking his pipe. What clues he expected to find were a mystery to Faro.

Lizzie had not heard from Faro since she left the report on Ida's disappearance at the Central Office. Sent to find her, Mrs Brown reported that she was not in the mistress's room. She wasn't in the kitchen either, and looking out of the window, Faro spotted her in the garden, hurrying across the lawn.

He went outside. With a sigh of relief she ran to his side.

'I must talk to you, Jeremy. This is awful, awful.'

Murder was awful. Faro nodded absently and she put an imploring hand on his arm. 'Jeremy, you must promise not to ask anything about me coming into the police station – about Ida being missing.'

'What on earth for? It was the correct thing to do. Besides, it's too late for that now—'

'I know,' Lizzie interrupted. 'But I've decided. I'm going to say I hardly know her.'

Faro gave her a stern look. 'I can't do that, Lizzie. It's my job.'

'And it's my job too. I had to tell the mistress that I came and told the police after Ida's mother came here in such a state. The master had to be told and he was beside himself, in such a rage as never was. Bringing disgrace on this house. Mrs Lumbleigh saved me, spoke up and insisted that I was to stay, that I was her servant and she couldn't allow him to punish me for what I thought was right, bringing a missing person to the attention of the police. Missing. How he laughed at that, just away having a good time, he said. Oh Jeremy, it's so awful, no one cares that poor Ida has disappeared.'

'It's worse than that, Lizzie,' he said grimly. There was no way of sparing her. 'I'm afraid Ida is dead – and it wasn't suicide as we thought at first. She was murdered.'

Lizzie gave a wail of horror, put a hand to her mouth.

'This is dreadful, Jeremy. Poor, poor Ida. Who would want to murder her? As for them' – she nodded towards the front door – 'all they will care about is the fact that there will be one almighty scandal when the newspapers get hold of the story and Lumbleigh Green's dragged into it.'

He put a gentle hand on her arm. 'Try to be calm, Lizzie, and tell me what exactly did Ida say to you? It might be important.'

Lizzie's voice was a whisper. She looked over her shoulder as if afraid she would be overheard. 'I had a message from her, she wanted to meet me – that afternoon.'

'Would that be Friday?'

Lizzie nodded. 'She had some good news: this fellow she was in love with, he was going to marry her, she said. She could hardly believe her luck. You see, she thought she was pregnant and that was why she was so sick in the mornings. Instead of being dismayed she was delighted. He would have to marry her now or, she said, take the consequences if he didn't. Those were her exact words . . . Sounded odd, didn't it?'

Faro nodded. Blackmail was not odd, it could be highly profitable or fatal, as Ida had found out. He did not doubt the identity of her killer, the secret lover, the rich fellow she had bragged about to her mother and confided to Lizzie. Without a name, alas . . .

They were still talking, walking towards the house, when Gosse approached. As Faro introduced Lizzie, Gosse's expression indicated he recognised the lady's maid as the detective constable's attractive young widow lady. He came to a sudden decision and, dismissing Faro, he said: 'I will take care of this.' And to Lizzie, with a bow and a beaming smile:

'Perhaps you would be so good as to answer some routine questions for us, miss. Is there somewhere . . . ?'

Lizzie murmured about the kitchen. 'Lead

the way, then, if you please.' And off they went, Lizzie giving Faro one scared glance.

Later, Lizzie told him how she had become involved. How it had all begun with Mrs Watts' panic-stricken visit. That she had been unable to conceal her anxiety from Clara, that her hands, usually so firm, were trembling and unsure. She dropped a hairpin or two when she was arranging her mistress's curls.

'Madam saw my face reflected in the mirror and wondered again if I was going to tell her I had found another situation. The very idea, Jeremy, when I'm so happy here. I told her about Mrs Watts. She had no idea who she was until I told her she was Ida's mother.

'Madam was quite cross. She wanted to know why I hadn't informed her – or the master, before going to the police. I reminded her that the master had one of his morning meetings in Edinburgh and she had taken the opportunity of the carriage to visit her milliner. I knew I should have waited, but it seemed so urgent. Poor Mrs Watts was absolutely frantic.'

Lizzie shook her head and said tearfully, 'Of course the master had to be told. He called for me and was so angry, he stamped his foot and shouted at me about allowing the misfortunes of a table maid to cause all this disruption to his household and for interfering in matters that did not concern me. Going to the police, he said, mentioning Lumbleigh Green – he made it sound like something sacred – in connection with a maid who had a nervous mother who regarded her absence as something to worry about.

'Madam was with me all the time and he said that these people were always up to something and that he had understood she was an orphan.'

Faro realised that Lumbleigh, like many of his kind, preferred to employ orphans from the workhouse. Less wages per annum and no family to expect a day off per month for a visit, or be meddlesome regarding the well-being of young daughters.

Mrs Watts was a prime example, he thought, as Lizzie went on:

'The master laughed at the idea of her having gone missing. As for me . . .' She shuddered. 'He said to Madam: "You had better start looking for another lady's maid. This one will have to go."'

Lizzie paused and looked at Faro wide-eyed. 'At that very suggestion, Madam implored him not to dismiss me. She burst into tears. And that saved me, but only just, Jeremy.' Lizzie had yet to learn that Clara had produced her one unfailing defence, her battle weapon: tears, which Archie had never learnt to resist.

'And now murder, Jeremy. Even Madam will not be able to save me. The master will say it's all my fault bringing Lumbleigh into disrepute. I know what he's like. He'll look for someone to blame.'

Faro restrained himself from stating the obvious.

During that first interview with Gosse, Lizzie remained silent about Ida's secret revelations, aware from Mrs Watts' visit that Ida was no pathetic orphan as she had claimed, but that she had not only had both parents alive and well in Bonnyrigg, but a host of relatives as well.

Later she told Faro: 'Of course, I didn't tell Sergeant Gosse about what Ida had said to me, Jeremy, it wasn't my secret. I had promised her, given my word.' And that was that. Keeping her word to Ida was sacred to Lizzie Laurie, even if she was dead.

In vain, Faro tried to make her understand that by telling Gosse it might help the police to find Ida's killer. But Lizzie was adamant. She shook her head obstinately.

'You must promise, Jeremy,' she pleaded. 'Don't you see, I could lose my job, my whole future is at stake. It was bad enough me telling the police poor Ida was missing, but now that it's murder, if the master finds I have been concealing anything else, it'll be the end for me. The mistress won't be able to intervene this time, he'll just send me packing and that's the end of it.'

Faro regarded her anxiously. Secrets were sacred to her, even though, he thought in exasperation, this particular one might lead to the capture of a killer of two women and the attempted murderer of an elderly man.

As for her future, he thought grimly, it was no consolation for him to realise that this was his chance – his only one to protect Lizzie's future – to ask her to marry him now and give her the security of a husband, where Lumbleigh and his kind could no longer destroy her.

CHAPTER NINE

Gosse was enjoying the prospect of another interview with the attractive lady's maid and Lizzie, with a final helpless glance in Faro's direction, knew that she must admit that Ida had been in touch with her.

'And what was this about?' Gosse demanded eagerly.

Now with a certain amount of delicacy she hesitated about telling Gosse about Ida's suspected pregnancy. But he was a married man, after all, and when he demanded was there any special reason for this good news, Lizzie sighed, and when she told him about the secret lover, his eyes gleamed. An unwanted pregnancy, here was the perfect motive for murder.

Faro was waiting in the hall. Lizzie's helpless, injured look in his direction indicated that she had broken her promise to Ida.

Gosse had a smirk of satisfaction, as if the interview had pleased him, and said that they would need to see the room Ida occupied in the house. At his request there was a murmur of disapproval from Mrs Brown, quelled by Gosse who said sternly that all places of residence linked with the victim were examined for evidence in murder cases.

'She was not murdered in this house.'

Ignoring that, Gosse said firmly, 'That is our rule and it is quite inflexible.' And to Lizzie: 'Did you share a room?'

Lizzie explained that Ida had shared a room with Betty, the other maid. 'We need to talk to her again then,' said Gosse and Lizzie was sent to summon the terrified girl, trembling in the darkest depths of the kitchen.

'It'll be all right, Betty, you have nothing to fear. It's just that poor Ida, well they think someone killed her.'

Betty gave a shrill scream of terror and looked ready to faint, despite Lizzie's warm hand in hers and her reassurances. She looked at the two policemen as if they were executioners waiting to lead her to the block. Scared and almost inarticulate, she answered Gosse's questions. Ida had kept herself to herself was all she could volunteer. None of us knew anything about her.

Yes, she would show them the room she had shared with Ida, and they followed her through a green baize door, along a gloomy corridor and up two flights of narrow wooden stairs into the attics, draughty, cold and inhospitable.

Betty opened the door into a tiny room with one bed which looked hardly large enough for two grown-ups to share. A small table, two wooden chairs, a broken-down set of drawers. When Betty opened the one which belonged to Ida and was intended to contain all her possessions, it was empty apart from a white apron and cap.

Betty said quite logically: 'As she was leaving she took everything else with her.'

There was a crucifix on the wall above one side of the bed.

'Yours, miss?' asked Gosse.

'No, sir, I'm not a Catholic. That's Ida's. She went to Mass at the church at St Leonard's. She wanted me to go with her.' A moment's hesitating, then she said: 'I don't think she would have committed suicide, sir. I mean, you see, Catholics don't allow it.'

'Did you ever play card games, miss?' Faro put in, ignoring Gosse's snort of disapproval.

Betty gave him a scared look. 'No, master would have dismissed us on the spot. Ida said she thought—'

But whatever Ida had thought they were not to know, for suddenly struck again by the awfulness of Ida's fate, Betty began to weep.

Gosse patted her arm, and said: 'We'll find our own way downstairs.'

Following him out of that desolate room, Faro hoped Lizzie fared better than the other maids. At least she had a room of her own.

There was still one member of the family remaining to be interviewed. Lumbleigh explained to Gosse that Paul was unavoidably detained at Surgeons' Hall, one of an army of medical students crowded round the operating table for an important anatomical dissection by the professor.

Gosse nodded. 'We will need to see him later.'

Lumbleigh scowled. 'My son will merely confirm his parents' comments. You are wasting your time and ours.'

Mrs Brown had returned and been told of Ida's death by Archie. She now stood with her hands clasped meekly before her, the picture of a dignified family retainer, and said in a clear, firm voice that although Ida was a bit lazy and slow and couldn't be relied upon and they had their

117

differences, she was, of course, sorry that the girl had suffered such a dreadful fate.

The housekeeper's face looked as if it had been carved out of stone. Did she ever smile, or laugh, or show any emotion? Faro had never before seen anyone whose countenance was so wiped clean of expression.

Of outside staff, Archie informed them there was only Eli Brown, coachman, gardener and general handyman. Having failed to find him at the cottage, Mrs Brown told Gosse that at this moment he was away down East Lothian buying spring bulbs for autumn planting. But, she volunteered, as he never crossed the threshold of the house, to her certain knowledge he rarely encountered the maids, so it was doubtful if he could be of any help with their enquiries.

Gosse added his name to be interviewed later. Asked if anyone shared their cottage, Mrs Brown said they had no children but boarded Laurie's schoolboy son Vince.

Faro's thoughts were on the conversation with Archie regarding Paul's alibi, which had been interrupted by Mrs Brown's entrance. He remembered Lizzie had said Paul was a bit of a flirt with the servant girls. He decided to keep that information to himself since he guessed, quite correctly, that the sergeant was hoping that Lizzie, who was keeping company with his detective constable, might be willing to gossip about other members of the household.

It gave Faro a sense of disquiet, aware that Gosse would regard such information as significant and, spider-like, weave a web around it. On the strength of being a known flirt, Paul might find himself in the role of prime suspect.

The mention of Ida's suspected pregnancy had been seized upon with delight by Gosse as the probable motive for her murder. She had told this mysterious wealthy chap who was her lover and he had panicked, like so many men did in similar situations.

'He lost his temper, that was it,' said Gosse. 'And when she made a fuss, he strangled her and threw her body over the bridge to make it look like suicide. The answer is easy, plain as the nose on your face,' he added confidently.

Perhaps in Ida's case it was, Faro thought, but it failed to explain the connection with the woman murdered in Fleshers Close or the attempted murder of Jock Webb strangled and left for dead. Nor did it explain the presence of the nine of diamonds playing card found under the dead woman's body, in Jock Webb's pocket and, most baffling of all, in Ida's reticule.

As for the devious Gosse, he had now decided

after that first interview that Mrs Lumbleigh's lady's maid was a stunner, wasted on his detective constable, and that he quite fancied her. Mentally he rubbed his hands with glee; talking to the lad Vince would also provide just the opportunity he was looking for to further their short acquaintance. He would unleash upon Lizzie all his charm and wit, which he believed was considerable and quite irresistible.

In his mind's eye he entertained a fleeting but blissful vision of walking with her on his arm in Princes Street Gardens, and seeing a scowling Faro in the background, smitten with a plague of envy and jealousy having been effectively pushed aside for an older man of more importance . . .

CHAPTER TEN

In his short stay in the Brown's cottage, Vince
had found a new friend. He had fallen out of a
tree and Paul Lumbleigh, riding back down from
Arthur's Seat where he had been upgrading his
shooting skills on rabbits and other small game,
entered the gardens by the back gate and found a
boy sitting on the grass at the base of a tall tree,
and nursing a bleeding knee.

The sight of fresh blood and possible injury
halted him, as became one on the threshold of a
medical profession.

'That looks nasty. Is it sore?'

Vince bit his lip, trying not to cry, as the young
man put aside his rifle and game bag. Kneeling down

beside him, he asked: 'Climbing, were you, and fell down the tree, did you? Know you're trespassing?'

'Of course I'm not. I live here,' was the indignant reply and as Vince pointed to the cottage, Paul looked round, nodded and said: 'Right. Come along and I'll bandage that knee.' Leading his horse he walked slowly, with Vince limping alongside. Tying the horse to the garden fence he pushed open the cottage door.

Vince's eyes widened in surprise. He hadn't even knocked first. What would Mrs Brown say? 'You can't go in like that,' he protested.

'And why not, pray? I can go anywhere I choose. Sit down!' He indicated a kitchen chair and laughed. 'Don't look so scared. It's only the coach house. Didn't know they had children. Is Brown your father?'

'No. My father is dead. He was a brave soldier. Killed in India.'

Vince was very proud of the father he had never met and whom his mother told him about. Now he looked nervously towards the window. The horse was clearly visible nibbling at the hedge. 'You're trespassing, you know; look at that horse of yours. Mr Lumbleigh is very hard on trespassers, especially ones with animals . . .'

Paul was filling a basin of water from the kettle on the hob. His lips tightened but he grinned. 'Is he now? Well, well, we'll see about that.'

'Are you one of his tenants?'

Paul didn't answer. After gently bathing the cut knee with one of Mrs Brown's kitchen cloths, Vince watched wide-eyed as Paul threw open cupboard doors, searching shelves. 'You shouldn't do that, she'll have a fit.' He didn't add that the warning was in his own interests as he, and not this kind man, would get all the blame.

'Who cares?' Paul shrugged, seizing a box. 'Excellent. This ointment will do splendidly. Hold on. This will sting a bit.'

It did. Vince bit back a yell as he watched more searching, opening of drawers, dragging out contents, then a cry of triumph, as the young man flourished a box containing lint and bandages.

Watching him skilfully dress his cut knee, Vince noticed that he had extremely gentle hands, but how on earth was he going to explain the array of wet cloths, a bloodstained towel and the general dishevelment of Mrs Brown's normally pristine tidy kitchen?

'That better?' said Paul, regarding his work with satisfaction.

'Yes, thank you. But how did you know where to find everything that was needed like that?'

Paul sat back and regarded him with a grin. 'I know enough about horses and coachmen to realise there will always be a plentiful supply of bandages and ointment on the premises. Stand up.'

Vince did as he was bid and said: 'Thank you. That's fine. But you'd better go before anyone comes.' He looked round quickly. 'It's a bit of a mess but they can blame me.'

Paul shook a finger at him. 'Listen, I can do anything. My father owns this cottage – the Browns are only his servants. So just shut up and stop worrying.'

Vince was impressed, and looking around at the disorder, he said: 'I'll tell the Browns I hurt my knee.'

Paul grinned. 'And did such a neat job of bandaging it too. Well, well,' he said mockingly. 'Must be off now. Bandage too tight or can you walk?'

'Of course I can.' Vince shuffled a few steps. 'Thank you again.'

Washing his hands at the sink, Paul said: 'Are you at school here?'

'St Leonard's.'

A quizzical glance. 'Like it?'

A shrug instead of the expected indignant schoolboy's reply. 'It's all right. I like some lessons, history and discovering things with a microscope, that's my favourite. I'd like to be a doctor when I grow up.'

Paul gave him a speculative look, a feeling almost of nostalgia. Once he had been like this boy; now he envied him the innocence before that other world, waiting with the years, destroyed it all.

Opening the door, he turned. 'Right. No football for a day or two and get your mother to have a look at the knee tomorrow, see that it's healing all right. Any problems and we have better things for bloody knees at Surgeons' Hall.'

'Surgeons' Hall?'

'That's right. I'm a doctor – or I will be in a year or two.'

'Do you live there?'

Paul shook his head. 'No, over there.' He pointed to the big house.

Vince looked at him. The rifle and the horse. This must be the son of the house, Paul. He remembered hints from his mother that this was the disreputable chap, gambling, always getting drunk, coming home and having to get someone to put him to bed.

This kind fellow somehow didn't fit that description but he had to be sure. 'Is Mr Lumbleigh your father?'

'Stepfather,' Paul said shortly.

'My mother is your mother's lady's maid.'

Paul looked sour. 'She's not my mother,' he said sharply. 'My mother is dead.' His tone was bitter, angry. 'Mrs Lumbleigh is not much older than me. And *he*' – he emphasised the word – 'he isn't any relation of mine. My father was a soldier, a colonel, killed in India – like yours.'

'Do you know my mother? Mrs Laurie?'

Paul shook his head and said almost apologetically: 'Not really. We don't know much about what goes on in the kitchen; as long as food is on the table when required and fires are lit, the servants are expected to remain invisible.'

Pausing he looked at Vince. Why was he telling this lad, a complete stranger, all this? Now, as he studied the boy with his mop of yellow curls, he saw a striking resemblance to one of the maids he had fancied. Lady's maid. He remembered meeting her in a dark corridor, standing in her way and trying to grab her and kiss her. She had slapped his face – hard.

He had been furious and said coldly, 'That could cost you your job.'

'Not if I have any say in it, Paul.' The voice was Clara's. 'Do go to bed, you silly boy, and leave the maids alone.' And to the woman, 'Come along, my dear.'

Rubbing his sore cheek, he watched her, hating her, swearing he would get revenge some day – on her and his stepfather. He wished they were dead, especially the man who had murdered his beloved mother, by keeping her to rot slowly, dying in a lunatic asylum. The rumour was that she had syphilis. He went cold at the thought – she certainly must have contracted that from her promiscuous husband, as so many wives did from theirs.

As Vince explained his bandaged knee later that day, Lizzie had been very concerned, made a great fuss, and while she was grateful to Paul she was also very curious when she discovered Vince reading a book by Sir Walter Scott, an author she knew little about except that Edinburgh was very proud of him.

'Where did you get that from?'

'Paul lent it to me,' said Vince. Paul had come by the cottage and seeing him sitting outside had asked after his knee. 'I was reading a book from school and he said he could do better than that. And he gave me this book. He likes books too. We're friends, Ma,' he added proudly.

Lizzie had doubts about that and some misgivings regarding this odd friendship, knowing the bad reputation of the profligate son of the house. But Vince was delighted. Paul had opened up a new world for him; he was to teach him how to play whist and show him card tricks to impress the boys in his class at school.

Lizzie met that piece of information with some anxiety. Paul was a known gambler – and loser.

'And he's going to teach me chess too. We both like puzzles.'

She refrained from reminding him that Faro had offered him what she called 'good' books, including Shakespeare's plays, many times, and to show him chess, but that had been met by a scowl, a shrug of disinterest.

Lizzie would have been even less happy had she known the outcome of Faro's interview with Paul Lumbleigh and the coachman. The latter was a mere formality, said Gosse, intending to donate that particular task to Faro while he engineered a chat with Vince as an excuse to further his acquaintance with the boy's mother, who had already stirred his senses.

While Gosse was having a smoke outside, he had met the returning coachman, whose enigmatic expression remained unchanged as he answered Gosse's questions.

'A satisfactory alibi. You can cross him off the list, Faro. Only one more and we're finished . . .' As he said the words, the front door opened to admit a tall, good-looking young man whose air of self-confidence proclaimed him to be Paul Lumbleigh. He was in his early twenties, but Faro recognised in his face the look that said he was already a man of the world.

He regarded the two policemen with

unconcealed disgust and, Faro thought, even a hint of anxiety.

Archie appeared at the study door and somewhat harshly introduced the departing detectives as being here on a routine matter. 'One of the maids has been murdered – but it's got nothing to do with the family.' Archie sighed. 'Nothing you need concern yourself about.'

Perhaps not an accurate observation, as Faro's sharp glance detected a certain tightening of the young man's lips. He made a mental note of a haunted expression that might well arise from feelings of guilt. Maybe he was innocent, but he did not share his stepfather's reassurance on the matter of concern.

The two detectives returned to the study where Archie and Paul sat down but they were to remain standing.

Somewhat reluctantly Paul asked, 'So what's all this about?'

Archie addressed Gosse impatiently. 'This is a mere waste of time, Sergeant.' And as Paul sprawled languidly in the nearest armchair, he added: 'This is a great inconvenience, Sergeant, my son knows nothing of our domestic matters—'

'At this stage it is a mere routine, sir. As I have already informed you,' Gosse said patiently, 'we are obliged to examine the deceased's place of employment in case anyone may be able to contribute further knowledge of activities leading to . . . er . . . possible suspects.'

But Faro was no longer listening.

He had made an important discovery of his own.

He knew the exact place where he had seen young Lumbleigh before. Outside the Vaudeville Theatre in Canongate, trying to persuade one of the chorus girls into his carriage. She was struggling and shouting and he, obviously very drunk, was laughing at her protests.

Faro had stepped forward and said: 'Let the young lady go, sir.'

Paul had glanced up at him, trying with some difficulty to focus his eyes. Then looking the girl over with a lewd expression, he grinned. 'I don't see any young lady here. And it's none of your business.'

Faro repeated, 'Let her go, sir. You're drunk.'

The girl had struggled free and Faro said: 'Off you go, miss.'

Paul scowled. 'Hold on there. I bought her a drink, a promise was made.' And to Faro, 'I know what you're up to. You can jolly well wait your turn, can't he, sweetheart?' He stretched out a hand to grab her, missed, and staggered.

Faro laid a firm hand on his arm. 'Leave her alone. Get yourself home and sober up, sir.'

'And who the devil do you think you are to give orders?'

'I'm a policeman.'

'Are you serious? You don't look like a policeman. If you're a peeler then I'm the Prince of Wales.'

Even out of uniform Faro had a presence and Paul tried to focus his eyes on this man who towered above him, tall, fair hair, with the kind of face he'd seen in pictures of Vikings. Sense filtered through the alcoholic haze as Faro produced a wallet, took out a card, confirming his identity. Not a man to tangle with.

As for the girl, she had seized the opportunity to escape and Paul suddenly lost interest. Angry, frustrated, he tapped the roof of the carriage: 'Drive on.' And Faro watched as this uncouth, educated lout shouted an obscenity at him as the carriage disappeared.

The memory of that encounter evolved into significance when he remembered taking Lizzie to the Vaudeville she loved. It was her favourite, the comics, the performing dogs, the acrobats, the dancers, girls with long legs in daring, glittering costumes, usually of scarlet satin.

Scarlet satin.

Like the woman they had found murdered in Fleshers Close, except that her dress was torn and muddied.

He felt the thrill of certainty.

Gosse was wrong. He had leapt to the obvious conclusion. Despite that scarlet dress and the face paint, the woman was not a professional prostitute but an actress, a chorus girl, a dancer. Perhaps out of work and starving she had had to seek survival on the streets. And a more significant memory: the woman in the tenement who had heard a carriage and drunken shouts that night.

Faro considered Paul with new interest. Should he confide his suspicions to Gosse, who wanted the woman in Fleshers Close to be a whore? He hated whores and had set his heart on that as the reason why she had been murdered. Bearing that in mind, Faro later felt bound to mention that Paul was a known flirt with the maid servants.

Gosse's reactions were exactly what he had expected. The sergeant's eyebrows shot skyward. A shake of the head, a mocking laugh. 'Are you hinting that the son of the house was Ida's secret lover? Paul and one of the maids! You must be insane. The idea is unimaginable – completely absurd.'

'It happens, sir,' said Faro. 'Every day.'

For him, remembering Lizzie's bitter past, the idea was neither absurd nor unimaginable.

Gosse gave him a pitying glance. 'Did you not see her lying in the mortuary – a plain little nobody? And him an educated, handsome lad, about to graduate as a doctor. What an idea.' And shaking an admonishing finger, 'And another thing. Don't forget Jock Webb. Why on earth should Paul attack an elderly man, a stranger?'

Faro suppressed a weary sigh. Despite the revelations of his interview with Webb, Gosse was still hanging on to his own theory, hoping that the murder might be pinned on the ex-boxer.

'And how do you fit all this in with the sinister planting of the nine of diamonds on the victims?' Gosse demanded.

Faro had to admit that the only link was that Paul was a known gambler. 'Jock Webb couldn't account for the playing card.'

In a voice heavy with sarcasm, Gosse said, 'Don't make me laugh, Faro. You're not using those much-vaunted powers of detection. It is a well-known fact that criminals do things exactly like that to divert suspicions from themselves. Wait till you've been tracking them down as long as I have, you'll see.'

It didn't divert from the fact that Webb had been injured, hit on the head by someone. But as Gosse said darkly: 'Webb is our prime suspect.' Only one thing still baffled him. He was as yet completely unable to fit Webb by any stretch of imagination into the role of Ida's killer, her rich young lover.

As for Faro, he knew from even the short experience of their dealings together that it would be useless to protest, impossible to dissuade Gosse from what he wanted to believe.

'Now that Wade is out of the enquiry,' said Gosse, 'for God knows how long – and if I know the inspector, he will be in no hurry to return to duty – all his work has fallen on my shoulders, so you will need to do the legwork, accept a bit more responsibility without me to look after you.'

This little speech brought Faro to a decision. Without Gosse looking over his shoulder, he would carry out his own search, beginning with the Vaudeville Theatre, to see if any of the girls were missing.

And time wasn't on his side. After more than a week in the cold store mortuary, unclaimed bodies found their way to Surgeons' Hall and the knives of the eagerly awaiting medical students.

CHAPTER ELEVEN

Faro's instructions from Gosse were to follow up
Jock Webb and interview him closely again. As
the sergeant had already made up his mind, in the
absence of any more suitable candidate, that the
ex-boxer was his prime suspect, it seemed to Faro
a complete waste of time and effort.

He had other plans. Lizzie had told him that since
her elevation to lady's maid, her generous mistress
was prepared to allow her extra time off duty, since
her services of hairdressing and robing could not, by
any stretch of the imagination, be required on those
domestic evenings, sitting by the fire reading a novel
or doing her embroidery, while her husband read
the newspapers or frowned over reports concerning

important financial activities he was involved in whilst keeping a strict eye on counting the pieces of coal the maid Betty had been summoned up from the kitchen to cast upon the dying embers.

'They don't go out much in the evening,' Lizzie told Faro, 'unless someone invites them to dine, that is. And the master disapproves of entertaining business acquaintances. Mrs Brown says he regards such hospitality very tiring and a waste of money, providing expensive wine plus lavish quantities of food which might go uneaten and have to be given to the servants.'

Lizzie sighed. 'Mrs Brown says he confines his own activities, such as lunches and dinners, to functions where, apart from his carriage and Mr Brown's miserable wages, expenses can be met by the organisers.'

Now that Lizzie's time off was not confined to weekends only, Faro could see her most evenings. This was to his advantage as he could combine official business with the pleasure of her company, in this particular instance, taking her to the Vaudeville Theatre which she loved. In the interval he would make an excuse to see the manager and ask if any of the chorus girls had gone missing, and with that information begin his own enquiries regarding the real identity of the murdered woman in Fleshers Close.

Suddenly fortune seemed to smile upon his plans, for there was another unexpected piece of luck awaiting him at his lodgings that evening. A note from his friend, retired detective superintendent Brandon Macfie, reminding him that he was due to have supper at Nicholson Square.

Faro always looked forward to those evenings, a cosy warm parlour, walls lined with shelves housing Macfie's library accumulated over the years, and where books could not be neatly accommodated, piled in every available corner.

In all other matters, except where his precious books were concerned, Macfie was well ordered and meticulously tidy. Books, he pointed out, were his friends, companions of many years and of far greater value, Faro often thought, than the huge mahogany sideboard on which were displayed all the medals and honours Macfie had received in his long years with the Central Office. One photograph of which he was immensely proud depicted a visit to Balmoral, at the side of HM Queen Victoria in her carriage in the castle grounds.

Part of the attraction of Faro's company was that he had become a link with Macfie's past life with the police and he liked to be kept up to date on the latest developments in crime-catching activities, information which had not yet filtered beyond the headlines of the news-sheets. All

Macfie knew of this latest violent death was that a woman had been found dead, apparently murdered in Fleshers Close.

As his housekeeper removed the soup plates and brought in the next course, Faro went over the gruesome findings, stressing that there was no identity as yet.

Macfie had also read a brief paragraph in *The Scotsman* about the more recent death, a young maid's suicide. He gave Faro a questioning look. Faro nodded and replied:

'That is so, sir. The girl's death was publicly notified as suicide; however, the police surgeon discovered that she had been strangled and her body then thrown over the bridge.'

'Strangled, you say. That is interesting, an identical cause of death to the first woman. Do they suspect some connection between the two killings?' was Macfie's shrewd question.

'Unlikely, sir. The first was a domestic murder, the husband gave himself up and is behind bars. The only connection between the two is a playing card found on the scene each time. The nine of diamonds.'

'The curse of Scotland, eh.' Macfie's eyes gleamed. 'That is extraordinary and implies that our killer has a knowledge of Scottish history and legends.'

'There was one other instance, sir, which has not perhaps been reported publicly.' And Faro went on to relate the murderous attack on the ex-boxer Jock Webb, with the identical playing card found in his jacket pocket.

'Indeed? How did he account for that?' said Macfie.

'He denied all knowledge of how it had got there. Very indignant too. A temperance man since his retirement, anyway, he went on at some length about the sins of gambling.' Faro paused. 'This did not satisfy DS Gosse, however, who is anxious to regard him as prime suspect.'

Macfie nodded. 'Exactly. The man he claimed to be his attacker could have in fact been his intended victim who turned the tables on him. It has all been done before.' He thought for a moment. 'Where was this discovery made?'

While Macfie topped up his whisky, Faro told him that it had been when his clothes were returned to him before leaving the hospital. Macfie frowned. 'I know something of the legendary Jock Webb, saw him in a great many fights years ago, and the police had reason to caution him on several occasions. Slightly addicted to carrying on his boxing activities with threats outside the ring, but alas, let us say all his power was in his fists and I doubt, indeed, whether he ever read more than the sporting news, much less grasped the significance of Scottish history relating to the nine of diamonds.'

Sitting back in his chair, he regarded Faro thoughtfully. 'How much do you know of this extraordinary legend which has filtered down the years?'

'Not a lot, sir. I had been led to believe that the order for the massacre of the McDonalds at Glencoe in 1692 was written on the nine of diamonds by Butcher Cumberland, who had his game of cards, where he had a winning hand, interrupted to write the order.'

Macfie smiled. 'That is the most popular belief; another is that it was the playing card used by Sir John Dalrymple, the Earl of Stair, to authorise the massacre – based somewhat loosely on the resemblance between the nine of diamonds and his coat of arms.

'There are several other legends. In the card game, Pope Joan, the nine of diamonds was mockingly called "the Pope", the antichrist of Scottish Reformers.' He shrugged. 'We must remember that diamonds imply royalty and there are royal connections. The nine of diamonds was the chief card in the game "Cornette" introduced into the Scottish court by our late unhappy Queen Mary. But according to an earlier account, her grandfather King James IV used it to draw up the battle ranks for that fatal field of Flodden.'

And Faro remembered from his Orkney schoolmaster, from whom he had learnt the magic of history and who would have shared Macfie's encyclopaedic knowledge, that Mary's father James V's last words, so sadly prophetic for the fate of Scotland, were 'It came wi' a lass, it'll gang wi' a lass.'

Macfie rubbed his chin thoughtfully. 'The woman in Fleshers Close – the one without an identity.'

'Her reticule has never come to light. Presumably it fell from the carriage and into the clutches of someone eager to purloin its contents.'

Macfie nodded. 'Most likely, considering the area. What did you deduct from her appearance?'

'A prostitute, according to Gosse. At first glance so much seemed obvious. She looked the part. A scarlet satin dress, powder and paint. But now, I'm not so sure.' Pausing he shook his head, not at this stage wishing to divulge his encounter with Paul Lumbleigh, so he said, 'I remembered seeing students outside the Vaudeville Theatre trying to entice one of the dancers into a carriage – she was dressed in scarlet, one of the chorus of dancers.'

Macfie thought about that and, leaning

forward, his dark eyebrows raised, he asked: 'The motive, Faro. Let us not forget that, lad. For all murders, there has to be a motive, and the inclusion of the playing card, the nine of diamonds, is a kind of autograph, a secret message from the killer.' He shook his head. 'These are not a madman's random killings, lad. There is a connecting link between the two murders of the young women and the apparently unsuccessful attempt on the ex-boxer.'

He paused to light his pipe, drew on it and then sat back in his chair, regarding Faro across the table. 'The card was found among Webb's possessions before leaving the hospital, you said?'

Faro nodded and Macfie thought for a moment. 'That might indicate, since our killer is an educated man, that he is to be found there.' He shrugged. 'Just a notion.'

And Faro thought of Paul, a medical student with possible hours spent at the hospital. Macfie continued: 'The small child you saw. Tell me about her again.'

'I was concerned about her because I was sure she had been a witness to the killing, and I went back to see the woman who had snatched her up from the horrific scene and promised to take care of her.' He frowned. 'I realised that this was no neighbourly gesture and that she did not know the woman at all. She had a purpose of her own for misleading me. She had quite a brood of small children, supposedly her own, but the child presented a valuable asset. There was money in this so-called act of mercy and my doubts about her intentions came from a fleeting remark, proving she was prepared – even eager – to sell the little girl to me.'

Macfie looked grim. 'Child labour – or worse. Poor wee soul. There wasn't much you could do, lad. It goes on and is ignored. The real curse of Scotland. So what clues do we have? A killer who leaves a significant playing card, which hints at a knowledge of Scottish history. So Gosse's favourite prime suspect is unlikely to be the elderly ex-boxer. The one clue we have is that our killer is an educated man. From what we know, I would stress again that these killings are in the nature of executions.'

Faro had an idea. 'In that case, could there be a possibility that the link with the nine of diamonds lies perhaps in the surnames of the victims?'

'Such as a McDonald of Glencoe descendant on the hunt for Campbells.' Macfie shook his head. 'An interesting conclusion but I fear rather too obvious and a little far-fetched.'

As he paused Faro put in: 'You maybe know that DI Wade is off the case, languishing with a broken leg in Inverness, and DS Gosse is now in charge.'

Macfie laughed. 'And not against the grain, I warrant. Knowing that gentleman, he will see hopes of promotion unlimited with one of his famous early convictions.' The retired superintendent was well aware of Gosse's regrettable tendency to nail evidence on his prime suspect.

Faro said: 'Since he now has a role of importance and has decided that Jock Webb is the killer, all responsibilities for proving his theory have been allotted to me, by regular interviews with his prime suspect.' He sighed. 'As I know the answers already, I have decided to pursue the matter of the unidentified woman on my own.'

'You have this theory that she might have been an actress?'

'I do indeed. Somehow she didn't quite fit the role of whore that Gosse was so keen to tag on to her.'

'So you think she may have been an unemployed dancer reduced to this unfortunate means of making a living.'

'Certainly, if the child I saw was hers. Perhaps that was not what she was doing in Fleshers Close. I suspect she was killed elsewhere; the woman upstairs claimed to have been wakened by a disturbance, a carriage outside during the night.' He shook his head. 'I have a gut feeling, sir, that she wasn't just someone the killer had picked up but that he was already acquainted with her, and in that costume, where better place to deposit her body than Fleshers Close with its notorious connections?'

'The important omissions from the discovery of the body,' he went on, 'were that, although it was a chill night, she had no cloak and, more importantly, she was empty-handed.'

'Precisely. The missing reticule. And is the playing card our killer's signature?' Macfie shook his head and sighed. 'It's quite a puzzle, lad. So what is your plan?'

'First of all, a visit to the Vaudeville Theatre. A chat with the manager, or some of the dancers, see if any of them have failed to appear for rehearsals, apparently left without giving notice. It is usual, I gather, as a matter of economics, for several performers to share lodgings, so hopefully I might get an address.'

Macfie looked grave. 'Again, remember the motive. The connection between the Fleshers Close killing and the maid from Lumbleigh Green, in her case a murder made to look like suicide. Both by an identical method – strangulation. As there was no weapon – no scarf or stocking involved, as is the usual case in such murders' – he paused, clenched his hands – 'presumably these were his weapons. Strong hands, adept, perhaps indicating a soldier.' He stopped and added grimly. 'Or a boxer. Except that he was a victim – or claimed to be.'

Pausing he nodded vigorously, 'Somewhere between all three there has to be a link.'

And they both knew without saying the words that to find that link, and the motive, they would have to put themselves inside the killer's mind.

Faro was preparing to leave when Macfie, aware that Lizzie was employed at Lumbleigh Green, asked him, as if in afterthought: 'How is your companion Mrs Laurie faring in all this sorry business?'

Faro was amused that he never referred to her as 'your young lady'. That would have been too informal. Macfie was scrupulous in such matters and would have viewed questions regarding any romantic attachment – which Faro had been careful thus far not to indicate, nor had he confided even vaguely any intentions regarding Lizzie – as vulgar curiosity. As far as Macfie was aware, he only knew, as did the rest of Lumbleigh Green and Faro's colleagues, that Lizzie was a widow he had befriended and that she had a young son.

'It is deuced awkward, sir,' Faro said, 'since she has recently been promoted lady's maid to Mrs Lumbleigh, and as you might imagine she found herself in danger of losing her situation by involving Lumbleigh Green with a police investigation. The maid Ida's mother had come to the door in a panic that her daughter had not arrived home in Bonnyrigg that weekend for her birthday celebration. She insisted that her daughter was devoted and dutiful. She was in such a state that Mrs Laurie felt she had no option but to come to Central Office and notify Ida as a missing person. Mr Lumbleigh, however, was angry to say the least that she had taken the decision, without consulting him, of dragging his very respectable household into sordid speculations . . .'

'To say nothing of reducing the value of his property's selling price, no doubt,' was Macfie's candid rejoinder, wishing him good luck and asking to be kept informed of developments, and Faro left fully aware that, whatever he learnt, Macfie's experience and his advice would be invaluable.

CHAPTER TWELVE

When Faro met Lizzie and they walked in Queen's Park that mellow evening it was to learn that the master had caused further ructions when he heard via his wife that her maid was keeping company with a police constable.

'He was terribly upset, Jeremy. Said to her that if that was not bad enough, worst of all,' she suppressed a giggle and eyed him proudly, 'this particular policeman was one of the detectives causing them so much personal inconvenience investigating Ida's murder.'

She sighed and took his arm. 'I am frantic with worry, Jeremy. If I am dismissed, what will become of Vince? That concerns me much more deeply than my own future. Doubtless I will get another situation as lady's maid in due course. Mrs Lumbleigh has been very pleased with my efforts and I'm sure she will give me an excellent recommendation to some of her friends.'

Pausing, she looked towards Salisbury Crags. 'But it is Vince I am so concerned about. If I leave Lumbleigh Green there will be no reason for him to stay with the Browns. And he is so comfortable in his wee attic in the cottage. It's a room of his own and he is well fed and cared for.' She shook her head. 'I dread having to take him away back to where we used to live, which is all I could afford. It was not the worst by any means, although now in comparison with the big house it seems quite dreadful.'

She stopped to retie the strings of her bonnet which had become undone and Faro's heart went out to her. She looked so pretty, so young and vulnerable; all his feelings were to protect her as she went on: 'When I think of being poor again and having to live in some loathsome close, I can bear it, but it is Vince I tremble for. Living in nice surroundings is so good for him, for his future, and all that will be taken from him. Oh, dear, that wretched old tenement was bad then, but it seems like a nightmare now!'

As far as Faro was concerned this conversation was a nightmare for him too; had Lizzie been able to see inside his head and read his thoughts, she would perceive how her words were once again a silent reproach, forcing him to consider how readily he could put an end to all her anxieties, her fears for the future – hers and her son's – by uttering four simple words: Will you marry me? Such easy words that would be what Lizzie imagined was an entrance to paradise. Walking at her side, her arm in his, he suppressed a weary sigh. One day, sooner or later, this seemed like the inevitable conclusion of their present easy-going relationship.

As for Vince's future, he was surprised to hear that he had been befriended by Paul Lumbleigh, who was apparently taking a greater interest in a twelve-year-old schoolboy than Faro could have ever imagined, considering his damaged reputation.

Lizzie was wide-eyed with admiration. 'Master Paul is a keen reader and is encouraging Vince to like great writers of the past, even Shakespeare.' She laughed delightedly as she added: 'Vince has been showing me some clever card tricks that Paul taught him. He is so deft with his hands. They played whist and Vince always wins – that amuses Paul since cards are absolutely forbidden in the house.' She paused and added guardedly, 'Master Paul lost a great deal of money gambling at college and at the master's club, which had to be repaid by his stepfather.'

'Indeed? A lot of money?'

She shrugged. 'Well maybe not a huge amount but we all know that the master is careful, very tight-fisted about money. Mrs Brown goes on about it constantly, saying this is a big house and she needs more staff, she is utterly worn out having to run it efficiently on her own. She constantly reminds me that matters have not been helped since I became Mrs Lumbleigh's personal maid, only to be seen in the kitchen these days preparing a tray to take upstairs to the mistress.'

The clouds moving over the heights of Arthur's Seat turned into a steady drizzle, and as they could find little shelter, their time together was cut short and he returned her to the house by the back gate. Vince came to the cottage door, obviously waiting for her.

Faro was feeling very despondent. He would have been even more so had he known that Paul's education of Vince was going beyond books and card tricks. Lizzie had omitted to inform him that his tuition also included the promise of how to use a rifle. He was very excited, as Paul was going to take him target shooting away from the house. Once he could handle the weapon properly, Paul told him, he would be able to shoot rabbits on the hill.

Watching the boy disappear inside with Lizzie, Faro had no desire to alarm her, but even unaware of these latest developments, this unlikely friendship and the association with playing cards brought back his earlier conversation with Macfie, who had emphasised that the killings had all the markings of an educated man, as did the attack on Jock Webb who claimed that the nine of diamonds had been planted on him. The possible significance of its discovery in the hospital had immediately occurred to Macfie: that maybe that was where they might find the killer.

Although Faro had not revealed to his old friend that he knew the identity of the drunk young man trying to lure the actress from the theatre into his carriage, its significance now weighed heavily upon him.

What if Paul was the killer? A twenty-year-old medical student who might well know how to strangle a victim efficiently. He remembered Macfie's words – that there had to be a motive. That was the only thing lacking, and for the life of him Faro could think of nothing to justify the two brutal murders. Unless young Lumbleigh was a madman. And there was a thought . . . hadn't his mother died insane?

He went on to consider Lizzie's observation of domestic life within Lumbleigh Green. Apparently everyone knew that there was bad feeling between Paul and Archie. The reason:

Paul blamed his stepfather for his mother's death. In the first place, for having her incarcerated in a lunatic asylum – although it was given a less startling title, a 'gentlewoman's retreat', that was undeniably what it was.

As far as the verdict went, she died there of natural causes, but if Paul was unbalanced he could see it as murder and believe that Archie had in fact caused her death by breaking her heart. He had been twelve years old, the same age as his protégé Vince, at a time of exploding emotions, resisting all attempts by his stepmother to gain his affection. Even mere politeness was an achievement, and hatred of Archie reflected on poor Clara. In a rare mood of confidence after a particularly disagreeable scene at the dining table, drying her tears, she had told Lizzie that she had tried everything without the least success to make Paul like her.

Domestic squabbles were one thing, Faro thought, but hatred of his stepfather was hardly a logical motive for sending Paul on a killing spree of two young women. That didn't make sense at all. Archie had never been in any danger. So for motive, he had to search somewhere else, but where?

He was still brooding over the possibility that the dead woman in Fleshers Close was a dancer.

He recalled Gosse's scorn, how he had demanded: 'Explain!' and apparently listened intently, his eyebrows raised in an immediate expression of mockery at the mention of the scarlet dress.

'Is that it?' he had said at the end of Faro's careful version of this theory which seemed so plausible and obvious to himself.

'Is that all you have to offer?' Gosse repeated, and regarding Faro over arched fingertips he added: 'Well, all I can say is that what I am aware of I know from my own experience – which is vast, Faro, quite vast! I know what Edinburgh whores look like, and so will you if you have a few more years with the force here. Maybe it's different in Orkney, but I would not hesitate to fit the woman we found into the streetwalking fraternity.' Pausing to let this sink in for a moment, he sighed and continued, 'I suggest you divert your energies and your imagination into digging deeper into the obvious – namely, Jock Webb's motives. He is, after all, our main and only suspect.'

With this pronouncement Faro had to be satisfied, realising that as far as Gosse was concerned the case was already closed and, but for a few minor details, he had his murderer and it would take a lot more than Faro's theory to persuade him otherwise.

Unless, and it was a very large and profound 'unless', he could prove it beyond question.

'Anyway, it's up to you now,' Gosse said dismissively, settling back into the comfortable armchair vacated on a temporary basis by Chief Inspector Wade. As he spoke, Gosse glanced across the highly polished surface of the curiously unlittered desk, smoothed the shining surface with satisfaction as if to remove invisible specks of dust.

'I hear from outside sources – my family connections,' he added importantly, reminding Faro that the detective sergeant was a distant cousin of Archie Lumbleigh's deceased first wife's wealthy family and therefore vaguely related to Paul, another reason why confiding any suspicions of the young man as the killer would be received not only with scorn but also with an angry response at the idea that anyone even vaguely related to himself could be guilty of such villainy.

Gosse shook his head. 'Aye, there are changes afoot, Faro.' A deep sigh. 'And when I get my long-awaited and I have to say, eagerly expected promotion, I will be on the lookout back down the ladder on which I have ascended to this elevated position, for the vacant role I have just quitted. Namely the role of detective sergeant . . .'

Pausing dramatically he looked intently at Faro as if expecting some rejoinder, perhaps hoping to detect an eager expression. There was none.

Gosse sighed and smoothed the arms of the chair as with a false expression of regret he shook his head. 'Unfortunately, I do not feel it is within my powers to be able to recommend you, Faro.' Another pause to be met once again by an expression which could not by Gosse's wildest imagination be the one he had been anticipating.

'To be quite frank, I have found you a disappointment, yes indeed, a grievous disappointment, Faro. You came to me with such high hopes from a source that was regarded as infallible . . .'

And Faro was in no doubt that the source was, in fact, Brandon Macfie, as Gosse went on: 'There are several possibilities that I am looking into. Constables who are even younger than yourself,' he added heavily, 'who would more efficiently fill the role of detective sergeant.'

Again he paused hopefully. But reactions there were none. Faro continued to listen politely and regard him enigmatically, oblivious to what Gosse saw as this bombshell launched at the detective constable's future prospects.

'You have all too much imagination, Faro, which is apt to overlook the obvious clues, as in the matter of Webb and the dead women.'

'Begging your pardon, sir, the only connection

regarding Webb's motives for killing the woman in Fleshers Close and the maid from Lumbleigh Green seems to be the playing card found at both scenes.'

Gosse shook an admonishing finger. 'Ah yes, Faro, but believe me there is a motive and that is for you to find out.'

Faro regarded him impassively. 'First of all, sir, I need to track down his present whereabouts. As you will remember, the address was an old one.'

'Ah yes, a typical piece of misdirection.' Gosse shook his head. 'Alas, I cannot direct you in this, these are matters I must leave you to deal with in the normal course of your duties. I now have much on my hands,' he said with a reproachful look across the almost empty desk, 'so I would advise you strongly against feeling free to explore a fantasy about a scarlet dress – thereby allowing precious time to elapse for the obvious killer to escape. A clever killer who has tried to divert our efforts, pulling the wool over our eyes with a playing card—'

There would have been more on these lines, Faro longing to point out somewhat mockingly the logic of the last rash statement, when they were interrupted by a constable who announced the imminent arrival of the assistant chief constable.

Dismissed, Faro left with a sense of injustice

tinged with relief, as he had no desire to remain in the claws of DS Gosse and could only hope that should he be promoted to inspector, then his successor would be more agreeable.

As Gosse trooped importantly after the constable and arranged his face prior to his meeting with his superiors, he felt intensely smug about the way things were working out. He had successfully put Faro in his place, but more importantly, had him off the scene. Faro going after Webb as well as scratching about for clues of a non-existent dancer would give himself more time and opportunity to begin his pursuit of Lizzie Laurie who, since their meeting at Lumbleigh Green, had been occupying a great deal of his thoughts.

He was beginning to feel that he was a little in love with her, and, after all, he was justified in his pursuit. Almost a bachelor, having a wife who had absented herself from the connubial couch and seemed unlikely to ever return, his feelings for this new conquest also allowed him to regard DC Faro in the additional role as a rival for her affections.

CHAPTER THIRTEEN

Almost a week since the first murder in Fleshers Close Faro considered the fate of the body in the police mortuary's cold store. To prove Jock Webb's innocence – or otherwise – he must first discover the dead woman's identity, so a visit to the Vaudeville Theatre was in order. Unfortunately, there was no one available there. The box office, said the notice, opened half an hour before the afternoon and evening performances. With a sigh he walked away, aware that his visit must wait until that evening, and provided Lizzie's services were not needed by Mrs Lumbleigh and she could be persuaded to have the evening off, he knew she would be delighted at this extra treat.

Meanwhile he must track down the elusive Jock Webb. His only link was still Liberton Brae, although the address had been inaccurate, but another talk with the voluble Tom at the Stag might offer some clues.

He was in luck. The old man came out of his cubbyhole on hearing Faro's voice, remembering joyfully that here was a listener interested in his tales of past days.

'You will never guess, sir – after all your enquiries we actually had a visit from the great man himself. He looked in to tell us all about his near fatal attack.'

And Faro gathered that the wily ex-boxer was taking full advantage of this drama by relating a full and somewhat highly embroidered account of his almost fatal attack, hoping that by choosing an evening when the bar was full of customers it would pave the way to free drinks to celebrate his remarkable survival, dining, or rather wining, out on the event and making sure that old acquaintances now greeted as bosom pals were not overlooked.

Faro gathered, reading between the lines of old Tom's account, that Webb had fallen on hard times and it was not, as he had told the hospital, his memory that was deserting him but that he had been ashamed to admit that he had no settled home any longer. The grand house had accompanied his local fame into sad obscurity and he had no fixed address. It was humiliating.

When the attack had taken place he had been on his way to his present lodgings with a lady, taking advantage of the fact that as she had once been enamoured of him she would be glad to offer him shelter under her roof until times improved. He had related this with a lewd and knowing wink to convey to the younger drinkers, who could not imagine Jock Webb, stout, old and bald, as a man irresistible to ladies, that he was still at the height of his sexual prime.

Faro interrupted Tom's temptation to break into a long catalogue of nostalgic memories by asking did he have, by any chance, Webb's present address? A scratch through the mass of papers, mostly bills, stuck behind the till with murmurings of 'It must be here somewhere' was followed by a triumphant cry. 'Here it is!'

To Faro's relief and delight it was a cottage just two streets away. With apologies he announced he must leave now, his departure watched by Tom, disappointed at the disappearance of his captive audience. Faro walked up the garden path to the door, which was opened by an elderly woman who greeted him cautiously. Perhaps she had been in domestic service, as she gave the standard non-committal reply: 'I will see if Mr Webb is at home.' It was unlikely that she was unaware of that fact seeing that the frontage of the property indicated a maximum of three rooms and a twitching lace curtain at a window facing the street . . .

'What name shall I say?' she added politely, but he was saved having to reply 'The police' because Jock had appeared in the narrow hall, overcome by curiosity from his vantage point. At discovering the identity of his visitor, by no stretch of imagination could he be described as overcome with joy.

'Oh, it's you again, is it?' he grunted.

'Shall I ask him in, Jock?' the woman asked timidly, as if Faro was invisible and not standing at her elbow.

'It's all right, Annie,' and Jock went into the kitchen followed by Annie and Faro. He pointed to a wooden chair at the table. 'You might as well sit yourself down, officer,' he said, and opening a cupboard produced a bottle. 'A drink?'

'Not on duty, sir.'

And Jock nodded as an ample supply disappeared into the depths of a large tumbler which he held aloft. 'First today.'

Faro decided the accuracy of this statement was in some doubt, considering the table contained evidence of tankards and empty bottles and the kitchen smelt almost identical to the atmosphere in the pub he had just left.

Jock took a large swig, wiped his mouth on the back of his hand and asked, 'What is it you want this time?'

In answer Faro produced his notebook and a pencil. 'This is just a routine matter, to check that you have recovered from your ordeal.'

Jock braced his massive shoulders. 'Fit as a fiddle, laddie. Take a lot more than that idiot to put me out of action. I well ken the times in the ring I had much worse—'

Faro cut short what threatened to be a tide of reminiscence by saying hastily: 'Glad to hear you are none the worse, sir.'

'Have you found the bugger yet?'

'No. Which brings me to the next reason for this call. Do you remember anything significant about your attacker which will enable us to apprehend him and make an arrest?'

Jock took another long drink. He frowned and said: 'Well now, I did remember one thing, but it didn't seem worth mentioning. I doubt whether it will be of any help to you. He was tall, as I told you, and he was wearing one of those Inverness capes, the kind that sportsmen go for. Cost a pretty penny, mind ye, I had one exactly like that myself, year when I was invited up to the Highlands to shoot over the Duke of Argyll's estate.' He sighed. 'I remember it well, the birds we brought down that day . . .'

Faro listened politely. The Inverness cape's original purpose had been to protect soldiers from rain but over the years it had caught on as a fashion, adapted in Harris tweed as a more practical garment than the sleeveless cape to become an accepted order of informal dress for both middle-class and wealthy Edinburgh society, seen regularly at race meetings and hanging in the cloakrooms of all the best gentlemen's clubs.

Webb was asking: 'Would there be any payment forthcoming, officer, for this piece of information? It would be greatly appreciated.'

Faro handed over a half-sovereign which was seized with delight. Detective Constable Faro was then ushered to the door with the understanding that he was to come back any time, any time at all. He was to consider Jock Webb a friend for life.

Making his way back to the Central Office, Faro decided this new evidence proved only one thing. Despite Gosse's efforts, as far as he was concerned Jock Webb was effectively ruled out as prime suspect. Reason: a lack of any credible motive. Unless he was a madman, what had this elderly retired boxer to gain by strangling two women? Another final question as he was leaving had decided him.

Did he ever go to the Vaudeville Theatre?

'Never that sort of thing,' had been the scornful reply. Watching a lot of pansy men dancing about. Give him something healthy, like the boxing ring. That was the proper place for real men.

As his road took him past Lumbleigh Green, and anxious to follow up his theory that the dead woman was linked to the theatre, Faro took the chance of seeing Lizzie. He was in luck. Lizzie was walking towards the gate, a basket over her arm, heading for the Pleasance.

Her face lit up with delight at seeing him, so unexpectedly. What was he doing here? He explained briefly he had business up the Brae and Lizzie asked no further questions. Tactfully, she never did; his police activities were private business and she had no wish to pry on that secret part of his life.

'Are you by any chance free this evening, Lizzie? I can get tickets for the Vaudeville. I hear they have a good show just now.'

Lizzie clapped her hands delightedly. 'Oh, Jeremy, that would be great.' A frown. 'At least I think so. Unless the mistress needs me.

But they are at home this evening, no plans for visitors, so she won't be needing her hair dressed.' She paused. 'Can you wait a minute, and I'll nip in and ask her? I'm heading to the shops, and as a matter of fact, I have forgotten my list.' She smiled impishly. 'A good excuse for going back.' Turning she said: 'You will wait, won't you?'

Faro nodded. 'I'm in no great hurry. But be as sharp as you can.'

She was back in two minutes, having met Clara in the hall. One look at her expression told Faro that she had got the evening off to go to the theatre. Feeling it inadvisable to say that she was going with her gentleman friend, the detective, since his enquiries about poor Ida had been so bitterly resented by the master, Lizzie told a bit of a lie and expanded his solitary presence to a group of friends.

Clara was pleased that her maid should enjoy freedom when her presence was not needed. Unlike many of the other wives in her circle, she liked to feel that her views about domestic servants were quite advanced: she was well aware that Lizzie, who Clara appreciated as such a treasure, in the service of another family might well have had her freedom restricted to one afternoon a week, expected to sit with the mending box, sewing on buttons, darning socks and repairing hems just in case the bell rang for her.

Clara sat mute through afternoon tea conversations with neighbours' wives, whose constant moans were about the unreliability of servants who wanted so much these days; she found their talk of nannies, children, and occasionally recipes, rather dull, since she never set foot in the kitchen if it could be avoided. Some of the more enlightened wives occasionally raised the risky topic of a book or a scandal, and only then did she listen a bit more eagerly as her insatiable curiosity also contained a clause for the possible use of a ripe piece of scandal to be stored away for future use.

At the theatre, which tended to be noisy as the enthusiastic audience were invited to join in the chorus of the popular songs, Faro patiently awaited the interval. Fortunately Lizzie spotted three of her acquaintances, and after an introduction and some admiring glances in Faro's direction, which Lizzie noted not with jealousy but with pride, he bowed and having provided the giggling young ladies with refreshments, declined the invitation to join them and returned to talk to the manager. Albert Migley was also stage manager, middle-aged, stout and balding, a commanding and arrogant figure in evening dress who was drifting proudly among patrons in the bar.

As Faro approached and asked for a private word, Migley nodded and indicated that he should follow him into a room marked Private. As the door closed, the manager looked Faro up and down with approval. The advent of this tall, handsome young fellow with thick blond hair and an actor's deep, rich voice was perhaps providential as he was searching urgently for a baritone to replace the one who had just left in such a disgraceful hurry. At least this one was better looking and younger; those looks alone would bring in the ladies – of all ages.

He indicated a chair at the large desk, its expanse almost empty but for a spread of solitaire, obviously Migley's method of filling in his leisure moments during the performance.

As Faro sat down, Migley said: 'What can I do for you, sir?' and pushed across a notice regarding auditions. 'I take it that you are a singer – and I would rightly guess – a baritone?'

Faro stared at him in amazement. 'I am sorry to disappoint you, sir, but I am not. I am a police detective.' Faro's identity confirmed in the usual manner, Migley's face fell, and consumed with disappointment, he said accusingly, 'You are not in uniform.'

Faro smiled. 'Not when I am off duty enjoying a night out with the excellent entertainment your theatre provides.'

Migley sniffed and looked less huffy. 'So what is it you require?'

'We are looking into a missing persons enquiry and it has been suggested that the young lady might be an actress. This is just a routine matter of asking at the local theatres,' he added hastily, watching Migley's lips tighten, 'and if any of your girls are missing perhaps you might be able to supply an address—'

There was a sudden change in Migley's manner. He stood up sharply, leaving Faro no doubt of the reply, and looking distinctly hostile, said coldly, 'I have no such incident to report.'

Faro probed further. 'None of your young ladies has left suddenly to take up employment elsewhere?'

Migley's face reddened; he was distinctly flustered by the question. 'Of course not, we offer excellent conditions of employment – the best in the country, I would add.' And walking towards the door he said stiffly, 'I am happy that I have no such incident to report as the one you are investigating.' And opening the door he added, 'I regret I cannot help you, officer.'

Faro thanked him for his time, bowed and left, not at all satisfied, for Migley's agitated manner hinted at either guilt or a condition he had come across often in his career – that he had something to hide.

He could do nothing more as the interval bell sounded and he rejoined Lizzie and her friends, who watched them return to their seats with shrill hopes that they would all meet again – and soon.

Faro paid scant attention to the remaining acts: cute animals well trained – little dogs and monkeys, some dressed as nursemaids, pushing tiny perambulators, which produced coos of delight from some, including much of the audience and Lizzie, but not Faro who had a deep-rooted disapproval of circus or show animals.

He was not required to engage Lizzie in conversation on the way back to Lumbleigh Green. She was still enraptured by the songs and jolly atmosphere they had left and his preoccupation went unnoticed. He resolved to return next morning to the pub near the theatre, which he had seen patronised by the performers, and chat to the man who as doorkeeper entertained fellow drinkers with a host of stories, mostly exaggerated, gossip and scandalous whispers regarding artistes – and the stage manager.

* * *

Next morning, when the pub opened, he found the theatre doorman, who went by the name of Jimmy, in full flood, almost invisible behind a cloud of pipe smoke in a heavy beer-laden atmosphere. With the doorman only too willing to gossip, this time Faro was more successful.

Yes, indeed, there had been a real panic. Not only had Beau Garde the main singer walked out, but two dancers had also left without notice. Stormed out in fact. Offered a chance of a season with a big show in Glasgow, they said.

So that was why Migley was so upset, thought Faro, not guilt after all, and he felt a moment's pity for the manager's feelings of being let down, of betrayal. No wonder he had been so eager to consider the prospect of a replacement baritone. Migley would have had to add disappointment to his feelings, since Faro couldn't sing a note in tune.

'These two girls, did they share lodgings?' Jimmy looked thoughtful as Faro went on: 'Can you give me an address? Their landlady might know their whereabouts, or have a forwarding address?'

Jimmy shook his head. 'Can't help you there, I'm afraid.' But a sharp look, eyeing him shrewdly, and Faro realised that his questions might be misunderstood, as the doorman went on: 'Have they done something wrong, then?'

'Not at all. It's a missing persons enquiry. Family anxious, you know the sort of thing.'

Jimmy nodded. 'That's it, is it? Aye, well as far as I know all three were heading for the Glasgow Hippodrome.'

Thanking him, Faro left considering his next move. Glasgow. That meant taking the train, a whole day there and back. But first he must report to Gosse and get his approval.

And that was easier than he had anticipated. As he told Gosse about the interview with the theatre manager, Gosse nodded, frowning, obviously preoccupied with other matters.

'Remember that Rickels fraud case we were investigating before these murders needed our full attention?'

And pushing across a letter, 'Well, here it is. Summoned by the court. Unfortunately I can't go and leave matters unattended at a crucial stage of our enquiries. So I have written a report and you will need to deliver it in my place. You can look into the Hippodrome, but I'll bet you'll find that both girls are there. So much for your wild theory that the woman in Fleshers Close was an actress,' he ended with a hoarse laugh.

After delivering last-minute instructions, the

sergeant watched him leave. As the door closed he rubbed his hands and chortled with delight. He had his own reasons for welcoming an excuse to send Faro off to Glasgow.

And that included his hopeful wooing of Lizzie Laurie.

CHAPTER FOURTEEN

Faro loved trains. They were the marvel of the age. Sitting back in a speeding carriage and being carried across the countryside through a constantly moving landscape without making the slightest effort was a rare luxury when every day's duty in Edinburgh meant walking mile after weary mile on foot.

The sun shone through the window, reflecting a glowing scene of tiny farms, tranquil hamlets and mellow fields surrounded by leafy hollows already making the dramatic change into autumn splendour.

Smiling to himself he decided this was bliss indeed as the palace of Linlithgow, birthplace of his beloved heroine, tragic, beautiful Mary Queen of Scots, filled the horizon to vanish behind a cloud of smoke as the train gathered steam.

Relaxing in his seat, he considered how long this journey would have taken by coach or horseback –the latter he avoided whenever possible, never having overcome his fears of the unpredictability of horses when faced with an emergency. A fear that had its roots in the childhood memory of his policeman father's death under the wheels of a runaway carriage on Edinburgh's Mound.

All too soon, as far as he was concerned, the journey was over as tall buildings and church spires staring down from either side of the railway line announced that they were approaching their destination . . . All that remained was the final negotiation on the track's approach through the Cowlairs Incline where the train was hauled up through a deep rock cutting and tunnel, by a cable attached to a steam winding engine.

A few minutes later and the train puffed to rest at a platform in the handsome surroundings of Queen Street Station. Originally named Dundas Street, opened almost twenty years ago in 1842 as the western terminus of the Edinburgh and Glasgow Railway, built on the site of the once opulent Crawford Mansion with its extensive grounds, the station stood on the northern threshold of George Square, the magnificent heart of the city of Glasgow . . .

As he stepped out into the sunshine on his way to the City Chambers, he remembered how proud Glaswegians were of this square laid out in the 1780s as an elite residential development on the city's western edge. It had been named in honour of King George III, and Robert and James Adam had prepared plans for a handsome terrace on its south side. It was never built and the last of the site's earlier impressive homes had disappeared when one-time residents, such as the thread-making Coats brothers of Paisley, had moved out. The private gardens were now used as a public thoroughfare while all that remained of the grandeur of the surrounding buildings was represented by the Georgian architecture of the Copthorne Hotel and the front garden of the City Chambers, where Faro was to present the report on the fraud case investigated by DS Gosse and himself earlier that year.

This should not take long, he decided, as he climbed the steps and was ushered in the right direction of the meeting. Perhaps half an hour and then he would be free to make enquiries at the Hippodrome Theatre regarding the three artistes who had left Migley's vaudeville show, hoping to discover that his theory was right and only two of the trio had ever reached Glasgow.

Ushered by a clerk into the boardroom where the meeting was taking place he went to join the men seated around the table. Taking a vacant seat, he glanced at the agenda and awaited his turn, finding the other topics were of local interest and some made little sense for him to follow even if he had so wished. The tendency was for the chairman to expound at length, and as several of the gentlemen obviously loved the sound of their own voices Faro began to despair at the passage of precious hours.

Whether his visit to the Hippodrome would confirm his suspicions with a sense of triumph or not, a prolonged meeting threatened to end a long-awaited chance of exploring Sauchiehall Street's elegant terraces and villas before catching the last train back to Edinburgh. It was not to be. When at last the Rickels fraud case was reached, there was an interruption and a note was delivered to the chairman. Looking across at Faro, he read out the message. Owing to the sudden indisposition of the defendant, this case on the agenda would have to be postponed.

Disappointed and preparing to leave, Faro was drawn aside by the solicitor who whispered that as the time had been reset for the following morning, he had better remain, take lodging for the night and that a telegraph explaining the situation would be sent to DS Gosse.

Outside with the sun still blameless in an azure sky and the mellow shadows of late afternoon across George Square, Faro gave a great sigh – of delight. Another day was an unexpected holiday, to explore the delights of a city so unlike Edinburgh. Somehow warmer, kinder he decided, with citizens who smiled upon this stranger who asked for directions to the theatre after he had twice got lost on the way.

At last, walking up the steps, he was told the matinee performance was almost at an end. As he was too late for that, would he care for a ticket for the evening one? Declining, he explained that he wished to speak to the manager.

He was in luck. Mr Dobson was to be found in his office. The welcome he received was polite and genial. What could he do for him? Mr Dobson was less shocked than Migley had been at the information that the enquirer was a policeman from Edinburgh.

'Sit ye down, officer. Something to drink, perhaps?'

A thirsty Faro declined alcohol in the course of duty. As he explained his mission, omitting that it was a murder case and explaining it was merely a missing persons enquiry, a soft drink produced from the cupboard was poured into a glass and set before him.

The manager listened, frowned. 'Aye, we have artistes just joined us from Edinburgh, right enough. Two of them, a singer and his lady friend, a dancer.' He shook his head. 'I'm afraid you've made the journey for nothing, officer. Your missing actress didn't come to us. You could try the Glasgow Fair, though.' He hesitated. 'They have sideshows, that sort of thing, a bit of a reputation. Maybe not the kind of setting for a reputable artiste, if you ken what I mean. Tell you what—' A distant sound of applause reached them. 'That's the show finished – you could speak to Beau and Jane, they might have some information that would help you. Come with me.'

Faro followed him into the wings, where the performers were taking their final bow. He had never been as close to a stage before and the excitement, the greasepaint, the drama of it all was a new and thrilling experience. As they all hurried past, chatting, laughing, teasing one another, curious and admiring looks from the dancers came his way. Stepping forward, Dobson congratulated a young man. 'You were in great voice tonight, Beau.'

Beau looked pleased as Dobson went on: 'Jane too. She's a great addition to our girls.' Then taking Faro's arm without mentioning that he was a policeman, he said: 'This gentleman is here about an actress who left Edinburgh at the same time as you.'

Beau smiled. 'You mean Doris Page.' He shook his head. 'She didn't come with us.'

A pretty girl on her way to the dressing room had seen them and, curiosity aroused, came over. Wearing the teasing bespangled costume of a high-kicking chorus girl, she was introduced as Jane by Dobson and also congratulated for her performance. She dimpled at that. She listened carefully as Faro's presence was again explained and the manager was suddenly called away by one of the stagehands.

Jane took Beau's arm and frowned. 'No, Doris didn't come with us. She wanted to stay in Edinburgh. She has a wee girl, you know.'

While Faro felt that this fitted neatly into his theory regarding the identity of the dead woman in Fleshers Close, Jane looked uncomfortable, by which he guessed that Doris was probably unmarried. 'Didn't want to leave her with strangers.'

'Have you any idea where she was going?'

Jane shook her head. 'She didn't get on with old Migley. He was always, well, chasing her, trying to get his hands on her.' Jane shuddered and Beau grinned. 'He was like that, always wanted his pound of flesh, if you know what I mean.'

Jane made a face. 'Well, Doris got fed up and they had a row. Told me she'd find something else. That was a couple of weeks before we left.'

Faro thanked her for her information, and given Doris's last address at the Edinburgh lodging she had shared with Jane, he took his leave. Mixed with a sense of triumph, he felt sadness for a broken life, and seeing again the face of that little girl at the murder scene, he determined to make further enquiries to see what had happened to her.

Walking back towards the square he wondered if they now had another murder suspect. Was it possible that Migley had killed Doris Page? Gosse, he knew, would jubilantly seize upon this new piece of information, but hopeful as it might be, it seemed very unlikely that Migley had also murdered Ida. He remembered that game of solitaire, the playing cards spread on the table. But that seemed an unlikely clue. Not by any stretch of imagination could Migley fit Ida's handsome, wealthy young lover (as whispered to Lizzie), nor did the description tally with the brutal man who attacked Jock Webb.

A stranger in this bustling city, he had no idea where to find cheap lodgings and as the Copthorne Hotel loomed ahead he decided to book a room for the night, hopeful that he could reclaim this as necessary expenses. If not, he did not really care – this was a once in a lifetime chance to enjoy the luxury of a splendid hotel.

As he made his way across to the reception area to book a room, a woman was walking in front of him towards the restaurant. A slim, young and lovely woman with long black hair.

His heart missed a beat. He knew that graceful lithe step. All his senses recognised this answer to all his dreams, and some of his nightmares too.

'Inga!' he called.

And Inga St Ola halted, swung round to face him.

CHAPTER FIFTEEN

Faro was speechless; he blinked again.

Inga? Impossible, a figment of his overactive imagination. But here she was, walking towards him, her light footsteps on the polished floor. She was smiling, holding out her hands in welcome.

'Jeremy Faro! What on earth are you doing here?'

Taking those warm hands in his own, his power of speech returned.

'I might ask the same.'

Her laugh as she tilted her head back was so familiar – he had heard its echoes throughout his long-lost Orkney years.

She nodded towards the restaurant and took

his arm. 'Come and I'll tell you about it.'

Shown to a table by the window overlooking George Square, sitting primly opposite one another, wasn't enough for Faro. Still wondering if this was a dream that he might prolong before waking up to reality, he longed to be at her side, touching her, holding her hand, breathing in the perfume she always wore.

Her eyes, blue as violets, smiled at him. 'I expect you are here on police business.'

When he nodded and asked: 'What about you?' she sighed.

'I have a job of work. A gentleman and his family were on holiday in Kirkwall. There was a sudden illness and they needed help bringing the family over to Glasgow,' she said briefly.

'How long are you to be here?' She began a long explanation, enlarging on the circumstances of the family crisis of this gentleman who was very important, a member of parliament.

He was no longer listening, his mind racing ahead composing excuses to send Gosse to extend his stay in Glasgow for several days, longer – indefinitely. A week, perhaps. A week spent here with Inga. He closed his eyes briefly, the answer to a dream.

She was shaking her head. 'I am not sure, it depends on Sir Hamish and how long his wife has to stay in Galloway.'

Her frown became a faraway sad smile. A sigh. 'Then it's back home again to Orkney.' She shrugged and her face clouded as if the prospect did not appeal to her and he said sharply and rather accusingly:

'You said once nothing would ever make you leave the island.'

She shrugged. 'I know, Jeremy, but that was a long time ago.' Was she reminding him of when he had asked her, begged her to be his wife, to return with him to Edinburgh, and her firm heartbreaking refusal?

Now she was saying: 'Circumstances change, you know.'

'You've obviously changed your mind,' he said, trying to keep the bitterness out of his voice.

Her eyebrows raised. 'I had it changed for me. A person in need, who needed my help. And it isn't for ever,' she said softly, giving him a teasing glance. 'Just a short while until proper arrangements for looking after the children can be arranged. Their nanny took ill, as I told you.' Had she indeed said that? He felt irritated, betrayed, confused.

'What with that, Jeremy, as if the poor souls hadn't enough . . .' She shook her head. 'Troubles never come singly, always in three, as we say back home.'

He nodded, not having heard a word she had been saying about that sick nanny, presumably why she had been recruited at short notice. She didn't like babies particularly, so how was she coping with this situation?

Silent now, she was staring out of the window, biting her lip, a habit he remembered she had when she was thoughtful. The sun had retreated leaving the tall buildings casting their long dark shadows across the square; the day would soon be drawing to its close, the romantic twilight hour.

The waitress came for the order. Inga shook her head. 'I'll be eating later, but tea and cake would be nice.'

'Same for me,' said Faro enthusiastically, although he would have preferred something much stronger than tea to steady his nerves. At that moment all appetite for food had been destroyed. It was something much more than food or drink for which his body hungered – to push aside the table and take her in his arms.

She had asked him how long he was staying and was waiting for an answer. 'Till tomorrow – at least,' he added hopefully. 'Will you be free this evening?'

She frowned. 'Maybe for a while. Are you staying here too?'

He smiled, said yes and at that moment he thanked destiny that he had to bring Gosse's report to Glasgow. He even added a silent thanks for Inspector Wade with his broken leg, all the threads that had destined him to book a room in the same hotel where Inga was staying.

'What would you like to do?' he asked eagerly. 'I don't know Glasgow but it would be pleasant to explore with you.'

She shook her head. 'I need to stay in the hotel – in case I'm needed by the children.'

He looked around the restaurant; people were arriving, looking for vacant tables. Soon it would be crowded. 'Difficult to stay here talking.'

She looked at him, smiled and understood. 'Agreed. We could go to my room and wait. They will know where to find me when they get back.'

Faro paid the bill and followed her upstairs, his heart racing. Not a single room in a corridor, however. She opened the door into a suite of rooms overlooking the square, the sky now wreathed in sunset. He followed her across a large handsome room, set with comfortable sofas and small tables.

Smiling, she opened the door into a smaller room, and Faro saw only a handsome bed, white pillows piled high – the perfect setting for love.

No sooner had she closed the door, than he took her in his arms. She did not resist, but she did not melt into them either as he hoped. Returning that first tender kiss, a little restrained, she moved away from him and said: 'So good to see you, Jeremy. Take a seat, will you.'

He saw the other contents of the room as she pointed to the window, with its two armchairs either side of a small table.

He remembered her well enough to recognise that this was all for the moment as she said: 'How's Lizzie?'

Lizzie was the last topic he wanted to discuss with Inga. He shrugged, and as she laughed lightly, his heart sank as miserably he realised there were to be no more passionate embraces. This romantic setting overlooking George Square was to be wasted for him, as sitting opposite him, Inga's talk suddenly became general, about Kirkwall and South Ronaldsay and the weather and not a thing he wanted to know about – not even about his mother, who was back in her own home in Kirkwall after a summer as housekeeper at Scarthbreck.

Mary Faro didn't like Inga and the feeling was mutual.

'Next time I see her, I'll tell her we met and that you were looking well,' Inga said, reminding him guiltily that his mother was overdue an only son's dutiful letter.

A halt in the conversation and she asked idly, 'Not getting married yet, Jeremy?'

'It's not Lizzie I want to marry, as you well know, Inga St Ola,' he said sharply. Suddenly her nearness was unbearable. He left his armchair and went over and kneeling put his arms around her.

'No, Jeremy, no!'

'Why not?' he said.

Moving away from him she sighed. 'You know why not. We've been through all this a thousand times. I can't marry you.'

'You mean you *won't* marry me.'

She shrugged. 'Put it that way, if you wish.'

Seeing his expression touched her heart; she stroked his cheek gently and whispered, 'It was never meant to be, Jeremy.'

'Why not?'

The same question but she shook her head, sighed. 'I can't explain, just that it isn't written . . . it isn't our destiny—'

'What nonsense you talk, my dearest love.'

'I'm not your "dearest love", Jeremy,' she replied indignantly. 'I'm a free spirit – remember?' She looked up at him and for a moment it was as if he saw clearly through her eyes and he knew again that among many other inexplicable things Inga St Ola, from his land of selkies and magic, had the ability to see into the future.

The sound of a man's voice, a door opening, footsteps in the other room. A tap on the door.

They both stood up as a man came in. A tall man, middle-aged but with good looks and presence outstanding.

And Faro, looking at Inga's face, saw something else.

The look of love, of absolute adoration. And in that moment, he knew that free spirit or no, Inga St Ola who had never been his, was lost to him for ever.

He hardly waited to be introduced. He was consumed with misery by this revelation, the confirmation he had never been willing to accept, that Inga had tried to din into him over the years. He had ignored the warning signs at his peril, that she would never marry him, that the wild attraction, the magnetism she had for him, was completely one-sided. She did not return it, had never done so and had never loved him in more than a friendly, companionable way, regarding him tenderly through the years as the boy she had initiated into manhood that long-lost night on a moonlit Orkney beach.

That and nothing more.

Now he had to face the truth, and that face of love he had glimpsed would remain indelible on his tortured mind. Clearer than any words, he had witnessed her adoration for another man and on both faces he had read all he needed to know: that they belonged to each other.

It was there for all the world to see. Marriage, a wife and children presented an ignored impediment to their relationship for they were consumed by an irresistible force, terrible in its intensity, the kind of love that could also destroy. The kind of love Jeremy Faro had never known and now would never know.

He thought he had bowed, shook hands, murmured goodbyes. He didn't know if either of them even noticed his absence, or whether they saw him leave. Their love wrapped them up and transported them to another dimension of time, inaccessible to ordinary mortals, and Jeremy Faro was as unimportant as a piece of furniture in the hotel's grand suite.

In George Square again he felt oddly naked and vulnerable, deprived of the dream of Inga St Ola which had been his for a decade, since he was seventeen years old. Tonight it felt like a death, but in spite of the terrible revelations of the last hour, his alter ego remained intact. The detective constable had not died in the assault to his emotions, and walking towards Sauchiehall Street he found a smaller, more modest hotel where he booked a room for the night.

Ahead next morning lay the appointment at the City Chambers and the statement he was to read out on Gosse's behalf, and then, with all desire for further exploration quelled in case he should meet Inga and her love again, he would return to Edinburgh by the first available train.

Meanwhile he discovered that he was hungry – it was some time since he had eaten – and he was given directions to a restaurant where, as some sort of consolation and healing to his bruised spirit, he ordered the most expensive course on the menu, helped down by a couple of large whiskies. Feeling better but realising he would sleep little in that tiny rather dark bedroom overlooking the hotel backyard, he decided to make notes regarding the success of his visit to Glasgow.

He had made one important discovery: he was almost certain that he knew the identity of the dead woman in Fleshers Close, an actress called Doris Page who had a wee girl and had not made the trip to Glasgow with Beau and Jane.

This was a triumph of sorts, being able to prove his theory was right, and he would enjoy proving Gosse was wrong. Having the name of the first murdered woman should put them a step further to finding the man who had killed them both.

He slept surprisingly well and, his appetite undeterred, he consumed a hearty breakfast and made his way to the City Chambers where Gosse's statement was first on the agenda and the hearing mercifully short. An hour later and he was seated in the Edinburgh train, the warm sun shining benignly through the carriage window, lighting up a landscape of undulating hills that would have inspired an artist had that been the role for which destiny had intended him.

As Edinburgh approached he thought fleetingly of the journey to Glasgow, how he had been unaware what lay in store. The final closure of a ten-year dream of a future, in which, despite all the odds, Inga St Ola would one day marry him.

He relived that moment before setting it aside for ever. The magic of seeing her walking towards him in the hotel, how his mind had raced ahead to conjure up the night before him in a wonder of fulfilment. That had passed away and he sighed, mentally saluting a youthful daydream, realising he did not even know the name of her lover, except that he was some sort of a politician.

But that no longer concerned him. He was unlikely to meet either of them ever again.

CHAPTER SIXTEEN

Leaving the train and heading up the Mound towards the Central Office, Faro prepared to put his new-found facts before DS Gosse and this gave him a twinge of self-satisfaction.

Gosse watched Faro as he outlined the proceedings at the City Chambers and how their report had been well received. He explained about the necessity for spending a night in Glasgow; Gosse was always ready to make a great fuss over claims for expenses, however the sergeant was less upset or querulous about this than Faro had anticipated.

'These things happen. At least this has finally closed the Rickels case. No more tedious visits to

Glasgow,' he added when Faro told him that they were to expect an official statement that the case was now closed.

Gosse had listened, frowning and nodding absently, but seemed to have lost all interest and his word of praise at the end of it was an unexpected bonus.

'Excellent, Faro. You did well, saved me a tiresome journey when there were much more important matters to deal with in my new capacity as acting chief inspector,' he reminded Faro again.

Gosse indeed had his own reasons for personal feelings of jubilation and Faro would have been surprised to know that these concerned Lizzie Laurie.

'There was something else, sir.' It was Faro's turn to drop a reminder, as Gosse looked at him and asked:

'Oh, indeed? And what was that?'

'I believe we now have the identity of the woman in Fleshers Close, sir.'

Gosse regarded him, smiling slightly, an expression of disbelief, and asked mockingly, 'Indeed. So you managed a bit of detective work on your own, did you?'

'Yes, sir,' was the eager response and producing his notebook Faro read out his account of the visit to the Hippodrome Theatre, his interview with the manager and his meeting with two of the three artistes, the singer Beau and the girl Jane, who had left Edinburgh for better prospects in Glasgow.

'The third member of the trio remained here. Her name is – or was – Doris Page.'

Gosse held up his hand, grinning. 'Sorry to destroy your moment of triumph and steal your thunder, Faro, but you are too late. We already have this information—'

'But how—?'

'Listen and I'll tell you. Yesterday afternoon, a man came in, looking for his missing wife, or rather to put it bluntly his common-law wife, for that was what she was, no legal marriage as proof of identity. His name is Len Page, his wife's name Doris.

'He had a little lass with him.' He paused and said, 'You will remember her, the wee one you were so concerned about at the murder scene. Well, she is their daughter. Apparently you were right about one thing,' he admitted reluctantly. 'Doris Page was an actress. I was wrong about that red dress and so forth, but she was also a whore, new to the game or not.

'Although Page had begged her to marry him on account of the bairn, she had always refused. They were living in Aberdeen at the time and after a big row, according to him, one day she walked out with the wee lass and disappeared. She usually came back but when a month went by he was determined to track her down. He wanted his daughter back whatever. It's taken a long while, until he got as far as Glasgow and discovered she had been working in the theatre there but some of her chums thought she might have moved on to Edinburgh.'

Gosse paused, shook his head. 'That was last week. He still couldn't find her, and as a last resort came in with a missing persons enquiry. As soon as I read the description, I knew it was her lying in the mortuary. Page was very upset, especially when we told him that she hadn't died naturally or by some unfortunate accident. She'd got herself murdered.'

He stopped, looked at Faro, and said: 'I can tell you this story raised all my hopes. A deserted husband is always the one we look for first, the prime suspect in a murder case. But no, not this time. It seems that she had a good reason for leaving him. He admitted to having a violent temper but when we found her in Fleshers Close he was safely behind bars, locked up in Glasgow police station. Seems he was charged with disorderly conduct, dead drunk and almost incapable of doing anything but knocking down the constable who came to arrest him and break up the fight.'

Gosse sighed deeply. 'Pity, isn't it? What a disappointment that we can't nail the murder on him. Would have been the perfect solution. Case closed. Instead, we still don't know who killed Doris Page and we still have a killer on the loose.'

'Even if it had been this man Page, sir,' Faro observed, 'it still wouldn't account for the assault on Jock Webb or the killing of the maid from Lumbleigh Green.'

Gosse looked exceedingly displeased at his detective constable's perfectly logical observation. Frowning, he said 'Ah well, not beyond the bounds of possibility,' and with a profound shaking of his head, he added solemnly, 'No, Faro, not by any means.'

And Faro smiled to himself. Surely fixing the blame on Doris's partner would have been beyond even Gosse's remarkable powers of invention.

He was saying: 'So we're not much further forward. You could have stayed here where the solution was waiting, if you'd had patience, instead of gallivanting away to Glasgow to track around theatres. Saved yourself the time, not to mention the expenses incurred by the Edinburgh Police.'

Having revived his usual lamentation on that

subject, another head shake. 'It will not look good in the report to the chief constable when he learns the answer was on your own doorstep, so to speak. These things are remembered, Faro, when matters of promotion are discussed, especially as all you have contributed in the Doris Page murder,' he added doubtfully and repeated, 'was wasting time going round in a circle.'

Faro listened patiently to this tirade, and when the sergeant paused for breath, he reminded him gently, 'There is still the business of the playing card unsolved, sir. We need an explanation for that too. Where does it fit in?'

'I've never believed that was anything more than coincidence, Faro, and I have more important matters to attend,' Gosse replied huffily, and gathering some of the papers on his desk he dismissed him.

Faro felt relief that the murdered woman's body had now been claimed for burial and that it would not suffer the indignity of ending up on a dissecting slab in Surgeons' Hall. Most of all, that forlorn, frightened wee lass who had had such a horrific experience in Fleshers Close would have a future with a caring parent.

'Wonder how the two of them met up again, sir?'

But Gosse wasn't interested. He sighed weary

and handed him a slip of paper. 'You talk to Page, see if there is anything I've missed – see if you can use those much-vaunted powers of observation and deduction to trap him into a confession,' he added mockingly. And as the door closed, 'But I doubt that. Another waste of time.'

Gosse's own time had not been wasted, however. He had seized the opportunity of Faro's absence in Glasgow to exercise his charms and ingratiate himself with the lovely Lizzie Laurie.

He found her polite, nice mannered and ladylike, but the awful truth was that he had not made much progress in the direction he sought, that was, to lure her into his empty bed. As a deserted husband he felt he was entitled to a little dalliance, even a mistress, although this would need careful concealment from the chief constable since any hint of a sexual scandal would considerably deplete his hopes of promotion. Bearing this in mind, he had taken care to craftily suggest that they meet away from Lumbleigh Green to continue his enquiries into her association with the maid Ida.

Lizzie believed him and over tea and a cake in the Royal Mile café she also feared that three visits to interview her at the big house might be subject to misinterpretation. Even with her mistress's kindly intervention on her behalf, she was conscious of the master's displeasure and his suspicious surveillance.

Watching her across the table with delight, Gosse was very pleased with his plausible explanation that no one could object to, especially as she anxiously confirmed that the presence of police detectives disturbed Mr Lumbleigh, to say nothing of his whole household, and upset him to such a degree that it put her own situation as lady's maid to Mrs Lumbleigh in jeopardy.

She sighed and told him that the master regarded her as a troublemaker who, instead of minding her own business, had brought discredit to his house by going to the police to notify them that Ida was a missing person.

As they talked over a second pot of tea, no expense spared, Gosse was mentally rubbing his hands with glee. It was all working out so well; he scrutinised every change of expression on Lizzie's face, and when she smiled into his eyes, he was certain that he was observing the onset of another emotion stronger, more daring than mere politeness.

And should she mention their meetings to Faro, he had no legitimate cause for complaint. DS Gosse was within his rights – as far as the investigation was concerned, he was merely doing his work, interviewing everyone who had the remotest connection with the murdered girl.

As Lizzie went over once more in scrupulous detail her vague association with Ida, he took out a notebook and wrote down once more in elaborate detail facts of which he could remember every word. Even he could not pretend there was anything further to be learnt from the murder investigation point of view. It was, to quote his own favourite phrase, a complete waste of police time.

Even had there been new information it would have taken him by surprise. He was no longer interested. His own goal had started out as merely to seduce this lovely woman, take her from Faro and score a victory over his detested detective constable. However, he was now completely obsessed by her. Love would have put a kindlier interpretation on the lust lurking in the darker regions of his heart.

On the evening of Faro's return, Gosse set him to work on some urgent reports in the Central Office, and while he was so engaged, decided to call on Lizzie at the coachman's cottage. She had been very accommodating and told him that their mistress allowed her to spend weekend evenings with her son when she was free of duties.

Gosse was grateful indeed for any venue but

the kitchen of the big house to further his cause, although his appearance caused an angry barking from the dogs outside and more than a flutter of annoyance inside. The coachman Brown and his housekeeper wife were at supper and quite plainly he was the last person they wished to see.

A more sensitive man might have thought that his presence, with its repercussions from earlier interviews at the big house, and the resulting displeasure of Lumbleigh himself on all the servants, might have been responsible for that sense of strain in Mrs Brown's cold reception.

'What do you want this time? We have told you everything you wanted to know.' Her husband barely glanced at him and continued applying his spoon to the soup.

Gosse had his excuse ready: it was Mrs Laurie he wished to interview. 'Again?' murmured Mrs Brown and gave him a look that he might have considered coy, as if she knew perfectly well what was going on and all about his intentions.

Brown's bewhiskered face raised briefly from his soup. Spoon in hand, he demanded: 'What's she done this time, then?'

'Nothing,' said Gosse. Conscious that this visit was doing his cause no good at all, he added righteously, 'A murder has been committed and this is merely part of our investigation.'

'Even though the girl wasn't murdered here on the master's premises?' said Mrs Brown. 'Seems your enquiries should be a little farther afield, officer.'

Gosse's response was a tight-lipped expression indicating that theirs was not to reason why, that this was duty and he was not prepared to argue about the merits or demerits of police procedure.

The housekeeper did not question his silence; she merely shrugged, extracted a pie dish from the oven and over her shoulder said: 'Mrs Laurie isn't here, as you can see for yourself. She came and collected the lad, taking him to the shops for new shirts. Said they would have their supper later.'

Gosse left polite but chagrined. Things were not going at all in the way he wanted and time was short. Not only for finding a murderer, but for his successful wooing of Lizzie Laurie.

CHAPTER SEVENTEEN

The possibility that Gosse was seeing Lizzie other than as an interviewing officer had not remotely occurred to Faro. Had it done so, he would never have entertained any fears of the sergeant as a possible rival for her affections.

To be honest with himself, Lizzie had not occupied a prominent role in his thoughts since his encounter with Inga in Glasgow. He knew he should get in touch with her, but decided to leave matters as they were at present until their next meeting.

Meanwhile, he would seek out Doris Page's common-law husband, see if he might provide some clues from her acquaintances and so forth, which would lead them to her killer. He doubted whether there was anything to be gained by this meeting. Reading between the lines of Gosse's account, he saw a dreary, often violent relationship and possibly the only reason the woman stayed with him was for the child's sake. Until that day dawned when she could take it no longer. Penniless, taking care of their small daughter, her distress must have been acute, Page a monster of cruelty, for her to take to the streets.

He went to the address near the Haymarket. A boarding house offering vacant rooms. A woman opened the door and before he could ask for Mr Page, a man appeared behind her.

'Have they come? Is it here – they're early?' he said, staring past Faro along the road.

It was obviously not a good time to conduct an interview about his dead wife as Len Page was clad in mourning; the black crêpe around his tall hat announced that he was awaiting the arrival of the hearse to accompany it to the cemetery. Faro held out his card and, offering his condolences, he had a quick insight into the misery, the distraught confusion of a bereaved man.

Page shook his head, stood aside, said: 'You'd better come in.'

The landlady ushered them into the parlour for receiving visitors and persons seeking lodgings.

As Faro took a seat at the round mahogany table amid a profusion of potted plants, large ornaments precariously perched on shelves and a galaxy of framed family photographs, there was little room to put his feet anywhere without some violent encounter with a tapestried footstool. The armchairs had protective antimacassars, and among the threatening dark landscapes on the walls, an occasional interjection of a cross-stitch text sternly warned 'Jesus listens to every conversation', which must have effectively tongue-tied lodgers inclined to frivolity. And over all the smell of beeswax polish indicated a clean and efficient landlady who took a pride in her home.

The door opened and a child's face appeared. The little girl Faro had seen before and recognised from that first tragic encounter in Fleshers Close. No longer poor and shabby but prettily dressed, she rushed towards Page and leapt upon his knee. The sight of a policeman's uniform aroused dreadful memories that had her burying her head in her father's shoulder.

Stroking her hair he said: 'It's all right, Jess, just a kind man come to see us.' And to Faro, 'It shouldn't be long now, Constable. While we wait, what can I tell you?'

Smiling at the wee girl, Faro whispered: 'How did you find her again?'

'God, I was so lucky. In despair, I was wandering down the High Street and there she was, walking towards me. She was living with this old woman who looked after her when Doris was – busy.' He shuddered. 'She had given her shelter – after—' His words failed. 'She won't talk about it, what happened – that night. Just shakes her head, poor wee sweetheart.'

Faro decided that if she had forgotten, then that was just as well. Sorrow clung round the man and his child and he thought beyond it to the events that had led to this tragic ending, the funeral of Doris Page. It had been a fraught time for Page, getting the legal matters settled, her body about to be removed from the police mortuary and delivered into the waiting hands of eager medical students at Surgeons' Hall.

As Page began to talk rapidly, the words tumbling out in a steady stream, the necessity to have someone to tell it all to, to unburden his shock at the killing of the woman regarded as his wife and mother of his child. As he talked the child sat thumb in mouth still staring, glaring suspiciously at Faro who smiled at her but she immediately hid her face.

Page said: 'When I saw you, I hoped you were bringing word that you had got him – the man, you know, who did it.' The latter words were in a whisper as he stroked his daughter's hair not wishing to use the terrible word 'murder' in front of a child who might well have witnessed the fatal attack on her mother.

'Can you tell us anything that might help to track him down?' Faro asked.

Page made a helpless gesture. 'I went over all I know with the other man, the sergeant. Do you want it all again?' he added wearily.

'Was . . . Mrs Page a gambler?'

Page looked bewildered, shook his head. 'No. She was just stage-struck, always had been, that's all.' He gave Faro a puzzled look. 'We didn't have money for gambling. Why do you ask that?'

Faro told him about a playing card that had been found beside her and Page shook his head. 'She was no gambler, just dying to be an actress.'

And Faro realised the irony of his words as he went on. 'We were in Aberdeen, I was a gardener with the parks. Out of work, so I took anything I could get, temporary labouring. That wasn't right for Doris and she would never have moved in with me, if it hadn't been she was expecting . . .' He paused and stroking the child's hair tenderly, whispered '. . . wee Jess here. It was an accident but although I wanted to marry her, make it legal and proper, like, in the church or registry office, she would have none of it. Said she would have the bairn first, then we'd decide what to do next.'

Pausing he sighed. 'She was mad about going on the stage, being a dancer, and she had a lovely figure, fine legs and a good voice. Everything that was needed. One day she met a fellow from the London theatre, up with a touring play, told her he had great influence in all the right theatrical places. Said he was right struck by her, with her looks and voice she was wasting opportunity. He could easily get her a job on the stage, even just in the chorus to start with, that was how most stars began.'

He looked thoughtful, shook his head sadly. 'Always a bit flighty, ye ken, and this was a chance she said she couldn't resist. Left a note saying to forget her. But I was determined to find her, talk some sense into her. And that has been my life for the past three months, trying to track her down. And now . . . this . . .' His voice broke and he dashed a hand to his eyes. 'Finding her too late.'

As Page talked Faro regarded him intently. It didn't take much reading between the lines to realise the story of this ill-matched couple. A middle-aged man, big and strong muscled who might have been good-looking long ago but was now stout and balding.

'She didn't like the only life I could give her,'

Page went on. 'I was often out of work and when we hadn't enough to eat she complained then that any money I earned I spent on drink. Drink was my escape but she didn't understand that. We quarrelled, she had a sharp temper and could say cruel things, telling me that I was old enough to be her father and she was wasting her life with me.

'And when I drank too much, I had a temper too and I would use my fists. God help me, I hit her often, and then, one day, it was too much and I came home to find that she'd gone, and taken Jess with her. I found an address in Glasgow among her things, I was there only last week looking for her.'

And Faro realised that this distraught man and himself had both been in Glasgow within a matter of days, each searching for a lost love. He gave a fleeting thought to his own disillusions, for this man's experience was the far greater agony.

'I didn't know what I would do if I found her, I just had to know, that's all. If she wanted to be an actress, I decided I'd let her go, I wouldn't stop her as long as I could keep Jess – I would manage. We were never right for each other and that's the truth . . .' He sighed. 'And I wasn't much of a provider.'

Faro guessed the rest, saw the curtains opened

on the life that was so familiar among most of the working men and women he met on his beat in Edinburgh. Men like Page, who asked not much of life beyond a working wage, an evening spent in the pub with wages left over from the rent, food and clothes for the bairns. Not much future beyond a few carefree hours, a pint or two of ale with mates and staggering home in an elevated state of pretending the world was a better place than the dreary streets, going home to a wife's arms and warm body for the comfort of the night.

Faro sighed. Whatever Page might be, he decided that this man might have killed his wife in a passion of rage but it was beyond the bounds of possibility that he had also killed Ida Watts.

'Have you found work in Edinburgh?'

'Aye, thank God. Used to be a gardener and I got a day's work with one of the big houses off the Dalkeith Road.'

'Was it Lumbleigh Green, by any chance?'

Page made a face. 'The very same. Hard, back-breaking work and a rotten boss, a miserly owner who worked us eighteen hours for a handful of coins at the end of it. One day was enough, I can tell you.'

Faro wondered if this was what the interview had been all about, the chance remark that often holds a hidden clue. 'Did you meet any of the servants, the maids . . .' He didn't want to ask directly. 'Did you know Ida?'

'No time for that. We were kept working well away from the house.'

Faro wanted to ask more, such as when was he there, but the sounds outside and the doorbell announced the arrival of the hearse, behind which Page would follow Doris's coffin, walking to the graveyard half a mile away.

The woman looked round the door, whispered, 'They're here.'

Page stood up and she took the now sleepy child from his arms. Jess awoke, shouted, 'Pa, don't go.' As if aware of what lay ahead for him, she struggled out of the landlady's arms, ran to his side and clutched his hand.

He kissed her, picked her up and handed her back to Mrs Reid, saying soothingly: 'Now you be a good lass for Pa. I'll be back very soon. I'll bring you sweeties,' he added encouragingly.

The word 'sweeties' worked wonders. Such treats had been few and far between in her short life. Now they seemed like landmarks and, consoled, she took the woman's hand and was led into the kitchen but still with that anxious backward look. 'Come back soon, Pa, you promised.'

On the steps, Page said: 'You're a good

listener, Constable. Sorry I had nothing useful to tell you.' And looking towards the hearse, the black-plumed horses, he grasped Faro's hand. 'Find the man who did it, will you?'

Helmet in hand, watching the sad cortège, Faro considered what he had learnt. Page had been a gardener at Lumbleigh Green. Was it true that he had never met Ida? Even though, after finding his wife again, he might have killed her, Gosse had checked his whereabouts. An unshakeable alibi, in a Glasgow jail at the time of her murder, locked up for the night, drunk and disorderly after a pub brawl.

But he had no alibi for Sunday in Edinburgh, possibly roaming about the area of the North Bridge, most likely drunk again. But the facts did not fit and Faro was glad they didn't. There was one vital element missing. Not by any stretch of imagination could this middle-aged, working man in search of his absconding wife fit Ida's description of her young, handsome and wealthy lover, wanting her to elope with him.

Making his way back to the Central Office he had one consolation. The fate of the wee girl which had so concerned him was now safely in the hands of her devoted father. And he decided to keep to himself that Page had been a temporary gardener at Lumbleigh Green. If Gosse had that piece of information he would be at Page's lodging with the handcuffs before the words were out of Faro's mouth.

And Faro remembered Page's comment regarding Doris's killer. 'I would bet that some man picked her up leaving the theatre. She would have gone for that. She knew what she was about and I know now that it wouldn't have been the first time, either. But this time something went wrong and he had to kill her.'

Even as Faro went over the words, he saw again vividly the episode he had encountered outside the theatre. The drunk young man trying to drag the protesting dancer in her red dress into his carriage. The abduction he had averted.

The evidence against Paul had steadily mounted since Faro first recognised him again at Lumbleigh Green.

CHAPTER EIGHTEEN

Paul was also playing a prominent role in Lizzie's growing concern about Vince. Faro came close in her list of worries, but only second. She loved him and longed to be his wife but in a straight choice it would always be Vince, even if that meant breaking her heart over losing Jeremy Faro, the only man she had ever loved.

She remained doubtful regarding Vince's hero-worship for the 'son' of the house. Delighted that Paul had taken such an interest in the twelve-year-old son of his stepmother's lady's maid, and conscious of a list of good things that might result, at the same time she was anxious; an ever-present worry nagged at her like a mild but persistent headache that refused to be ignored – a feeling that something was wrong but she didn't know how to talk to Vince about it. The reason, she guessed, for his intense friendship with the older man was that Vince had never had a father, only the fictitious one she had invented, a brave soldier killed fighting for country and queen in India, and this was a common link, a bond with Paul.

'Just like my father, Ma,' Vince had sighed proudly.

Lizzie groaned inwardly. Her lies had come home to roost with a vengeance. She hoped she would never have to reveal the dreadful story of his conception – certainly childhood and adolescence were not the right times. Maybe wait until he was older, grown up and aware of the true facts of life, and that other world that existed beyond a mother's devotion and protection.

Lizzie was aware that as far as Vince was concerned, Paul Lumbleigh was perfect, he could do no wrong, and already the boy was heavily under his influence. Most of it, she had to agree, was hopeful and helpful, especially since Paul was clever and knew about books and the kind of things like art and music and history, subjects of which she was almost totally ignorant; famous people of the past that Jeremy also liked to talk about, a bewildering world she had never had time to explore as an overworked maid bringing up a small boy. Her reading matter was limited to occasional romance stories.

She didn't mind the card tricks. She was lost in admiration for Vince's quick-moving fingers as, by demonstrating, he explained away the apparent magic of making cards disappear and reappear thanks to the sleight of hand Paul had showed him. Proud of her clever son, she laughed delightedly. Her only fear in that direction was that Vince might also use his skills one day to be a gambler. She shuddered at the thought, remembering rumours that Paul and the master had quarrelled over Paul having suffered heavy losses at the gaming tables, and that he was only saved from jail by his stepfather having to settle all his debts.

There was a more pressing reason for her anxiety. Vince was being taught how to use firearms to shoot over the hill, using guns Paul took from the big house.

One day, Vince showed her the handgun that had replaced the rifle, a more efficient weapon Paul had told him. And when she gave a shriek of horror, Vince put an arm around her and smiled sadly.

'Men have to know these things. No need to be scared. Pa would be proud of me. I bet he always

218

wanted me to be a soldier.' He kissed her cheek. 'There now, Ma. Paul is a good teacher and I'm very careful. I know what I'm doing.'

Those words from a young boy. Lizzie shook her head, she could think of no suitable reply, and felt only misery for that lie once told. Vince believed in anything that brought him close to the fictitious father she had invented for him.

And Lizzie felt she had to do something, tell someone who would understand. That man was Jeremy and she brought it up that evening when they were walking together in Queen's Park.

To her surprise Jeremy merely laughed. He obviously didn't think it a matter for concern, and he certainly did not share her fear about accidents.

She looked at him a little sadly. He seemed different, a bit distant since his return from Glasgow, and she suspected more preoccupied than usual with the details of the murder of Ida Watts. To be truthful, he had very little interest in Vince's activities, which came well down the list of important and urgent matters like finding the killer of two women.

His sole concern about Vince's new friend was how it would affect Lizzie if she knew that Paul was the prime suspect in the murders of Doris Page and Ida Watts.

As Lizzie went on about her fears for Vince, Faro wondered what she expected him to do. Of course she felt helpless and was pleading for his support. Was that what Lizzie was hoping for, that he would sit down and talk sternly to Vince? He almost laughed, it was so ridiculous and unimaginable, a cosy chat between them. He certainly had no intentions, nor was he even willing to consider confronting the boy who loathed him and made no secret of it. Surely Lizzie was aware of the tensions between her suitor and her son, that any advice Faro offered would have exactly the opposite effect.

At the moment he wasn't prepared to take her fears seriously. If he had concerns they were about his own relationship with Vince's mother. What was he going to do about their future after the bitter revelations of his encounter and rejection by his own true love, Inga St Ola? In vain, he tried to thrust out of his mind that disastrous meeting.

Had it changed his feelings for Lizzie, somehow revealed her in a new light? He shook his head. The fact that Inga did not love him, had never loved him except in his wild imaginings, did not automatically upgrade Lizzie and make him fall wildly in love with her.

* * *

Inside the big house all was not well. The absence of policemen lurking about and making enquiries had done nothing to soothe Archie's indignation and outrage at the invasion of his privacy. The impeccable reputation he had been at such pains to build seemed likely to topple and he was hurt and bewildered at finding Clara's reactions were not as sympathetic as a husband would have naturally expected. Sometimes he thought he hardly knew her at all. She had a habit he found particularly irritating of attempting to soothe away his fears with a plea for a better understanding of those beneath them. In fact, showing an alarming tolerance for human nature.

Nervously he wondered if she was aware of his long-standing relationship with the madam of a brothel. He shuddered at the idea but she was certainly displaying much more compassion for the lower classes than seemed right and proper for a lady in her position in society.

Archie had good reason for bewilderment. Behind those gentle smiles Clara still lived on a knife-edge of keeping hidden the secret of her own reinvention. Maids come and go without reason or explanation at regular intervals in big houses, but the upheavals in the calm of Lumbleigh Green over the table maid's disappearance and the shocking evidence of her killing had taken their toll on

Clara's sleeping. She had firmly believed that the girl who had once been Ethel Wyner had passed into oblivion and would stay there safely buried for ever. At least that was so until Ida's murder, an event which had opened several cans of worms in the Lumbleigh household, and the house teeming with policemen (according to Archie) had jolted her back into memories of an unsavoury past.

Conversations with even the most polite policemen she found quite unnerving, although she had reason to regard DS Gosse with disquiet – his young and very attractive assistant, DC Faro, she learnt, was walking out with her maid Laurie. She approved of that but was at pains to keep this information from Archie. At present the mention of Laurie brought a frown of anger, a furrowing of his brow, and to add romantic entanglement with one of the policemen who had cast such a blight upon the sacred precincts of his home might well have sealed the immediate dismissal of her precious maid from the premises.

Laurie was not the only cause of Clara's sleepless nights. She had other pressing worries. The sight of two policemen striding across the lawn towards the house had reawakened long-buried memories of a previous encounter with the law after the prison fire that had enabled Jabez Bodvale to escape.

Clara remembered being the object of long interrogations in the hope that she might have information regarding his whereabouts. Now those memories reawakened and became ghosts to haunt her rest, taking shape in nightmares about her terrifying stepfather . . .

In them she saw a resurrected Jabez rushing across the lawn towards her, with his evil grin, while she stood paralysed, unable to flee. The front door had opened to admit him and she heard clearly his footsteps on the stairs.

She woke up sweating with terror. Of course it was impossible, to imagine him lurking about outside Lumbleigh Green. How long was it since she had heard of his dramatic escape? Years since the police had arrived at her door with the dreadful news and the suggestion that she might be hiding him, her movements regarded with suspicion. At long last they had accepted that he had other plans for his escape and his stepdaughter was not involved. Still she had waited in terror for the policemen's return or, what was far worse, the appearance of Bodvale at her door. Time passed without any news of his recapture. But if he was still alive and free, roaming about the country somewhere, there was not the slightest doubt in her mind that his uppermost thought would always be to track her down.

Obsessed by nightmares, the vivid memory of which clung to her even during daylight hours, terror lent a pressing urgency to share her fears, to tell someone. She needed a confidant, someone to soothe her fears. The most natural person would have been Archie, but that was out of the question. The whole unsavoury past would have to be revealed, and shuddering, she imagined his horror.

In that fact alone she was mistaken. Her concerns about what Archie's reaction would be were quite without foundation. In her husband's eyes she was a beautiful and priceless ornament and he would have been as indifferent to her past as he would to the past owners and often bloody histories of those large, and she thought preposterously ugly, Chinese vases which he boasted had cost a small fortune.

But just as his wife had dismissed him as her confidant, so Archie had also turned to someone other than Clara to listen to his troubles. Had Clara made a small calculation she would have wondered at the fact that, never famous for an ever-open purse, Archie was uncharacteristically generous in keeping her very well provided for. And it was on his regular visits to the perfumer's establishment in York Square that Mavis – keen to maintain her own small allowance from Archie

– listened and shook her head in eager sympathy.

Having firmly decided in her ignorance that Archie was the last person in whom to confide, Clara considered her women friends. No, they were acquaintances, really, that she encountered in her small social world. There wasn't one of them with whom she had anything in common or that she warmed to. Their backgrounds belonged to another world from hers. Thoughtfully regarding the ladies sitting around the table with her, she guessed that they had never known poverty, hardship, the sexual violence of a cruel and brutal stepfather. Their main concerns over afternoon tea or the dining table in the evening were money, their husbands' elevated ranks in Edinburgh, dressmakers, milliners, parties, children and servants – a considerable time was spent moaning about the latter – all topics, with the exception perhaps of clothes, which had a very limited interest span for Clara.

Idly she wondered if any of them had a husband with a long-term mistress like Archie. She had known about Mavis for a long time. Had she loved him more she might have been hurt and shocked, but instead this was a piece of knowledge to store away at the back of her mind. It might have its uses later.

In desperation, Clara realised, there was only one woman with whom she identified. And that was her maid Lizzie Laurie, from whom she could not conceal the dark circles around her eyes brought about by lack of sleep.

Lizzie was also concerned about Clara. Considering her mistress's reflection in the dressing-table mirror, she said: 'Madam is looking so pale today,' and added anxiously, 'Is there something wrong?'

And that was enough, the decision was made. Clara moved over to the sofa and indicated Laurie sit beside her so they were less likely to be overheard. Hairbrush still in hand, looking somewhat bewildered, Lizzie followed.

Clara smiled. 'Leave my hair, it will do for now, Laurie. There is something very important I have to say to you.'

At her solemn expression, Lizzie laid aside the brush with a trembling hand. She felt suddenly sick. Had the master won? Was she to be dismissed? Oh dear, what was worst of all, what would become of Vince deprived of his lovely secure new existence? But her beloved mistress was taking her hands, saying: 'What I am about to tell you, Laurie, you must promise never to tell a living soul. It has to be

226

our secret. Will you promise me that?'

Lizzie promised and her eyes widened considerably as, almost in disbelief, she listened to the terrible story of the mistress's fearful childhood, the disgusting, brutal stepfather; the following years after her escape from his clutches, awful to guess at, and which were tactfully skimmed over, and then how she had struggled to survive before she met and married the master.

Lizzie blinked; it was like something from those novels she read but much worse, because this wasn't fiction . . . this was real.

She was, however, less shocked than Clara had expected. In return she could have shared her own secret that she was not in fact the widow of a brave soldier killed in India, but that Vince was illegitimate, fathered on her at fifteen by a guest, identity unknown, in the Highland mansion where she was a maid.

She might have told Clara, exchanged confidence for confidence, secret for secret, but she thought better of it. There were so many other people involved for whom such knowledge of her past might have repercussions – most importantly, Vince himself, being told that his whole life story, the father of whom he was so proud, was in fact a lie invented by his beloved mother. Only one person, Jeremy Faro, knew the truth and Lizzie knew that she could trust him with her secret more than anyone else on earth.

So she closed her lips firmly and lent a sympathetic ear, aware that Clara had told her just enough to shed a little of this intolerable burden in a secret bond that made it marginally easier for her mistress to bear.

CHAPTER NINETEEN

When Faro reported his interview with Page, Gosse commented dryly: 'Pity you didn't think to go to the funeral with him. Funerals, I have discovered from my vast experience, are places to pick up clues. Family mourners often reveal surprising things about their relationships in the stress of the moment.'

He paused, adding grimly, 'And funerals are often visited by murderers. God knows why, perhaps to make sure their victims can't jump up and denounce them, or out of a sense of curiosity that they have got away with it. Safe at last.' He shook his head. 'But one thing is sure, it's a time of high emotions all round and the most unexpected people can be overcome and give away useful details for a murder investigation.'

Faro listened patiently and as Gosse paused for breath he took the opportunity to interrupt: 'I could hardly walk behind the coffin with the bereaved and grieving husband, sir. He didn't suggest that I accompany him and there weren't any other mourners with whom I might have mingled unobtrusively. No one. As far as we know from Page's statement, he had just arrived in Edinburgh and his late wife hadn't been here long.'

Gosse held up his hand. 'I don't agree with your objections, Faro. Page claims he wants to know who killed her. You could have kept a sharp look out and made a note of any curious observers.'

This seemed another one of Gosse's tedious arguments bent on getting nowhere and Faro said sharply, 'I must confess it never occurred to me, sir. It would have seemed an unpardonable liberty to intrude on the poor man's grief with my presence any longer.'

Gosse looked at him silently for a moment, then sighed. 'You are far too sensitive, Faro, as I have said before, and this, I fear, will be a great impediment to your career. I can visualise you still being a detective constable when you're past fifty and ready to retire. Police business, catching criminals, comes first, before personal feelings if you want to succeed. Try to remember that.'

And picking up some papers on the desk, he added, 'So don't let it happen next time.'

'Next time, sir?'

Gosse sighed wearily. 'Yes, indeed. You are to go to Ida Watt's funeral. There will be plenty of mourners there, local people as well as the servants from Lumbleigh Green.'

Faro had in mind a kirkyard where the Watts lived in Bonnyrigg when Gosse said: 'You'll be saved all the footwork. Catholic church at the Pleasance have their own burial ground. See if you can have a word with the priest, prise any information out of him. Confessions and all that sort of thing could be a mine of useful information. Fill in those vital missing details. He's our best bet, Faro, so see to it.'

Faro thought that prising information out of the priest was highly unlikely. His knowledge of religion was sufficient to tell him that the secrets of the confessional were sacred and unbreakable.

Observing his doubtful expression Gosse pressed on: 'For God's sake, man, show some enthusiasm. Stress that this is a murder case and he will be more than willing to help us find the killer. A young woman from his congregation.

Priests are human beings, after all.'

Gosse sat back in Wade's comfortable armchair. 'I have a lot on hand, Faro.' And consulting a note, 'The funeral's this afternoon. See if you can make a success contributing something to our investigation for a change.'

Faro hated funerals and decided against wearing his uniform. This was agonising enough for the dead girl's family without a reminder that she had been murdered, her killer still at large.

The fact that the servants from Lumbleigh Green were likely to be there and that would doubtless include Lizzie, well to the fore and marked down as Ida's friend, did nothing to cheer him. He wasn't looking forward to meeting her at the graveside.

Gosse had got the time wrong and the Requiem Mass in the church redolent with incense – as a non-Catholic, a ceremony way beyond Faro's Presbyterian upbringing – was almost over, and he decided to head on to the graveyard a short distance from the church. Under the lofty shadow of Salisbury Crags, it offered little shelter for grieving relatives.

Mercifully, this was a clear, sunny but cold afternoon, and after a short wait, the trail of mourners arrived, headed by the Watts behind the coffin followed by friends and members of the congregation. He went forward and offered condolences to Ida's parents; her distraught mother looked as if she had not stopped crying or slept for a week.

In a tearful acknowledgement to Faro, she was leaning on the arm of her husband, who was losing the battle to keep a stiff upper lip on the loss of a devoted daughter. He asked sharply and somewhat accusingly: 'Well, have you got him yet?'

Faro shook his head. Never had he felt more helpless. The grief of those two, as well as the memory of Doris Page's bereaved husband, strengthened his resolve to find the killer, see him brought to justice and hanged for his crimes.

Listening to the committal service at the graveside, he was surprised to see that the priest was a man younger than himself: tall, athletic-looking, with exceptional looks and a splendid voice that would have served him well in the theatre. Faro thought wryly that such attributes were lost in a life of celibacy.

He looked round the mourners. Lumbleigh Green was represented by Clara in a respectful black bonnet, with Mrs Brown, Betty and Lizzie, who wore dark clothes as their servants' uniforms, and had added black ribbons to their bonnets. The four women were driven over the short distance but Brown did not join them at the graveside, remaining with the carriage nearby. In the traditional manner of coachmen used to coping with Edinburgh's uncertain weather and chill winds blowing from the Firth of Forth, Brown sat muffled up and, as fashion dictated, abundantly whiskered. Faro preferred to remain clean-shaven and thought that having so much facial hair must have seemed like regarding the world from behind a thick hedge.

Clara's arrival had been greeted with courtesy and bows from the women and raised tall hats from the men. Alongside the chief mourners, Mrs Brown at her side appeared regal and dignified, hands clasped, suitably respectful.

Lizzie was looking pale and sad in her servant's dark costume; mourning had demanded that those rich, fair and abundant curls be securely bonneted. Her arm supported Betty, sobbing uncontrollably and distraught as befitted the chief mourners, despite her short acquaintance with Ida.

Faro was conscious that Lizzie was gazing in his direction, but with a feeling of helplessness he avoided her eyes and concentrated on the heartbreaking scene being played out before him. Despite Gosse's instructions, it was impossible to see among some forty strange faces surrounding him, a loyal turnout of the church's entire congregation, as well as local friends of the Watts, whether they included a murderer lurking in their midst.

And suddenly it seemed no longer important. Ashes to ashes, dust to dust, a flower thrown into the grave by Ida's father and it was over . . . the benediction.

Lizzie lingered; her eyes tear-filled, she came towards him.

'It is so sad, Jeremy . . . I am so sorry . . .'

Although he took her hand, bowed briefly over it, so cold in the warm depth of his fist, she was conscious that he was hardly aware of her. He indicated the priest shaking hands with the mourners, anxious not to lose contact with him.

'I can't talk just now, Lizzie. I will call on you in the next day or so.'

Raising his hat politely he bowed and hurried away. Feeling let down, rejected by his manner – so alarmingly casual – and with tears for her own sadness and disappointment now, needing his comforting presence so much at this tragic time, she watched him approach the priest.

It was time to return to Lumbleigh Green in the carriage, with Brown, patient for so long in the cold, trying to calm the horses stamping their feet. At last, trotting briskly, they passed Faro in earnest conversation with the young priest. He did not glance in their direction and that hurt Lizzie too.

Clara sitting at her side took her hand in a wordless gesture of comfort while Betty continued to stare out of the window, her eyes red with weeping, her frightened glance indicating a very uncertain future of possible murderers lurking around Lumbleigh Green.

Fr Burren's first question to Faro had been: 'Are you a friend of the family?'

Faro shook his head. 'No, Father.' Out of uniform and in the midst of the mourners he was reluctant to declare himself as a policeman, although the Watts were aware of his identity. 'Just a word in private.'

A hand touched the priest's sleeve. It was a woman, come to thank him. Ida's auntie from Kelso.

The priest stopped sharp, his eyes flooded with tears. 'Dreadful, dreadful.' He put a hand briefly on her shoulder, she turned away and he looked blankly at Faro who repeated:

'I was hoping to have a few words . . .'

The priest regained his composure, stared wildly ahead and said: 'I cannot talk to you just now – I have daily offices, you understand.

Perhaps you could come across to the church in an hour or so.'

Faro duly presented himself as the priest had requested, after spending that hour sitting on a wall nearby and taking the opportunity to make notes of his somewhat unhelpful observations to present to Gosse.

The church door creaked open. It was dark inside after the sunlight and at first glance seemed empty, apart for the serene faces of the saints looking down on him, the lingering smell of flowers and incense.

'Hello!' he called, and as his voice echoed round the walls, another sound: Fr Burren emerged from the direction of the vestry, donning his white surplice over his clerical black garb.

Smiling gently he invited Faro to follow him and indicated a pew in the aisle. Adjusting the sacred velvet stole around his neck, he laid it reverently to his lips and asked: 'What can I do for you, sir? Is it confession you are after, then? Friday is the normal day . . .'

Faro shook his head in embarrassment. 'No, Father. I am not a Roman Catholic. I'm a policeman – Detective Constable Faro – and my presence at the funeral is to further our enquiries into the death of the young woman.'

Again the priest seemed overcome by emotion.

Lowering his head, he nodded a few times as if shaking away those terrible thoughts, then recovering he said stiffly, 'I am not aware how I might help you, Constable. I only knew Ida' – pausing he took a deep breath – 'the young lady, as a parishioner. I am new to the parish and indeed to Edinburgh. I came over from Dublin a few weeks ago to take up this parish.' As he spoke Faro noticed again the fine voice, the pleasing Irish brogue.

That was indeed a setback but Faro went on: 'I wish to get to know those of her circle who were acquainted with her movements. Perhaps you could give me some advice in that direction.'

The priest looked at him intently and frowned. 'I am not sure what you mean by "advice".'

Faro took a deep breath. 'We have been led to understand that Ida was in a difficult position, regarding her family, and she had no one in whom to confide her problems.'

Burren bit his lip and thought about that for a moment. 'And what sort of problems would they be, now?'

'She had some wealthy young man who she claimed wanted to marry her. On the night she . . . disappeared, she was intending to elope with him.'

The priest was watching him, hands clasped so

238

tightly his knuckles shone white, but his face gave nothing away.He took a deep breath and asked softly: 'And how is it that you think I can help you?'

'If you could give us the name of this young man . . .'

Burren seemed startled by the question. 'Was he not present at the graveside, then?'

'Not that I am aware.'

'Then how do you think I can help the police?' He stood up sharply, bowed towards the altar – a clear sign of dismissal. 'I am sorry.'

'A moment, Father. Did Ida come to confession regularly each week?'

'Of course.' And Burren realised too late that he had fallen into a trap. His shoulders slumped but he regarded Faro sternly. 'Such matters are not for public scrutiny. What is revealed in the confessional is sacred between priest and penitent and God's forgiveness.'

'But she did tell you something of her intentions?' Faro insisted.

The priest shrugged, folded his hands before him. 'Perhaps so,' he said uneasily. He did not want to lie.

There was a moment's uncomfortable silence before Faro said: 'I realise you are in a difficult situation, Father, but you must realise that if you know and are withholding some detail of importance regarding Ida's unfortunate death, your silence is hampering police investigations and the capture of a murderer. I might add that he has already claimed two women victims and might well claim more.'

The response was a shudder of horror, a genuflection, then in a calm voice, Burren repeated once more: 'I can tell you nothing, officer. I am responsible to a higher authority than the Edinburgh City Police and to break the Church's vows is to sacrifice the future of my calling as well as my immortal soul.'

'Then you do know something,' Faro insisted.

A shake of the head. 'I cannot discuss this but I can assure you that Ida Watts is – was – a God-fearing young girl, a good Catholic, and I do not believe she would have given her heart to an evil killer.' He made a move towards the door. 'You must look elsewhere for your information, Constable.'

Faro stared at him. Incredible that he was stubbornly refusing to help by telling them the name of Ida's lover, her killer who had probably also murdered Doris Page.

'Now I must leave you,' the priest said sharply. 'I have offices to perform.'

Watching him walk firmly towards the altar,

Faro thought of his eloquence, those exceptional good looks, somehow wasted on this servant of God, with his splendid reverberating voice, that lilting Irish brogue.

As he walked away from the church he thought that this short acquaintance with Fr Burren had made a rare and lasting impression on him. Remembering that first sight of him at the graveside intoning the solemn words of the burial of the dead, yet stumbling through it as if for the first time, reading from the book through suppressed tears. The handsome young man, strong, virile-looking and less like a celibate priest than any cleric he had ever encountered. Faro was curious as to what, when he had so much going for him, had made him choose such a profession.

Later he would learn that Burren had said: 'We do not make choices, God chooses us to do his work.'

And on his way back to the Central Office, a new thought struck him: the emotions that mention of Ida had aroused in Burren, who had known her so briefly. Remove the clerical garb of this unlikely priest and he fitted neatly the description of the mysterious, handsome young man who wanted to marry her. Wealth was the only missing ingredient.

However, was it possible that after seducing her he had suffered an attack of conscience and murdered her?

And a final thought. Did he have a pack of cards hidden away in the vestry, including the nine of diamonds? But unless that priestly garb concealed a ruthless killer, he could think of no possible motive to link him to the murder of both women.

CHAPTER TWENTY

There was a message awaiting Faro at his lodgings. It was from Macfie, inviting him to dine that evening, and, always glad to see his old friend, Faro was even more pleased at the offer as the funeral and the aftermath of his unsuccessful interview with the priest had left him depressed.

An evening with Macfie was something to look forward to with even more than his usual pleasurable anticipation. Dining and wining with his old friend was one of the highlights of his present sorely troubled existence.

Macfie would want to know all the latest developments at Central Office, his crafty means of keeping in touch with the police whom he had never quite forgiven, after serving for so many years, for forcing him reluctantly into retirement when his faculties were sharp as ever, his physical strength undiminished.

Faro felt a sense of relief that here was a man whose experience of the criminal world might well be of assistance to the police in this particular case, detecting what was beginning to look like a spate of serial killings. If Jock Webb's testimony was correct, as Faro believed, then he had narrowly escaped becoming the second victim.

Over a dram, the two men sat by the window in the handsome parlour overlooking the ancient wall which once marked the boundaries of the city and was built to keep the English king's army at bay after the Battle of Flodden.

Fascinated by living in the lap of history, Faro found it strange to sit in this elegant house in the tranquil surroundings of Nicholson Square. Often he wondered what poor, unhappy ghosts still haunted the nearby buildings of Edinburgh University raised on the rubble of what was once Kirk O' Fields – in the sixteenth century an ecclesiastical site high on the breezy outskirts of the city and noted for its health-giving properties but to be forever associated with the murder of Lord Darnley, unhappy Queen Mary's insufferable second husband.

As the rosy glow of an autumn sunset touched the skyline of Salisbury Crags and slowly faded, a cheerful fire cast its gleams beyond the new gaslight which had replaced the candle sconces still lining the walls. They remained Macfie's preferred illumination, disliking the gas mantles which he claimed were an abomination and an irritation, their constant hissing disrupting consecutive thought processes.

Realising the value of Macfie's advice built on his thirty years with Edinburgh City Police, Faro produced his notebook. Faro explained that he had just come from the funeral of the last victim, the maid Ida, and as he described the young priest who conducted the service, Macfie looked up and gave him a questioning glance.

'Something troubling you?'

Faro shrugged. 'I wasn't prepared for a priest like Fr Burren conducting a funeral service, a burial. He seemed . . . well, just out of the seminary. I expected priests to be older somehow, more experienced and much less handsome and worldly.'

Macfie smiled. 'We all have to start somewhere – even the clergy – and detectives, when they emerge into the world, are very young.' Pausing he gave Faro a wry glance. 'And some are very good-looking too.'

Faro said: 'That may be so, but detectives begin as raw young peelers, start their apprenticeship on the beat seeing all the worst aspects of human nature.' He shook his head. 'This fellow seemed so ill-equipped for my idea of a priest, but he already had what I call the voice of authority. You know what I mean, the accent of the well-to-do, used to issuing orders.'

It was Macfie's turn to shake his head; he clearly didn't see what Faro was getting at or what all the fuss was about.

'Wish you could have seen him. Even his looks, the physique of a man of action. A superb voice as he stumbled through the prayer book, losing the place at the graveside, as if it was the first time he had read the words, like an actor forgetting his lines.'

Faro paused thoughtfully. 'Very emotional too. Once or twice I thought he was going to burst into tears – and this, remember, was just for the member of a congregation he had only been with for a few weeks.' He frowned, again that helpless shrug. 'All this . . . somehow didn't quite add up, if you know what I mean, sir. Just a feeling that it didn't fit, an instinct that there was something wrong, that I was missing something important – some fact I should recognise that was missing.'

Macfie had been listening carefully. He knew

Faro's observations and deductions well enough not to ignore these signals. Now he regarded him intently. 'Right from the beginning if you please, lad.' As he tried to describe the scene at the graveside in detail, Macfie was arching his fingertips together in a manner Faro was familiar with. An attitude of deep concentration. At the end he sat back and smiled.

'Ah, now I realise what is troubling you. Our young priest fits remarkably well into the description the girl Ida gave your young lady companion. That is so, is it not?'

Faro didn't answer and Macfie continued consolingly. 'But let's face it, lad, you must realise that this is an unlikely and difficult role for a killer to adopt. Of course, it has been attempted and does exist in the annals of crime, the perfect disguise for the perfect crime which no one would suspect.' He laughed. 'Never a priest, a man of God!'

Macfie paused. 'Perhaps you are being unconsciously influenced by the idea that this particular priest's appearance suggested an actor, and actors lead you to the Vaudeville and the first murder of Doris Page. You are applying logic in a baffling case – all those playing cards for instance – and perhaps looking for a killer with theatrical connections. Am I correct?'

Faro hadn't actually got that far in his assumptions. He said: 'It is an interesting theory, sir, and the description also fits Jock Webb's description of his attacker as a tall, strong man who he wrestled with.'

'A young man?'

Faro shook his head. 'Webb didn't specify age. Asked, he merely emphasised the man's physical strength but his actual age and appearance would be difficult seeing that he was tackled from behind, and as it was dark, he never actually saw the man's face clearly.'

Macfie sighed. 'We will need to know a great deal more about Fr Burren and I think I can help you there. The head of the Catholic Church here in Edinburgh is an old friend from a fraud case I investigated some years ago. Perhaps any information he can obtain will confirm or put an end to your suspicions.'

There was a pause in conversation as Macfie's housekeeper came in. Miss Agnew, a middle-aged spinster of ample proportions and a genial but respectful disposition, who, Faro suspected, absolutely doted on her employer, removed their soup plates and replaced them with an excellent beef steak pie. Murmurs of approval came from both men as they ate in silence.

Finally Macfie laid aside his fork and knife, refreshed their wine glasses and continued: 'Now, about this actress you were clever enough to work out as the killer's first victim. Well done, lad. As you know, observation and deduction never go wrong. How was Glasgow? I knew it well in the old days before so many changes had been made to George Square. The city centre was more like a country estate.'

'I'm afraid it was a wasted journey, just a small expedition of my own after delivering Gosse's report to the City Chambers. When I got back to Edinburgh it was to learn that the victim's husband, one Len Page, had informed the police that she was missing and identified her body just as it was about to be shipped off to Surgeons' Hall. When I interviewed Page at Gosse's request all my instincts said that unless this ordinary middle-aged widower was also a consummate actor, I would swear that he was not her killer. Just a poor, unhappy man, wasting his life by loving the wrong woman.'

As he spoke Faro felt again overwhelmed by the surge of his own anguish, his unrequited love for Inga St Ola.

He paused and Macfie nodded, said softly, 'Almost as though you had been through it all yourself.'

'Something like that, sir.' Faro sighed and put down his glass, then continued hastily: 'Page has an unbreakable alibi: during his search for his missing wife he got into a pub brawl and, fortunately for him, as it happened, was locked up in a Glasgow jail that night, as drunk and disorderly.'

Macfie smiled. 'Fortunate indeed. Otherwise he would have been marked down by Gosse as the prime suspect.'

Faro wasn't smiling. He was frowning. Suddenly the need to share his distress was compelling. 'When I was in Glasgow, sir, I met someone again, from Orkney . . .'

Macfie's head jerked upwards, a questioning look as Faro went on. 'Yes, my first love. I have never forgotten her and always hoped that we could be together some day.' He shook his head. 'But she was at the hotel where I intended staying – she was there with . . . someone – an older man, she claimed was her employer. I gathered he was of some importance, a politician.' He paused, reliving that painful scene again. 'And I knew instantly that it was too late. They were in love. I read it in their faces as if they had shouted the words at me.'

Another pause as the housekeeper brought in the Scotch trifle, a favourite with both men. They ate in silence, replacing spoons on empty plates, and ignoring Faro's earlier outburst of confidence, Macfie asked: 'Has Gosse finished his interviews at Lumbleigh Green?'

'He continued some of them while I was away, I believe.'

Macfie smiled to himself. So that explained it – or did it? How he had seen Gosse and Mrs Laurie having tea in his favourite café in the High Street, which seemed an unusual setting for a police interview rather than the place where she worked, the scene of the maid's disappearance.

From a shrewd observer's point of view it also seemed that DS Gosse, laughing, smiling, leaning forward to whisper, laying the charm on thickly, was very taken with this particular member of the Lumbleigh servants. Tactfully Macfie decided to keep that information to himself and merely remarked: 'How is Mrs Laurie?'

Faro responded that she was well, and happy at having been promoted recently as Mrs Lumbleigh's personal maid. 'That also offers extra facilities – living in for her, and also for Vince to be boarded at the coachman's cottage. It's a great improvement on the tenement room she had in the Pleasance.'

'That is good news,' said Macfie. 'Perhaps you would like to bring Mrs Laurie to tea sometime.'

Faro realised that Macfie was keen to meet Lizzie and said, 'I'm sure she would be delighted, sir,' leaving Macfie to wonder whether the wily sergeant was playing some unsubtle game trying to drive a wedge between Faro and his young lady, as Faro added: 'Sir, I don't know what to do about her at the moment. My emotions are all topsy-turvy. I am very fond of her and she has had a rough time.'

Macfie nodded. In common with everyone else he knew nothing beyond the fiction that the very attractive Mrs Laurie was a soldier's widow with a young son, as Faro continued hesitantly, 'You see, sir, the boy Vince is the main problem to our relationship. He makes no secret that he detests me.'

The older man smiled. 'That is not surprising, lad. Often the way with a lad seeing his mother with a new man in her life and feeling that he is being replaced in her affections, and worse, that this fellow is going to try take his father's place. I shouldn't let that worry you too much.' And with an abrupt change of subject he said, 'We still haven't solved the playing card conundrum. The curse of Scotland. Where does that fit in? Do you think it is a clue?'

They discussed that for a while. The possibility, however remote, that the killer had some link with past family grievances.

Macfie nodded. 'It doesn't make sense; it could be a madman, very highly educated but obviously insane, to have such a concept. But we never know until it is too late, mostly, that motives like revenge can have terrible consequences – on the innocent as well as the guilty.' He looked thoughtful. 'On the other hand it could be merely something put on the scene of the crime to distract the police from the real purpose behind the killings.'

Faro left him that evening, making his way back to his lodgings and wondering whether he should have told Macfie about Paul Lumbleigh being the drunk young man at the theatre trying to drag a dancer in a red dress into his carriage. Especially as that was what had led him to suspect that dead woman in Fleshers Close might not be a prostitute, as Gosse maintained, but a member of the chorus from the Vaudeville Theatre.

It had paid off. And now, until Macfie had found out more about Fr Burren, Paul Lumbleigh was his prime suspect.

CHAPTER TWENTY-ONE

Faro awoke next morning determined that an immediate interview with Paul Lumbleigh was a vital stage of the murder investigation.

When he mentioned this to Gosse without giving his reasons, the sergeant shrugged. 'I had a quick word with young Paul and he had an alibi. You'd be wasting your time – and police time too. And let me tell you, once again, there has been enough ill feeling with our dabbling inside Lumbleigh House without having his father issue an official complaint for harassment against the Edinburgh City Police – as he has threatened. And he has friends in high places.'

He sighed wearily and fingered the papers on

his desk in a manner of urgency. 'So just leave it alone, Faro, and keep looking in more likely places.' Pausing he shook his head. 'I haven't quite given up on Webb, or even Page for that matter.'

So Faro left him. He certainly wasn't persuaded to give up on Paul but he was still pondering on what plausible excuse he could invent, when opportunity came for him from a most unexpected quarter.

Clara Lumbleigh had been delighted to discover that she shared a birthday with Lizzie Laurie. She had never met anyone with the same birthday before and it seemed such a good omen, the reason she felt more drawn to her maid than to any of the other women she'd ever met. Not that she had been on intimate terms with any of them to discover such personal information.

She decided this was the mystical bond that explained why she had so much in common with Laurie and had trusted her with a few of those secrets from her past. She would have been even more surprised to learn that, had Lizzie vouchsafed her own particular confidences in return, they had even more in common than she could have imagined.

Clara's scheme began with a gentle reminder of the approaching birthday to Archie, who never remembered or even tried to remember such occasions. Too busy, was his excuse. However, although he winced at the prospect of another expensive piece of jewellery for his beloved wife, he realised that good form and their social position demanded the obligatory celebration. As this year was not a milestone, a small dinner party with some of their friends – notably those business acquaintances who he hoped would ease his foot a rung further up the social ladder – perhaps eighteen filling the chairs around the long mahogany dining table would be adequate, a table that rarely saw more than himself, Clara and Paul as the sole diners.

Arranged as a surprise, he had the invitations printed and presented Clara with his list. She hardly knew any of the invited guests; a trio of the women she met for afternoon tea summarised her circle. Others like Mrs or Lady so-and-so were strangers to her.

Nevertheless she surveyed the list critically, concealing her feelings with a gracious smile saying how she appreciated Archie's thoughtfulness, and she added sweetly:

'There is one extra person, dear, someone who shares my birthday and I would love to include her.'

Archie looked up from his desk. 'Of course, my

dear, this is your party, you may include anyone you wish. What is the lady's name and address? I will have an invitation sent to her.'

Again Clara smiled, and leaning over him, put an arm around his shoulders, kissed his cheek. 'There is no need for that, dearest. I will deliver it by hand. She will be quite charmed.'

Archie frowned. 'Indeed? Are you seeing her imminently?'

Clara laughed delightedly. 'I see her every day.'

'Every day? I don't understand . . .'

'Of course you don't. It is Laurie.'

'Laurie? Laurie – not your maid, surely?' Archie looked shocked.

'The same, my darling. You see, we have the same birthday.'

'You do? How incredible.' How incredible, he thought, that a mere servant should share the same birthday as the lady of the manor. It didn't seem quite decent somehow. But worse was to come.

'I would like her to be my guest.'

'You mean – at the dinner?' And Archie's mouth fell open in astonishment.

'Of course.'

Archie stared at her in amazement. She must have lost her wits, to even think of making such a request. Her servant sharing the dinner table with his list of some of the cream of Edinburgh high society.

She was standing there, smiling at him so eagerly, awaiting his reply.

He shook his head. 'No, my dear. It is impossible, quite impossible.' And as she began to protest he said: 'No, my dear, surely you must realise that we cannot have a servant dining with us. We would be a laughing stock.' He added stiffly: 'That is all I have to say on the matter. I am sorry to disappoint you. No – wait, my precious—'

But with tears in her eyes, Clara was already on the other side of the study door. Disappointed, maybe, and let down by her husband, but certainly not defeated. Laurie should have her party and she herself would be her guest.

Accordingly it was arranged with Mrs Brown, who baked a cake and made all the preparations for the birthday evening. Clara's celebration was arranged for 8 p.m. but before that, at 6 p.m., she would be in the kitchen sharing a birthday party with dear Laurie.

Lizzie, who knew nothing of Clara's original intention to have her included at the event upstairs, was immensely flattered that her birthday should have been considered so important to her mistress.

'You are to invite whoever of your friends you

would like to have, as well as, of course, Betty and the Browns.'

Lizzie did not need to consider a list. She had only two requests: Vince and, she added shyly, 'My friend, Detective Constable Faro, if you please, madam.'

Clara wasn't put out by this request. Patting Lizzie's hand, she said: 'Of course,' determined, however, to withhold this information from Archie who she suspected would get very angry indeed at one of those wretched snooping policemen being entertained in his kitchen.

So the plans were made. Vince mentioned it to Paul who said rather grimly: 'It will be more fun than Clara's official one, I can tell you that. My stepfather's collection of friends are quite dire.'

'Why don't you come to Mamma's then? I'm sure she would love to have you.'

Paul looked at him. In his innocence Vince was quite unaware of the notorious reputation Paul had among the female servants. He felt very wistful. Perhaps Laurie wouldn't remember that amorous overture and the slapped face he got in return.

Noticing his hesitation, Vince said: 'Please come, Paul. It won't be much fun without you. And we could do some of your card tricks. Oh, please, please.'

Any plea from his young friend was quite irresistible. So Paul promised, as long as Vince consulted his mother first and she approved.

Lizzie wasn't taken aback by Vince's request. She tried to set aside her initial misgivings, her suspicions that, in Vince's eyes, Paul was rapidly filling the place of an absent father. A fact that was, in truth, hardly surprising seeing that she was just seven years older than Paul and to a boy of twelve they must have both appeared as quite old.

While recognising that hero-worship was important to a fatherless boy, she could only hope and pray that some of the less agreeable aspects of Paul's character, like gambling and shooting, would not do any lasting damage.

And so, on the evening of Lizzie's birthday, Mrs Brown having overseen that everything was present and correct in the drawing room for the arrival of the birthday guests, at 6 p.m. Clara made her way down to the kitchen where the housekeeper had spread a handsome white tablecloth on the wooden table and put flowers and candles as adornments beside a birthday cake, a tiny replica of the one that would be displayed on the sideboard in the dining room upstairs.

Lizzie looked very pretty in her best dress, a turquoise silk gown trimmed with lace, and that little boy Vince looked quite grown up in a dark-blue suit with white shirt and cravat. He would be a handsome young man some day, resembling his mother with his blond curls, and Mrs Brown decided she must ask Laurie more about his father. He had the look of quality, well bred and instinctively polite, as fitted the son of a gentleman rather than a common soldier.

Detective Constable Faro arrived. Out of his policeman's uniform she was immediately struck by his good looks. As he took a seat next to Lizzie, Clara knew immediately, without anyone saying a word, that her adoring looks in his direction declared to all the world her love for him, and blowing out the candles on the cake, she would make a wish that all would work out well for her dear Laurie.

Betty and Mrs Brown were making the final preparations at the stove. She took a seat at the table and fell into polite conversation with Vince – the usual topic he was so used to from most of the adult world. How was he enjoying school and what subjects did he like best? He was spared the usual polite answer by the sound of manly steps approaching along the stone corridor. Clara took a great gulp of air and gave up a silent prayer that this was not Archie with some reason for visiting the kitchen.

The door opened to admit Paul. Vince, Faro and Lizzie sprang to their feet. Betty and Mrs Brown, looking confused, curtseyed.

Paul smiled and handed Lizzie a posy of flowers. 'Happy birthday, Mrs Laurie.' He looked at Clara, for once a smile without hostility.

'Do sit down, sir,' said Lizzie.

Clara gave him a puzzled glance. Vince smiled. 'Paul is my mother's special guest.'

Vince had painted a birthday card, which was viewed by all with great admiration. Faro, who had little experience regarding presents for young women, had remembered that females liked wearing lace shawls and there was just such a shop on his way along the Lawnmarket.

Lizzie was delighted, and thanked him shyly as he draped it around her slim shoulders, other females exclaiming: 'How lovely! It suits you!'

Faro relaxed and gave a sigh of relief as they took their seats around the table. The only missing member was Brown; his wife said he'd begged to be excused and in a whispered aside to Lizzie explained: 'He can't take rich food. Has awful trouble with his stomach, has to be careful what he eats. His digestion is chronic, it's all that waiting about in the carriage in all weathers.'

A light supper followed, but all eyes were concentrated on the iced birthday cake. As they ate, Faro now a keen observer found himself for the first time on common ground with Vince, discovering things they shared and his remarks greeted with smiling interest, without unconcealed hostility. The boy was intelligent and looking forward to reading one of Shakespeare's plays, thanks to Paul, who laughingly confessed that he dabbled a bit in the amateur dramatic society at the university. Faro found himself making a mental note of that for later.

The conversation was among the three males; the females had little to impart, Mrs Brown and Betty attentive to food and drink while Clara merely gazed from speaker to speaker in an attitude of listening intently without any apparent desire to be drawn in, and as topics moved to poets, artists and music, ready with a gracious smile to any whose eye she caught across the table.

Faro sat back amazed. The first surprise was the sudden transformation in Vince from a sullen, uncommunicative schoolboy to a friendly, highly intelligent young lad. Doubtless this owed much to Paul Lumbleigh's influence on him, and there lay the second surprise. Apparently there was a great deal more to the son of the house than the dissolute wastrel he had been led to believe he was.

But when Paul produced a pack of cards and invited them to take one, put it back and then amazingly produced that very card, watching his deft movements vaulted Faro back into the realisation that he was in fact on a murder investigation. And the young man with his magician's tricks who was also his prime suspect had now added another dimension to the sinister presence of the nine of diamonds at the murder scenes. A possible link with the theatre.

CHAPTER TWENTY-TWO

The evening vanished almost too quickly; all too soon one of the line of bells high on the wall alongside clanged noisily, summoning Mrs Brown. She curtseyed briefly to Clara who stood up and sighed. It was time for her to return as hostess of her own birthday party. Her wry shrug indicated more than any words that it would not be nearly as much fun as the one she was leaving, Vince lamenting the fact that she had not seen Paul do some of his card tricks.

Paul stood up, bowed to Clara and Lizzie.

'You're not going so soon, please stay,' Vince said to him.

Paul shook his head. 'Sorry, lad. I have to go. Duty calls.'

A look exchanged between Paul and Clara, fellow sufferers on friendly terms for the duration of the evening at least; whatever their relations when they returned to the family fold, it expressed their regret at leaving this cheerful informal birthday feast.

But their departure had signalled its end. Lizzie remembered that it was past Vince's bedtime and there was a sudden return to the sulky schoolboy with his shrug of indifference. Mrs Brown and Betty remembered their duties too and began to silently clear the table, removing the dishes to the sink, the housekeeper whispering a promise to Vince that she would bring some of that cake back with her later.

Lizzie looked across at Faro. 'I'll walk Vince back to the cottage.' Her pleading glance begged him to accompany them.

Here was the opportunity to talk to Lizzie that Faro had dreaded, although there would be little chance of more than polite civilities in Vince's presence. They emerged into a moonlit evening with a star-spangled canopy over Arthur's Seat and Vince lapsed into silence in the short distance to the cottage.

As they approached, a large black dog rushed

over. Faro's policeman's instinct was to distrust all large dogs that bounded towards him. He gave a sigh of relief that this was one of the guard dogs Lumbleigh insisted was necessary to patrol the grounds. They lived in the stables and Vince, the object of the dog's attentions, was greeted effusively.

Vince patted him and grinned at Lizzie. 'This is Boy, he sometimes goes with Paul and me catching rabbits on the hill.'

Then politely listening to stern instructions to do his homework properly, Vince smiled, kissed his mother: 'Goodnight, Ma,' and instead of ignoring Faro in his usual manner as if he was invisible, he held out his hand and with a slight bow said: 'Goodnight, sir. Thank you for coming to Ma's party.'

Faro replied in kind. 'It was a good evening. You'll soon be top of the class in English, if you like Shakespeare. Well done – keep it up.' Another grin and Vince disappeared indoors.

Faro turned to Lizzie and took her arm. 'Now it's my turn to see you home.'

She laughed. 'Hardly! It's only a few hundred yards away,' but she took his arm fondly. 'I do love my new shawl. You are so clever to choose exactly the right kind.'

They had been walking smartly and were

within sight of the entrance to the big house. Lizzie looked back towards the cottage, candlelight in the attic window indicating that Vince had taken her advice and retired to his room.

She sighed. 'I'm so glad Paul came. I felt so honoured. And he is so kind, really fond of Vince. He calls in most weekdays to help with his homework. Like having a private tutor,' she added proudly. 'I've decided he is, at heart, a good young man.' She paused. 'A bit of a flirt, but then all students are a bit wild. I think he'll be a fine doctor some day, don't you think?'

Faro merely shrugged and Lizzie looked disappointed, obviously wanting him to share her good opinion. Would they linger in the moonlight and talk for a while? But Faro was suddenly bereft of suitable topics. He kissed her gently and said: 'I'll see you on Saturday as usual, shall I?'

'Of course, Jeremy, that would be lovely.' Lizzie sounded delighted, as if this was some new arrangement. 'You must tell me all about your visit to Glasgow.'

'If I can remember,' lied Faro. As if he would ever forget. 'It seems like long ago.' That at least was true. 'Goodnight,' and leaning down he kissed her cheek, aware again of that familiar fragrant perfume.

He watched her disappear inside and began his walk back to his lodgings, the moonlight gleaming on a setting built for a romantic evening, mocking a wretched would-be lover. His thoughts turned miserably to the new version of Paul he had just encountered.

How could he tell her of his secret anxiety? He had looked at Lizzie wanting to say something, a warning to look at what may lurk beneath the polite, friendly veneer. If Paul was the women's killer, then it was a lot more sinister than a rich lad's tendency to flirt with the maids. And if his growing suspicions were proved correct, he thought of the effects of this catastrophic revelation of lies and deceit on a twelve-year-old boy.

His hero, his first friend, the young man he had set up in his imagination as akin to the brave soldier who had been his father, suddenly revealed to all the world as a callous, brutal murderer of two young women. One of them, the maid Ida, he had seduced and promised to marry until, believing her to be pregnant and she threatening to blackmail him, in a panic he had killed her.

Faro's imagination failed to deal with the results. And looking further, what of Lizzie who also had another devastating blow awaiting Vince? That she did not even know the identity of his father, an unknown rapist, and that the brave soldier he had come to venerate and whose example he wished to copy was a work of fiction, of lies and deceit.

He sighed. And at the end of this nightmare how would such revelations affect his own relationship with Lizzie? He could sense that it was crumbling. He could see her life ruined, and not even marriage could restore what would die for her the disastrous day Vince came to know the truth.

While his thoughts were turning back to Paul again, Lizzie had said: 'He's a bit of a flirt – and not the only one.' She had laughed gently. 'Policemen like to flirt too.'

Puzzled he said: 'You mean me? I don't—'

She laughed, took his arm. 'No, not you. Your sergeant.'

'You mean DS Gosse?' He stared at her. 'You amaze me.' He shook his head. It was unbelievable; he couldn't imagine an amorous Gosse flirting with any female. There must be some mistake, but Lizzie was smiling gently.

She had decided she should tell Jeremy. 'He has invited me out to tea a couple of times.' After the first time, she knew that there was more in this than a mere police interview which could have properly taken place in the kitchen at Lumbleigh

Green. She had a woman's instinctive awareness of a man's lust, something left over from thirteen years ago, and had always avoided arousal in the men she had encountered.

As for Jeremy, he was no seducer, respected her even if he was not madly in love with her, she sighed, as she was with him. And at times like this, despite her hopes, he seemed so far away, preoccupied, and she felt no longer close to him, their easy friendship fading, slipping away, soon to be lost for ever.

The one night when they had slept together, briefly become lovers, had given her so much hope for the future. The ecstasy of those hours, once so real . . . now she wondered if she had dreamt it all. Or if it was real, she thought guiltily, had it created a barrier between them, a decent man's fear of being trapped into marriage?

While these were Lizzie's anxious thoughts, Jeremy was merely wondering if she was trying to make him jealous. But he was not one to brood for long on anything except an unsolved mystery. And there were more important issues than Gosse's conduct with a witness. Pushing aside problems regarding his love life, or absence of it, his remarkable memory with its complete recall presented the events of the evening, particularly Vince's transformation, and prayed that the good terms established between them would last until their next meeting.

A friendly exchange with the new version of Paul Lumbleigh, also revealed at Lizzie's birthday party, was indicated. And one more ominous detail bounded to the front of his mind. That Paul, with an interest in university dramatics, was an amateur actor.

Was this fact relevant, the vital clue to the murder of Doris Page?

Approaching the Pleasance, he passed by the Catholic church, ominously aware of a new face among the possible suspects.

Father Burren, a handsome young man with a splendid voice who wore the role of parish priest so uncertainly. Another actor perhaps?

A call at the rectory tomorrow was also required.

CHAPTER TWENTY-THREE

Arriving at the Central Office next morning, Gosse was seated as usual behind the inspector's desk. He looked up and pointed Faro towards an impressive number of papers on the opposite desk.

'These are for you to deal with.' Faro scanned through them. Edinburgh criminals had been busy. Attempted burglaries in Newington, domestic brawls with neighbours in the Pleasance, drunken fights in the High Street closes. A bank customer reporting a suspicious fraud case.

He sighed and Gosse said, 'That'll keep you busy, and if you have any spare time,' he added sarcastically, 'don't forget there are a lot of loose ends still to be followed on our murder cases.' Head down, bent over the desk, he seized some documents with an air of frantic impatience, indicating clearly that Faro was not to expect much help.

Deciding that the sergeant was making heavy weather of his important new role as temporary inspector in Wade's absence, Faro said: 'I thought I might look in and see Fr Burren.'

Gosse's frown deepened as he looked up from the desk. 'A waste of time, Faro. Another of your impossible theories.' He shook his head firmly. A lapsed Roman Catholic, it was many years since he had set foot in a church or attended Mass, but the early training of regarding priests, with superstitious dread, as being next to God still lingered.

The routine duties of a detective constable dealing with matters arising from the daily reports took some several hours. With nothing but untidy loose ends and sore feet to show for his day's activities, late that afternoon Faro wearily made his way down the Pleasance towards the Holy Virgin church.

The door was firmly closed. With no idea if that was usual when there were no services, he considered leaving a message at the rectory next door.

He was out of luck. Once again, a closed door and no answer to the bell which he heard clearly ringing through the house. Faro was about to scribble a note and push it through the letter box, but second thoughts suggested misgivings about how this might be received, alarming the sensitive young priest, so he decided to call tomorrow instead.

He sighed. There remained one possibility at the end of a disappointing day of making even a small amount of progress in the murders of Doris Page and Ida Watts. The latter lay in the direction of Lumbleigh Green and walking as briskly as weariness permitted he headed towards the garden entrance at the base of Arthur's Seat, praying that his visit might coincide with Paul tutoring Vince at the Browns' cottage.

At first it seemed fortune was with him, but it was soon evident that Paul was not pleased to see a uniformed policeman, as he came not from the cottage but off the hill. Vince at his side, both were carrying guns and a shooting target. Boy bounded towards him but the dog's welcome was the only one on offer.

He waited, and as they approached he greeted them cordially. Paul hardly glanced in his direction and staring ahead looked annoyed as with an effort at politeness Vince asked: 'Chasing criminals, sir?'

Faro muttered a smiling acknowledgement in a desperate effort to make this sound like a casual encounter, without any excuse that would have been a lie.

Vince nodded briefly and turning to Paul continued a conversation about adjusting the shooting target next time, leaving Faro bereft of any of the friendly overtures he had come to hope for and expect after the genial friendliness of Lizzie's birthday party.

Paul walked on steadily ignoring them both and Faro sighed inwardly. Had it after all been merely a polite show put on for Lizzie's benefit, and had Vince also stepped back into his normal role of resentment?

He watched Vince race ahead with the dog and said desperately: 'I'm glad to see you, sir.' Paul turned, regarding him with some effort, and received this statement coldly, his manner suggesting that this sentiment was not mutual. Determinedly Faro pressed on: 'It will save me another journey, if it is convenient to have a few words, sir.'

Paul sighed, stopped in his tracks. 'Well?' he said heavily.

Encouraged, Faro took out his notebook. 'DS Gosse is finalising enquiries, making sure they are right in every detail. As you probably know much of the law, sir,' he added, hoping a touch of flattery would not come amiss, 'you will be aware that it is a routine matter to establish alibis – just to ensure where everyone was in Lumbleigh Green when—'

Paul, interrupting with an impatient gesture, said sharply: 'Yes, yes. Get on with it.'

Faro consulted the notebook as if reading its contents for the first time, conscious of Paul's impatient expression and that Vince had moved in closer to his friend making it clear, whatever the verdict, whose side he was on.

'I was at home, as my stepfather informed you,' Paul said wearily.

Faro looked up. 'Is that so, sir. Mr Lumbleigh said—' and as if reading from the notes, 'he said that you were at Surgeons' Hall.'

Paul shook his head. 'That was incorrect. He was wrong,' he added, as though proving his stepfather wrong gave him a certain amount of pleasure. 'That was only until early evening. Then I came home and went directly up to my room without seeing anyone. I stayed there and missed dinner.' Pausing he shrugged. 'I was feeling a little off colour.' And trying to repress a shudder, 'Dismembering and cutting up a corpse can have a destructive effect on one's appetite, as you will probably know in your own profession, Constable.'

He sounded sincere enough and Faro said, 'So no one can vouch for your presence that evening?'

'No one. I had left instructions not to be disturbed and went to bed early. I remained there until next morning.' He said it firmly. 'You must take it or leave it, I'm afraid,' he added, his shrug implicating that he cared not one jot either way.

With no excuse or invitation to linger, Faro bowed and left, his feeling of depression more about Vince than Paul – certain he had lost the ground he had gained momentarily at Lizzie's party and when walking back to the cottage with them both. But more important, he saw again the tragedy that lay in wait for the boy who was also Lizzie's son if he proved that Paul was a murderer . . .

Faro made his way back to the Central Office and read through the reports. A morning of tying up more loose ends on the domestic dramas, and soothing the suspicions of the bank customer. The burglary at Morningside was the work of an old lag newly out of jail but undeterred. Not prone to feats of ingenuity he was easily tracked down, as Faro suspected, in the tenement of the woman he lived with in periods of freedom. There Faro made the arrest, put the handcuffs back on him, regardless of noisy protests of innocence, one of the accompanying constables emerging from the bedroom with the bag of stolen jewels. After meeting the bank customer and with some difficulty persuading him that he was not being robbed, a somewhat weary Faro went in search of Gosse for further instructions. The sergeant was not at his temporary desk and Faro would have been surprised to hear that he was in his favourite café on the Royal Mile.

He was awaiting the arrival of Lizzie Laurie to take tea with him in this informal atmosphere, pretending to himself and any who might believe him that he found this method of interrogation easier with the fairer sex. Far more successful, he maintained, than the intimidating atmosphere of the interview room at the Central Office for taking down statements from witnesses.

At that moment in the café, Gosse was consulting his timepiece with an uneasy feeling that the early progress he had envisaged with Mrs Laurie was fading and that she was not returning his ardour. This did not make him feel more favourably disposed to Faro, now regarded by him as a serious rival. He consoled himself with the thought: how on earth could such an attractive young widow prefer a lowly detective constable to a sergeant, especially as he had hinted strongly that he was about to be promoted to inspector?

Faro meanwhile stood outside the church in the Pleasance reading a notice in large letters beseeching 'All Worshippers Welcome. Please Come In.' Deciding that the locked door would be a disappointment to those religiously inspired or with consciences overburdened and in sore need of confession and absolution, he read a further notice in smaller letters: 'If closed, intending worshippers should apply to the rectory.' An arrow pointed towards the tall thin house with narrow windows that Faro had visited earlier that day.

There was an apology of a garden and the open door unleashed a strong aroma of incense and a hallway decorated, if such a frivolous word could be applied, by a profusion of saintly images as well as paintings and candles which had apparently overflowed from or sought a warmer refuge than the chilly atmosphere inside the church.

A stout woman of middle years and motherly aspect eased her way through this medley, her eager expression vanishing as she gazed past him down the road. It said clearly that he was not the visitor she expected. In answer to his question, no, the father was not here; her accent, identical to the priest's, proclaimed that she was also from Ireland. Concealing her emotions she was regarding Faro's uniform as if a policeman who was not of the Holy Virgin's congregation was contaminating the rectory's sacred threshold.

Eager to close the door, she asked politely: 'Can I help you, Constable? I'm Mrs Casey, the father's housekeeper.'

'I don't think so, madam. A few words with Fr Burren is all I require. When will he be back?'

The housekeeper shook her head, bit her lip . . . 'Who knows? He has parish matters to attend to and this is his day for the infirmary visits. He has evensong then, confirmation classes this evening, and tomorrow morning—'

'Thank you, madam. Please give Fr Burren a message. I will call again tomorrow,' said Faro, cutting short what promised to be a long list of the priest's more pressing engagements.

Turning at the gate, he was conscious of the woman's watchful gaze. Not upon him but anxiously on the empty road beyond.

Although he was reasonably near Lumbleigh Green, Faro was suddenly anxious to return to his lodgings and get out of uniform in preparation for meeting Lizzie, hoping as always that she would provide the calm his soul so weary of crime needed.

She came to the front gate to meet him, wearing a new bonnet and cape handed down from her mistress. Faro's reaction was a mere: 'You're looking very pretty,' which was true. In his eyes, she was revealed as sweet, radiant and loving, a refreshing antidote to sordid danger and murder.

At his side, her step light and looking so happy, as always at the prospect of spending an hour with him, she took his arm and he made a sudden decision.

Hailing a passing hansom cab, he put her inside and said: 'Princes Street.'

She looked at him in amazement at this extravagance and said in reproach: 'This isn't my birthday any more, Jeremy.'

He laughed and put an arm around her shoulders. 'Isn't it? A pity. Then I think you should have a celebration every day.'

She gave him a quick, rather anxious glance. Had he been drinking? He smiled and leaning down, kissed her cheek and sighed, 'Had an awful day, Lizzie, that's all.'

Leaving the cab as it turned into Princes Street, he ushered her inside the Balmoral Hotel. Wide-eyed she was led towards the restaurant. The waiter bowed, showed them to a table, and once seated, presented the supper menu.

Up to now Lizzie had been too taken aback to do more than murmur a protest. Looking around she whispered: 'It's very expensive, Jeremy.' And scanning the menu, she whispered, 'Can we have something light?'

'No. This is my special treat.' Ordering the set supper, Lizzie sighed, and listening to the quartet playing a Strauss waltz, she sat back, feeling more like Clara Lumbleigh than her lady's maid as she looked around at the well-dressed, well-off customers.

'Oh, it is so lovely. Thank you, Jeremy.'

Leaning across the table he took her hand. 'I'm the one to be grateful, Lizzie. Grateful to have such a friend as you.'

She smiled gently, only slightly put down that he had used the word 'friend' when she would have preferred a stronger, more lasting word for their relationship. 'Wouldn't it be wonderful,' she said at the end of the delicious meal, 'if there were special moments we could keep for ever? Like those snowstorms in glass paperweights, bring them out, give them a shake – relive them over and over.'

There were many moments in Faro's life that

he would not care to relive. Moments from hell in the past and he was keenly aware of deadly perils that awaited hidden by the future. But this present hour was not one of them, this was an evening he was to look back upon, when his heart raced ahead and made its own decision.

As for Lizzie, walking on air remembering that goodnight kiss, her only thought was regret for the first time that she did not have a home of her own. Even the deadly tenement had its one precious memory of that solitary night of passion they had spent together.

In her life now, there was no such place for lovers; even if Jeremy had been so inclined, they could have hardly gone to his lodging under the eagle eye of Mrs Biggs. As for her own room in Lumbleigh Green, Mrs Brown never missed anything either and discovery would be not only humiliation and embarrassment for them both but, for her, instant dismissal.

Even Jeremy's love was too great a risk, too high a price – not only for her own sake but for Vince's future.

CHAPTER TWENTY-FOUR

Collecting his reports next morning, one look at Gosse's grim expression told him not to expect anything cheerful. 'Well, making any progress on our murder enquiries?'

When Faro shook his head, Gosse's eyebrows raised mockingly. 'Really? Thought by this time you would have had our killer in handcuffs. Obviously those rumours of what to expect from our splendid new detective constable were somewhat overrated—'

Interrupting this flow of sarcasm, Faro quickly outlined his visit to the church, telling him that he had been unable to contact the priest yesterday but was returning immediately.

Gosse sighed deeply. 'All right, get going. Don't waste my precious time standing here talking.' And indicating the papers on his desk, 'I have more than enough to keep me here.' As Faro was leaving he shouted encouragingly, 'And come back with some results this time.'

There was no evidence of life in the empty church. The priest had not returned and Faro's footsteps echoed hollowly on the stone floor as he called 'Hello?' several times, not really expecting any answer.

At the rectory, the door was opened by Mrs Casey, a very different, tearful version of the cautious housekeeper he had encountered yesterday. Attired in cape and bonnet, fingering the crucifix about her neck, flustered and distraught, she said: 'Oh, the Lord be thanked, it's yourself, Constable. You've saved me a journey this very minute, going to the police station.'

Suspecting the report of a burglary of some sorts, Faro asked: 'What has happened?'

'It's the father, Constable. He's gone missing' – a sobbing breath – 'that's what. And I don't know what to do,' she added, wringing her hands in agitation.

In an effort to calm her, Faro said gently: 'And what makes you think that, madam?'

She pointed towards the staircase. 'He comes and goes a lot, trying to make meals for him is a nightmare, I can tell you. I'm getting used to it now, though he says the Lord's work comes before meals. But . . .' She paused, looked around with a bewildered expression. 'He's usually back here at nights. He'd gone out, but I didn't actually see him leave—' An anguished sob. 'I was a bit concerned when I saw that his bed hadn't been slept in, but I thought he'd been held up somewhere. But when he didn't come back last night—' And wringing her hands she regarded him tearfully. 'Oh, Holy Mother of God, save us. I don't know what has happened to him.'

'When I was here yesterday, you said he was visiting the hospital.' Giving that a moment to sink in, he shook his head. 'You should have told me of your fears, Mrs Casey. This is an important piece of information you were withholding,' he added sternly.

'I just didn't want to believe there was anything wrong. But I should have known better. I'm sorry, Constable.'

'Has he never done this before, perhaps been delayed with someone who is ill?' he added weakly.

'Never,' she said firmly. 'If it was last rites, he'd always get a message to me to let me know.'

And leaning weakly against the banister she whispered: 'Oh, dear God, I know something dreadful has happened to him. I just feel it in my bones.'

'May I look in his room?' Faro asked.

'Yes, yes, anything,' she said as he followed her up the stairs. The room was spartan, indeed, and suggested a monk's cell rather than a parish priest's bedroom.

'I changed the sheets the other day and the bed's just as I left it, never touched. See, his nightshirt, just lying on the bed where I left it for him.'

Faro looked round the room: a crucifix, a picture of the Sacred Heart and a shelved cupboard, known locally as the 'Edinburgh press'. The housekeeper opened the door and looked inside. 'He took nothing with him for an overnight stay, just went out in ordinary clothes—'

'Ordinary clothes?'

'Yes, he never wore his clerical garb – look, here it is – when he went out at night, taking God to the heathen, visiting the less privileged members of our society, as he called the down-and-outs.'

'In Edinburgh?'

'Not always. He often went down the coast, to Musselburgh and beyond.' She sat down on the

bed, smoothed the immaculate covers. 'He has few possessions, Constable, and I could swear that he did not have one solitary piece of luggage with him, not even his case he carried for the last rites.' And shaking her head, 'Not even a clean collar or shirt, and he's very particular about that every day.'

Faro looked at the empty table. 'His diary?'

'His appointments, you mean. I keep that for him. He needs reminding every day.'

'Did he have many casual callers at the rectory here, without appointments, I mean?'

She frowned. 'Oh, quite often. Always on call, available to his parishioners, and anyone else who needed help.'

Faro felt it was a useless question but he asked: 'Any visitor you can remember before you last saw him?'

She bit her lip, thinking for a moment, then said: 'There was one. A nice young chap came to see him. I showed him into the study.'

'Did you know him?'

She shook her head. 'He wasn't one of us, from our church, if that's what you mean,' she added in faint tones of disapproval, and frowning. 'Tall, well-spoken, good-looking.'

'And did he have a name?' Faro asked gently.

'No. Just said the father was expecting him.

When I took the tea into them, they were talking about a drama group needing a place for practice. The hall over yonder, behind the church – the verger Mr Mundy lets it out from time to time. The money's useful. He lives just across the road, in number 17, if you're interested.'

Faro made a note of it. He was very interested, particularly in her description of Fr Burren's last visitor before he disappeared. He left with a pointless reassurance not to worry, that the police would do everything they could to find Fr Burren again. Meanwhile should he reappear she should let them know.

At the Central Office, Gosse was installed behind the desk as usual and looked up briefly from his papers as Faro entered. 'Back so soon, Constable?'

'We've got another missing person, sir.'

'Nothing new. That'll be the third in the past two days.'

'But this one may be related to our murder enquiry, sir,' he said passing over his report.

Gosse's head shot up as Faro continued, 'Fr Burren, the priest.'

And as Faro related his conversation with the housekeeper, Gosse thumped his fists together with an air of triumph.

'By God, by God, maybe this is our answer, what we've been looking for.'

'I don't see—'

'Of course you don't,' was the curt reply. 'So much for your observation and deduction.' And tapping the report, 'This tells me, before reading a word, that we have our killer. He knows we're on to him and he has scarpered. Cleared off. Probably on his way to a ship back to Ireland or God knows where, at this moment.'

As Faro listened, his eyes narrowed at Gosse's predictable reactions, seizing an answer, a peg at last to hang the murderer on, preparatory to the gallows.

'Perhaps, sir, that is one answer,' he put in. 'The other is also obvious.'

'Well?' Gosse demanded.

'The priest is the killer's fourth victim,' he said slowly.

Gosse's eyes widened in disbelief. 'Nonsense! How do you come by that idea?'

'Because Fr Burren received Ida Watt's confession before she was murdered. And she revealed to him the identity of this secret lover – who we suspect killed both her and Doris Page.'

A little deflated, Gosse growled. 'Perhaps you're right but I wouldn't bank on it. Well, as a missing person we have to find him, dead or alive,' he added grimly. 'So we'll set the usual search procedures in operation. You'd better get back to the housekeeper, find out everything she knows, last seen and all that sort of thing.'

At the rectory, Faro stood by the closed door which remained unanswered. He was about to cross the road to number 17 and speak to the verger when the door suddenly opened and a flustered Mrs Casey appeared carrying a basket of washing. She regarded him anxiously. 'Oh, it's yourself, Constable. Any news?'

Faro told her it was all in hand and sighing she said: 'Come in, come in, the kettle's on and I'll make you a cup of tea.' Laying the basket aside, she shook her head and sighed. 'I was doing the washing. Can't sit around just praying. Have to keep busy and leave it in the dear Lord's hands, that's what Sean – the father – would want us to do.'

Putting cups on the table, she looked tearful, red-eyed with lack of sleep. Leaning on the table she smiled sadly. 'Sean's just like a wee bairn, not my parish priest at all. Known him all my life, I have, since he was a babe in arms. Same village in Connemara; the Caseys always worked for the Burrens. His father was Sir Aidan.'

Then she was sitting down opposite and Faro was hearing that Sean Burren had his reasons for the priesthood: a high-born father whose lifestyle he deplored.

'Sir Aidan's heir, the elder son, would inherit more than the title. The very spit of his father in every way. Ten years older than Sean. Everything went to him and he was no model for the younger son. He had inherited all his father's love of rich living: money, gambling, drinking – and women,' she added grimly.

'Sean wanted none of it, he had high ideals even then. He was to make his own way in the world. Ireland was a troubled place and he believed that God had called him so he took holy orders and came across the sea to Edinburgh. When he got this parish, he needed a housekeeper. We had kept in touch . . .' She paused, smiling gently. 'And I needed no second bidding. You know the rest. And if you think I'm going on a bit, being only a servant, to Sean I am the mother he never knew.' Crossing herself, she said: 'She died giving birth to him, God keep her.'

There was one serious omission in Faro's report to Gosse regarding his interview with Mrs Casey.

As she was showing him out of the rectory, she said, 'Wait a minute, Constable, that young chap I told you about. I remember his name now; the father called him Paul.'

And that description, fitted very precisely one man . . .

Paul Lumbleigh had been the priest's last visitor before he disappeared. And what did that signify, Faro thought grimly as he went across the road to talk to Mr Mundy?

Thankfully the elderly verger, a businesslike picture of cheerful, bright-eyed efficiency, was at home. Oh yes, he remembered the young gentleman. Enquiries about an amateur group involved looking for a suitable hall. Shakespeare, they were doing.

He made a face. 'A bit ambitious for the church hall, but this young chap' – pausing to consult his ledger – 'Mr Paul Lumbleigh, he was very enthusiastic, had great hopes for them.'

Faro had decided that the most effective way of a meeting with Paul was in the informal atmosphere of one of his fairly regular after-school visits to Vince, at the Browns' cottage. But how to disguise a searching interview with the boy doubtless hovering on the sidelines?

He sighed wearily. Vince's antagonism was the last thing he wanted, losing whatever friendly ground he believed had been recently gained.

As he made his way back to the Central Office, the weather was worsening. A heavy mist was descending, a thick white shroud already covering Arthur's Seat. The weather conditions emanated from the Firth of Forth and could render the south-side suburbs invisible regardless of sunshine in the city a couple of miles distant.

'Seen the weather?' said Gosse looking out of the window. 'This will hamper the search for the priest, I'm afraid.'

The police routine began at the last known sighting of the missing person. In this case the rectory in the Pleasance, under the shadow of Salisbury Crags, already vanished beneath the enveloping mist.

'If he's been killed as you suspect, Faro, then the hill is the most likely place where his body has been concealed,' Gosse said grimly, consulting a police map of the area. 'A favourite place for malefactors to hide their evil deeds.'

Faro knew that was sadly true. The extinct volcano held many hollows and deep secret caves, some only revealing themselves by the accidental movement of the glacial deposits which every decade or so came loose and thundered down onto the Duddingston Road, a dreaded avalanche and a mortal danger to travellers.

Late afternoon was most promising for an encounter with Paul. Heading towards Lumbleigh Green, ignoring the weather conditions, he decided to take the short cut across the hill to the back gate.

On his way, occasionally visible looming out of the mist, were a group of constables who shook their heads and, shivering, complained bitterly.

Weather was never on the side of the police; it always seemed bent on aiding and abetting criminals. Unless the conditions improved, the search would have to be abandoned for the moment, since the result would be general confusion with chilled, angry constables losing each other and in imminent danger of injuries from a treacherous terrain of unseen hazards.

'Useless looking up there in this weather,' one grumbled, pointing in the direction of Hunter's Crag.

'We're more likely to be the casualties,' said another.

'Aye,' said a third, 'nearly broke my ankle in a rabbit hole.'

Faro commiserated with them, deciding that the search also provided an excellent excuse for his 'accidental' encounter with Paul.

The weather conditions were getting steadily worse and by morning Edinburgh's Newington residents would wake up trapped in a cotton-wool world, with visibility no more than a few feet beyond their windows. He pitied the men who had to make their way to work amidst the unseen traffic hazards, as carriages collided with horse-drawn tramcars, the carriage horses, scared and uncontrollable, upsetting pedestrians.

In the railway station, stately trains puffed away like outraged dowagers, marooned at platforms or in sidings, waiting for signals, at present rendered invisible, to proceed with their journeys while irritated passengers lamented at such enforced delays.

Faro was also now considering the folly of having taken the short cut when it would have been more sensible and much safer to walk on the main Dalkeith coach road and enter the house through the front gate. However, as he walked towards the familiar part of the steep incline which led directly to the garden gate, the mist thinned momentarily, the lower reaches of the hill becoming visible again.

Confident, he walked faster now, his mind very much on what to do about Lizzie for again the accursed weather was a blight on their future activities – no more countryside walks as winter approached, and the shorter hours of daylight would also cut short their options of what to do with dark evenings and no place to go.

Deep in thought, suddenly he realised he had missed the path. Where was it now? He stopped, considering. Turning, searching, looking round for the landmark, a large boulder he remembered.

That second's hesitation saved his life.

Had he not stood still, he would have died on the spot, killed by the bullet that ricocheted off a boulder above his head. Instinctively, he threw himself down, lay silent, heart thumping, awaiting the next shot.

It did not come and cautiously he lifted his head, rose to his feet. The chill, clinging mist was the only thing that moved in that desolate scene. And suddenly he had a sense of triumph.

This attempt on his life meant that the killer realised that DC Faro was on to him, and getting closer. Someone who knew his movements, and what better way than to use the mist as a screen for a shooting accident?

But who? Suddenly a black shadow emerged from the mist. The killer? It grew into a big dog, hurtling towards him.

'Boy! Here, Boy!'

A human voice, and then a tall man became visible.

Paul Lumbleigh, carrying a rifle.

CHAPTER TWENTY-FIVE

A few steps behind Paul, a small figure. Vince with the shooting target. If Faro's sudden appearance had shocked Paul – was it to find him still alive? – then the sentiment was mutual.

'A bit off your beat, aren't you, Constable?' said Paul eying the uniform.

'We have a missing persons enquiry, sir,' Faro said shortly. There was no point in pretending otherwise, seeing that Paul would soon know the truth, he thought grimly, if he was not aware of it already.

'Indeed?' Paul looked around as if the mist might provide an answer. Then with a shrug he said: 'Best of luck, then,' and turned in the direction of Lumbleigh Green.

Vince indicated the target and added proudly: 'Makes it harder to hit when visibility is poor.'

'I gather you are improving,' Faro said and Vince nodded eagerly.

'Paul says I'll be a crack shot when the circus next comes to the Meadows. I'll win all the prizes. I'd like something nice for Ma,' he added wistfully.

Paul smiled. 'She will be very proud of your progress.'

Faro doubted that and as the two prepared to walk on, Faro said: 'A moment, sir, if you please.'

Paul stopped, sighed and shivered. 'Not more questions, Constable, we're off home. Vince is straight from school, hungry as a hunter and needing his tea.'

Faro ignored that and said: 'This won't take long; perhaps I might walk with you both as far as the cottage?'

'As you wish,' Paul said shortly as Faro fell into step alongside.

'I understand that you are interested in running a drama group.'

'True.' Paul turned and Faro noted a look of sudden anger. 'Are you interested in joining such activities? We are always on the lookout for new members,' he continued. 'And males are harder to recruit than females.'

As Faro shook his head and replied, 'Sorry to disappoint you, sir,' Vince put in:

'I'd be keen to join. You know that, Paul.'

Paul laughed. 'Wait a few years. You're too young for Othello.'

As Vince began to protest about suitable young roles in Shakespeare, Faro interrupted and said seriously: 'This matter concerns the hall at the Catholic church, sir.'

Paul stopped. 'Indeed. We are desperate for suitable premises for our rehearsals.'

Faro put in quickly, 'The priest, Fr Burren, is missing.'

Engrossed in watching Vince throw sticks for the dog, Paul shrugged. 'So?'

'I understand from the priest's housekeeper that you visited him two evenings ago, just before he disappeared.'

Paul stopped, shook his head. 'That is so. But I don't understand why that should be of interest to me, Constable.'

Faro took a deep breath. Either Paul was innocent or he was a good actor. 'The priest has been reported as missing, sir. The circumstances surrounding his disappearance have aroused some concern. They indicate that he has either suffered some accident or has been abducted.'

'Abducted!' Paul whistled. 'Who would want

to abduct a priest, for heaven's sake?'

'I doubt that heaven was concerned in this matter,' Faro said gravely.

'Indeed?' Paul frowned. 'This is a serious matter, but how does it concern me?'

'As possibly the last person to see him, sir.' Faro said carefully, 'It is a purely routine matter for us to talk to you in the hope that you might provide some information that might help us to trace him.'

Paul groaned. 'More of the same tedious procedures we have endured at the house, eh, Constable? Well, I can save you a little legwork. My visit was to see if our drama group might hire the church hall. I was with him about ten minutes and then I crossed the road and called on the verger to book the hall.' Pausing he sighed. 'Does that satisfy requirements, Constable?'

'I shall make a note of it, sir. Might I ask, was there anything that seemed to you odd in his behaviour that might be evident to a doctor – such as yourself?'

Paul, resisting this flattery, shook his head. 'Seeing this was our first and only meeting, I had no means of judging his mental condition. He seemed a nice enough chap, earnest and eager to be helpful. A bit highly strung, perhaps,' he added as an afterthought.

They had reached the garden gate where Vince

was waiting for them. Paul turned. 'Well, once again, good luck with your search. Hope you find him soon.' And looking up to the hill: 'Hope the poor chap hasn't come to some harm. The rabbit holes are a curse.'

'What's happened?' Vince asked.

'Someone gone missing on the hill,' said Paul.

There was one more vital question. 'Did you see anything just now, sir? I mean, did you see any of our lot?'

Paul shook his head. 'Not really. We were just at the base of the hill. But just before we met you, I saw a shape in the mist. I called out to him in case he was lost. Presumably one of your constables.'

Vince said: 'Paul said we had better warn him. It's dangerous if someone got between us and our target.'

This remark received a rather irritated glance from Paul as Faro went on: 'You didn't by any chance take a potshot at this shape, sir, mistaking it for a rabbit, of course?'

Paul laughed. 'A man-sized rabbit! Now that would be something new, one of these mysterious beasts of local legends.'

'Like the hounds that reputedly sit by King Arthur's side inside the hill,' Vince put in eagerly. 'I'd love to see them ride out in full armour, wouldn't that be wonderful?'

'A bit scary, I should think,' said Paul. 'They might mistake us for their enemies—'

Faro interrupted. 'I heard a shot.'

Paul nodded and indicated the game bag over his shoulder. 'One for the pot, Constable. Good day.'

'Bye, sir.' Vince waved as he disappeared in the direction of the cottage.

Faro was still shaken. Someone had tried to kill him – and perhaps thought they had succeeded, given he had thrown himself to the ground and remained there playing dead, preparing all his muscles and sinews to spring up and fight for his life had the killer come over to make sure he had hit his target.

As he headed back toward the Central Office, a deadly thought persisted. What if Paul had intended to kill him and was accused of attempted murder? He would produce Vince, a twelve-year-old boy, to convince the jury that this was an accident, a stray shot on a misty hill.

What horrors might then lie in wait for Lizzie and her future?

CHAPTER TWENTY-SIX

The following day Archie was at home, recovering his good spirits. His faith in the power and social benefits that money could achieve had been dented but not destroyed by what he regarded as a mere interlude. The unfortunate episode of the table maid's suicide would have been bad enough, but to then have it declared as murder, that was too much, followed by the unpleasant surge of policemen with their incredibly prying questions into his private life which was completely unrelated to the crime.

Clara, he observed, had also resumed her smiling exterior, her quiet submissive existence as a beautiful ornament in his priceless collection. It was to his advantage that she never expressed the slightest interest in his life before they met.

Or so Archie fondly believed. The truth was rather different and would have disturbed his tranquility, to say the least. Under that smiling exterior displayed to all the world, there lurked a resourceful curiosity. That was not remarkable if one considered the details of her own past and her struggle for survival. Spending most of her days within the confines of this vast house, with a husband whose only interest in her was displayed behind the closed doors of their adjoining bedrooms each night, she had few friends – only mere female acquaintances whose husbands were involved in Archie's business circle, which he so assiduously nurtured in his constant strive to climb the ladder of Edinburgh society.

Daily life against such a background was predictable and monotonous; with no reason or opportunity for exploring the vast city outside Lumbleigh Green, she felt trapped, a bird in a gilded cage. Anything locked became her absorbing interest. She enjoyed a secret exploration of locked cupboards and drawers, with a particular fascination for the forbidden mahogany desk in the study.

One day Archie had been called away and carelessly left a set of keys on his desk. After a trial, one fitted, and after some effort opened a rather difficult lock.

Clara's curiosity was rewarded with a large envelope file. A quick look inside revealed it contained information about Archie's past. Details of court proceedings along with newspaper clippings, perhaps retained on the off chance that some future proof or defence might be needed.

The sound of Archie's voice in the hall announced his unexpected return. In danger of being caught red-handed, she panicked, flung down the keys and with no time to fumble with the lock of the stubborn drawer and replace the envelope, she carried it upstairs and, trembling with guilt, thrust it away to await an opportunity for its return.

In common with eavesdroppers who hear no good of themselves, the proceeds of her idle curiosity made her painfully aware of the transience of her own future should her past be revealed.

However, she was also aware of the value of what she held as a possible means of preservation, aware that as a woman she was utterly dependent on her husband. By law everything she possessed, every piece of jewellery down to the very clothes on her back, belonged to Archie. He could send her out into the world stark naked if he decided she was no longer useful, his heart set on a new, more exciting woman in his life.

Her brief glimpse of the envelope's contents had also produced a bundle of letters which were of more immediate interest than dull court proceedings. A legal document concerning Mavis Rayne, a perfumer, and her property, owned by Archibald Lumbleigh. From the date, Mavis had been on the scene long before Clara made her appearance – a threat should a day come when her beauty faded and with it her husband's fascination and interest.

Clara was aware that Archie's mistress lived in a handsome house in York Square. By chance Clara had been visiting her milliner who lived opposite, and looking out of the window she had seen Archie's carriage arrive and wait on the other side of the street. She had been a little surprised; perhaps he was calling for her and had got the address wrong, but no, he looked around, ran up the steps, pressed the bell and was admitted.

Noticing Clara's interest, Adele, a lady who enjoyed a bit of gossip, whispered: 'That gentleman is a frequent visitor. And he is not there just to buy perfume.'

In no time at all, Clara heard the full story. The house, which carried on a flourishing business as a perfumery, was also rumoured to be a high-class brothel, and the madam was a middle-aged woman called Mrs Mavis Rayne.

The milliner went on to say that Mrs Rayne had some very pretty young employees, two of whom were also her own clients. Apparently the gentlemen were all well off and paid for their pleasure in the quiet middle hours of the day when their wives could presume that they would be sitting in their business establishments, poring over dull documents in banks and offices rather than poring over the naked charms of ladies of ill repute.

Adele, without the faintest idea of the reason for Clara's interest in the house across the way, was always eager to gossip to Mrs Lumbleigh, who was fast becoming her favourite customer. She didn't belong to those high-and-mighty Edinburgh ladies but had an easy-going manner that made her feel instinctively that they were equals.

A lie from Archie about how he had been visiting his banker that afternoon confirmed Clara's suspicions. She now knew about Mavis and made it her business to keep a careful eye on that part of Archie's so-called business life. She decided to hold on to the envelope, certain that Archie would not miss it before she had a chance to peruse its contents, sadly aware that her husband might be far from the respectable model he was so eager to present to Edinburgh society.

And so it was on that day, while Archie was basking in his regained sense of security, Clara sitting by her window upstairs was intrigued to see a well-upholstered veiled lady emerge from a carriage and stride purposefully towards the front door.

The sound of the bell clanged through the house, followed by Mrs Brown's footsteps through the hall. As she opened the door, the newcomer's ringing tones echoed upstairs to the banister where Clara stood concealed.

Mavis Rayne – for she it was – demanded to see Mr Lumbleigh immediately.

Mrs Brown gave the standard reply: she would see if the master was at home.

To her horror, the stout woman rudely pushed past her and marched in the direction of Archie's study. The door opened and banged shut again before Mrs Brown, scuttling behind the interloper, could protest. Raised voices too indistinct to interpret reached Clara's ears. She hurried downstairs to where a very flustered, outraged housekeeper was heading back to the kitchen.

'A moment, Mrs Brown. Who was that?'

Mrs Brown, recovering her dignity, said stiffly:

'A business acquaintance of the master. No name was given, madam.' With a brief curtsey she retreated into the kitchen. Let Mrs Lumbleigh sort that one out.

Behind the study's closed door, Archie was on his feet. He could hardly believe his eyes.

'Mavis!' he croaked. 'What the devil are you doing here? I have told you over and over; never – I repeat, *never* – are you to come to this house. This is totally against our agreement,' he thundered.

'Whoever made that agreement,' Mavis said angrily, 'they didn't include one that promised protection if my life – *my life*,' she repeated, 'was to be in danger.'

Archie sat down like an exploded balloon. 'What on earth are you on about?' he gasped.

Mavis had taken a seat opposite and was unveiling her bonnet. 'I've just been attacked on my way home, outside my own door, returning from an exhibition in George Street. There's a terrible mist outside which you might not have noticed and a man sprang out from one of the basement areas, where he had been lurking, no doubt. A tall man in a cloak. He grabbed me from behind, tried to throw me down. I expected rape, and as he tried to fling me to the ground, I screamed and prepared for action. I've learnt a thing or two about dealing with attempted rapists in my time.'

She stopped for breath, gave him a triumphant look and added, 'My scream was sufficient, my knee was not needed. A whistle, footsteps, and he was off. A policeman ran towards us and that saved my virtue, if not my life. He had a gun – did I mention that?'

Archie could only listen, shaking his head in horrified bewilderment. 'This is dreadful, dreadful, Mavis.'

'Is that all you can say?'

His thoughts were racing ahead. Had Mavis been killed, his secret life would have been revealed. All those cursed policemen invading his privacy once again. The scandal, the newspapers.

He felt suddenly sick.

'Did he take anything?'

'He grabbed my reticule, but he dropped it when he ran off. The policeman got it back for me. No time to steal anything valuable—'

Something to be grateful for at least, and Archie interrupted: 'You must not be seen here, Mavis.' He gulped. 'My wife – she must not know of your existence.'

It was too late. Overcome by curiosity, her presence shielded by their angry voices, Clara had opened the door a fraction and listened to the conversation.

Armed by a false sense of security, Archie said to Mavis: 'Come, I will take you home.'

Mavis smiled. 'I hoped you would. I kept the carriage. It's waiting.'

A sigh of relief. Brown was away on an errand, and he could rely on Brown who was honest and reliable. Thank God, he thought, heading back home again and paying off the hiring cab. Brown knew about those visits to York Square, but the coachman's discretion was well paid for, and he also benefited from expensive second-hand clothes from his wealthy employer's extensive wardrobe, the envy of Mrs Brown, who observed elegant items from Mrs Lumbleigh's wardrobe, which would have never fitted her by any stretch of imagination, all heading in the lady's maid's direction.

As Archie went indoors, he regarded the front windows anxiously, hoping that Clara had not been in the garden and would not question him as he considered a selection of valid excuses. What would a veiled lady want with him? Perhaps the widow of a business colleague with shares to invest, in need of helpful advice.

Yes, that would do excellently, that was the most convincing, but as they sat down to dinner he was relieved that no excuses were needed. Clara never mentioned the incident. He sighed with relief, perhaps she had been taking an afternoon rest and had missed the disturbance entirely.

Paul joined them. 'Heard the latest?'

Archie, involved with his own troubles, looked up anxiously for an instant. 'Don't tell me you haven't seen the police out on the hill, swarms of them?' said Paul.

And before Archie could digest that monstrous presence so close to home once more, Paul picked up his knife and fork and said: 'The local Catholic priest seems to have gone missing. I met DC Faro roaming about near the back garden. I gather he hasn't been seen for a couple of days.'

A sharp exclamation of concern from Clara who wanted to know more. 'I met him. He conducted Ida's funeral service. Just a young fellow. Seemed so nice and sensitive. Oh dear, I wonder what can have happened to him.'

Archie groaned at this painful reminder. Damn Faro and all the rest of the Edinburgh City Police. Was Lumbleigh Green never to be free of association with a table maid's murder?

Paul was saying: 'Searching the hill in the mist hasn't been much use.' And looking at Archie: 'The gardens will be in line for a search – just a routine matter,' he added, enjoying his stepfather's discomfort.

'Can't we be spared that?' Archie said angrily and Paul smiled and left them.

Some time later, Brown reported to Archie that Master Paul had met him parking the carriage and that they had made a thorough search of the extensive gardens. There was no place where the missing priest could have hidden had he wanted to do so.

'I reported this to the beat constable, sir, and this information was duly noted. He assured me that we would not be troubled any further, sir.'

This reassurance fell a little short of its mark and Archie merely shook his head and murmured: 'When will it all end?'

And in the Central Office, PC Jansen, who had saved Mavis in the nick of time, had duly reported that incident. It was now reposing on the desk between Faro and Gosse who thumped his fists together in a gesture of triumph: 'At last – a breakthrough. We've got him at last.'

'Have we, sir?'

'Don't you see? Sounds like the man who attacked Jock Webb,' he said eagerly, then frowned. 'Maybe it *was* Jock Webb. Have you thought of that? Never been sure of him, high on the list of suspects. Get down there and check his movements last night. And see this woman – this Mrs Rayne.'

Meanwhile, at home with her girls, who had listened horrified to this story, Mavis, who was removing the contents of her retrieved reticule into another, discovered something she had overlooked the first time.

A playing card. How on earth had it got there? She rarely played cards at all and it was the first time she had used this new reticule, an accessory bought specially to match her new velvet outfit for the art exhibition.

She looked at the card with distaste. Her attacker must have put it in there. But why?

Who knows and who cares, she said, and flung it into the fire.

CHAPTER TWENTY-SEVEN

Faro was on his way to York Square to interview Mrs Mavis Rayne. As he climbed the front steps of the handsome Georgian house, somewhere inside a dog barked shrilly and the door was opened by the lady herself.

His uniform explained his presence, no explanation was needed.

'Come in, Constable. I was expecting you.'

She gathered up the tiny white poodle and he followed her down through the hall into her study, somewhat overwhelmed by the heavy odour of perfumes and the vast array of scent bottles and other evidence of female toilette around him.

Noticing his somewhat startled glance she

smiled. 'You will have observed, no doubt, that I am a perfumer by profession, Constable. Do sit down.' She took a seat in the armchair opposite, and cradling the little dog she looked him over candidly. Always glad to appreciate the presence of a handsome young man, this one was exceptional. However, she decided that the circumstances demanded that she sternly control her natural impulses and she must not flirt or even flutter her long eyelashes.

Faro was finding the atmosphere of femininity daunting enough but he already knew a great deal about Mrs Rayne. He was aware, as were most of his colleagues, that this business also concealed one of Edinburgh's high-class brothels. But this was not his concern as Mrs Rayne said:

'The attack was an attempted rape, Constable.' With a shuddering sigh she added, 'And the man also held a gun to the back of my skull. I will not easily forget the feel of that either. I was fortunate to escape with my life as well as my virtue . . .'

As Mavis went through the details she had given Archie once again, Faro carefully made notes, and at the end of her account, since it was almost identical to that of PC Jansen, he asked: 'Was there anything particular you observed about this man's appearance, madam?'

Mavis laughed scornfully. 'I was not in a

position for observation, Constable, since he was behind me with an arm about my throat.'

'Are we to understand, then, that you might not be able to identify him, should we succeed in arresting him?'

Mavis shook her head. 'When your constable approached, he ran off, looked round briefly and, although I was unable to see his face clearly, he was tall – about your height, Constable. And I thought he had a cap pulled down well over his eyes, the lower part of his face hidden.' She thought for a moment. 'One thing I did notice, though: if you will forgive the indelicacy, he was more than a bit smelly. He stank.'

As she made a face, Faro said: 'Was it alcohol, or just uncleanliness, body sweat?'

Mavis shrugged, stroking the poodle. 'More like a dog, like Pip here – when he gets wet. Yes, that's it – wet wool.' Faro's eyebrows raised at that and she laughed. 'I have an exceptional sense of smell, Constable, that is why I am a perfumer. I can instantly detect the merest hint of any odour and also identify it,' she added.

And Faro, hoping that he smelt of shaving soap and keenly aware that he was only two days away from Mrs Biggs' sternly regulated bath night, solemnly wrote 'the attacker smelt of wet wool' in his report.

Closing his notebook, about to leave, he turned at the door and thanking Mrs Rayne for her assistance, said: 'Should you remember anything else, however trivial, please let us know, as it may help us to track this man down.'

Mavis thought for a moment. 'There was something . . . well, rather odd. He snatched my reticule as you know, but PC Jansen recovered it a few yards away. When I checked the contents there was nothing missing only' – she shrugged – 'there was something added. A playing card.'

On the step Faro turned swiftly. 'One of yours?'

Mavis shook her head. 'No, I'd never seen it before. I don't carry packs of cards in my reticule, Constable.'

'What kind of a card was it, madam?'

Mavis shrugged. 'A red one, hearts? I'm not absolutely certain but I think it was a diamond.'

'The denomination?' Faro asked sharply, the nine already taking shape in his mind.

She shook her head. 'All I recognised was that it wasn't one of the face cards. A number.' She shrugged. 'I just threw it in the fire. But odd, isn't it, how it got there?'

Odd indeed, thought Faro. And sinister too for he did not doubt that the card had been the nine of diamonds. Touching his helmet, he left Mrs

Rayne, who watched him go with some regret.

She didn't meet young men like this every day and would have enjoyed his company over a cup of tea, or more, over a drink.

As for Faro, he was wondering what would have been her reaction to the knowledge that her potential rapist had already killed two young women, had been frustrated in his attempted murder of an elderly man and was perhaps the killer of a missing priest.

CHAPTER TWENTY-EIGHT

In the Central Office, Gosse poured scorn on Faro's report of his interview with Mavis Rayne.

Faro insisted: 'I feel there is more in it than attempted rape. Those individuals might carry a knife just to press the point, as it were, but not a gun. Then there was the playing card.'

'Which the lady was unable to identify for certain, just vaguely – hearts or diamonds.'

'I still feel that its existence at the scene links her attacker to our murderer.'

Gosse waved a dismissive hand. 'What kind of evidence is that, pray? A playing card she threw into the fire. You're wasting your time again, Faro – and mine,' he added, although Faro would have thought the latter was far from evident since Gosse seemed quite happy to spend his days comfortably seated in an armchair, apparently brooding over a mass of paper on Inspector Wade's desk.

When the sergeant said: 'You'd better get back on the track of Jock Webb, check his alibi for the time of the assault,' Faro had a shrewd idea that Gosse had already made up his mind on the killer's identity, hoping that his detective constable would solve the crimes, and ready to claim full credit for anything that Faro unearthed as evidence.

What Faro did not know as he made his way towards Liberton Brae was that Gosse had been humiliated by Lizzie; his one move at extending their policeman-witness relationship on to a more personal basis by kissing her had received an angry retort, a sharp slap. Her face scarlet, her voice cold, she fought off his embrace. All friendly smiles had vanished for ever as she jumped out of the carriage and said:

'May I remind you, Sergeant, that you have overstepped the line between witness and policeman. I have verified in our meetings all the evidence you could possibly require and that, as far as I am concerned, is the end of it. I shall not be available for further meetings with you.'

Rubbing his still stinging cheek, Gosse was furious and the failure to seduce Faro's young lady, his original spiteful plan for ousting Faro, had blossomed into something deeper, an obsession, an infatuation that might be regarded by some as love for Lizzie Laurie. His feelings were those of a rejected lover and did not endear him to his bitter rival whom he now blamed entirely for Lizzie slapping his face. How dare Mrs Laurie prefer Faro to himself?

On the way to Liberton Brae, the rain that had been threatening all morning turned into a deluge. With no place to shelter, Faro looked round as a carriage stopped alongside. The driver was Brown, under a large umbrella. The door opened and Clara Lumbleigh looked out, Lizzie at her side.

'Can we drop you off somewhere? We're heading to Bonnyrigg.'

Lizzie looked over her shoulder, smiled at him.

'Thank you but I'm just a step away, up the hill here.'

'Then jump up, get under Brown's umbrella.'

Faro was grateful for that brief shelter as a hundred yards ahead he indicated Jock Webb's door. As he stepped down Lizzie leant forward and blew him a kiss. He shouted: 'I'll see you this evening.'

'I'll be waiting for you.' And Lizzie sat back, smiling, content. 'If that is convenient for you, madam,' she added anxiously.

Clara nodded and smiled. 'Of course, my dear. Glad we were able to rescue your young man. Not much fun having to walk miles in the rain.'

Lizzie sighed, wishing her young man was more than that, wishing with all her heart that she had a more official public role in Faro's life. Then the horrible embarrassing incident with the sergeant might not have happened. She told herself that the future did not really matter as long as all her days continued to be linked together, strung along with the prospect of meeting Jeremy. She closed her eyes; today was enough and tomorrow was still all she had to hope for.

From the doorway Faro watched the departing carriage through the rain. With that unexpected meeting, just those few words between them, he was overwhelmed by a sudden longing to be with Lizzie again, a need for her tender, gentle presence in this turmoil of his life.

Footsteps approaching and the door was opened by Annie who regarded his uniform and the request to see Mr Webb somewhat doubtfully.

'Just a few words to finalise our report. I won't detain him long,' he added encouragingly.

'Then you'd better come in. Jock's having a wee nap.' She stood aside and led the way into the kitchen, its atmosphere heavy with the smell of drying clothes, the fire totally obscured by a clothes horse. Pointing to it she said: 'This weather's just awful and Jock's cape takes up all the fire drying. Won't be parted from it, got soaked through twice. Last night he was out again drinking with friends.' Faro detected a note of disapproval as she sighed.

'It'll never dry in time. We're off shortly to an anniversary party in Penicuik.'

A door opened and Jock emerged, bleary-eyed, his dishevelled condition suggesting a more than ordinary hangover.

'Oh, it's you. Thought I heard voices. And what d'ye want this time, Constable?' he demanded shortly.

There was no way of phrasing the obvious question. 'We wondered if there had been any follow-up to the attack on you, sir. If you'd had any reactions, or possibly even remembered something about your attacker. That he might be local and you had seen him around.'

Jock laughed harshly. 'If I'd seen him around you'd have heard about that, Constable. I'd have knocked the bugger's head off, that's what.'

'Sorry to disturb you like this, sir,' Faro said

apologetically, 'but there has been another incident.'

Jock was interested. He said sharply, 'Has there? Where?'

'He's attacked a woman in York Square and her description fits closely to the one you gave us.'

'York Square, eh?' Jock laughed. 'Well, well!' A nod and a wink. 'Known for its upper-class whores, even in my day,' he chuckled.

'The lady was lucky to escape with her life,' Faro said.

'Wait a bit,' said Jock. 'Now I know why you're here. What you really want to know is whether I was telling the truth first time round. You and that sergeant never believed my story, did you?'

Faro looked embarrassed, somewhat taken aback by this astute rejoinder as Jock continued: 'I was out with my cronies. Went to a pub or two – or three. They'll tell you, that is if any of them can remember.' Pausing he scratched his head. 'And I'm damned if I can remember myself, who was there or where any of them lived.'

It wasn't much as an alibi and it would be tortuous indeed to verify. As Faro again apologised for disturbing him and prepared to leave, Jock said forgivingly: 'All I still remember that sticks in my mind was when I was attacked this man was wearing an Inverness cape,' he pointed to the clothes horse, 'like mine over there, Harris tweed, best there is but takes a devil of a time to dry.'

Heading out again into the rain, faced with the rain-soaked walk back into the city, without hope of a rescuing carriage this time, he went over what Webb had been saying. And in the deep roots of that retentive memory, something clicked . . .

The rain had eased and meeting Jeremy was for Lizzie the one gleam of sunshine in a grey dismal evening. Her smile was radiant as she walked out of the door of Lumbleigh Green and saw him waiting at the gate. The feeling was mutual, but there was an unusual awkwardness and conversations begun eagerly died suddenly. Topics were searched for, picked up and dropped. Silences only broken by the sound of their footsteps across wet pavements.

Faro remembered their last meeting, how elated he had felt, almost ready to ask Lizzie to share the rest of his life. That moment had vanished and now Lizzie seemed almost a stranger. Oddly enough, if they had been able to read each other's minds, Faro would have found Lizzie having the same thoughts of being somehow let down. In her case, with a sense of generosity regarding Jeremy's shortcomings as a suitor, she put it down to preoccupation regarding some new investigation, details of which he could not, of course, share with her.

The rain, which they had regarded as a threat to the evening together, began again, increasingly heavy, and sheltering in a doorway Faro shrugged.

'It's no use, Lizzie. We will have to call it off. We're both getting drenched. Best head home.' He stepped forward, hailed a passing hiring cab. Pressing a coin into the driver's hand he said: 'Take this lady to Lumbleigh Green, if you please.' Ignoring her protests, he kissed her, handed her into the cab and whispered: 'I will see you again very soon.' With that she had to be content.

Faro returned to his lodgings. As he was removing his wet coat Mrs Biggs looked out of her parlour and said: 'You're like a drowned rat, Mr Faro. Let me take that coat. I'll put it by the fire and it will soon dry. What awful weather, even for Edinburgh.'

Thanking her, he received a disarming smile. 'I've just made a pot of tea.' And pointing to the kitchen, 'And there's a slice of pie needing eating,' she whispered. 'But don't tell the others. A good landlady doesn't have favourites, you know.' But the arch look which accompanied that statement belied her words.

For once, he found it easy to talk to Mrs Biggs,

easier in fact with this woman he hardly knew at all than with his Lizzie, much to the landlady's delight. She encouraged him to a second cup of tea and watched him finish the pie which he proclaimed 'delicious'. Questioning him about Orkney, she leaned forward across the table, listening wide-eyed as if it was an unexplored planet, further away than darkest Africa.

An hour later, footsteps outside declared the noisy return of his fellow lodgers, so snatching his jacket he thanked her and fled upstairs before the first key had turned in the lock.

The weather was abominable, even worse than usual with eternal rain or heavy mist, and with images of constables unhappy as drowned rats searching for the missing priest, of Clara and Lizzie in their carriage, the meeting with Jock Webb, coming home drenched, glad of Mrs Biggs' restoring cup of tea, the warm fire and smell of cooking and drying clothes, Faro tried to order his thoughts.

Troubled, he was becoming increasingly aware that he was getting precisely nowhere with this murder investigation in which Gosse seemed to have lost all interest, but would doubtless put in an appearance to claim he had solved it – eventually.

As he prepared for bed, he solemnly regarded his still damp jacket, his mind going over the day's events, the thought niggling away at the back of his mind that he had touched the first clue of any significance that led to the killer's identity. Fighting off the desire to sleep, he picked up a pen, and as was his method with all cases, he drew out a sheet of paper, took out his notebook and went back to the beginning, trying to give substance to an idea built out of circumstances surrounding the killings.

A few minutes later he sat back, yawned. A church clock nearby struck eleven; an early start called next morning at 6.30. It was useless. His mind refused to function, his eyelids grew heavy. He couldn't fight off sleep any longer. It overwhelmed him, he knew when he was defeated. The vital clue remained a vague shadow.

CHAPTER TWENTY-NINE

Next morning he awoke refreshed and knew he had to talk to someone. And the only person who could help him, who had the wisdom and experience of many years, was Brandon Macfie. If there were no urgent reports awaiting his attention at the Central Office he would call on his old friend at Nicholson Square.

At ten o'clock, he rang the bell. Macfie opened the door and smiled. 'My dear lad, what a pleasant surprise. Come in, come in.' And as Faro followed him into the kitchen Macfie said: 'You were lucky to catch me at home, I'm off to Newcastle for a couple of days, giving a talk about the differences between English and Scots' law.'

'In that case, sir, I will not detain you.'

But observing Faro's anxious expression and the early hour for such a visit, Macfie realised the matter must be serious and immediately said: 'I have a couple of hours until my train. Do sit down.'

As Faro sat at the table, Macfie's housekeeper appeared as if by magic and put down coffee and bannocks. Smiling, Macfie thanked her and looking across at Faro, he said:

'Problems, lad? Personal or is it the murder investigation?'

Faro shook his head. 'The latter – my personal problems do not deserve intruding on you at this hour of the day.'

Macfie poured the coffee, sat back in his chair. 'Go ahead, I'm listening.'

'Truth is, sir, we . . . or rather I am getting nowhere with this investigation. I am in a complete muddle, things that don't seem to fit in anywhere, like the nine of diamonds—'

Macfie held up his hand. 'Let's have it, then. Right from the beginning, that first murder in Fleshers Close, if you please.'

'Gosse and I were called out. He presumed the dead woman was a prostitute since she was wearing a red gown. But the condition of her body, the presence of the small girl hovering about, suggested something else to me. I recalled seeing a woman similarly attired leaving the theatre after a performance and a young drunken fellow attempting to drag her into his carriage.'

Faro paused there; he was not ready to impart his suspicions of Paul who he had recognised as the drunk in a subsequent visit to Lumbleigh Green concerning the murder of the maid Ida.

'My theory that the dead woman was possibly an actress proved correct. Enquiries at the theatre here led to Glasgow and I learnt that her name was Doris Page and that her husband, who had been searching for her, had just arrived in Edinburgh. For Gosse, Page was an immediate suspect. However, he had a perfect alibi – he was in a Glasgow jail after a fight on the night Doris was killed.'

'You told me earlier about the playing card, the nine of diamonds, found under her body,' Macfie interrupted.

'There was no explanation for that, or for its appearance at all three of the subsequent incidents.'

Macfie nodded. 'We'll get back to that. Carry on.'

'The second attack was on Jock Webb, the ex-boxer, also in the Newington area, quite near where Doris Page was found. Webb described a tall, strong man, face hidden, who he fought off. But his injuries were enough to put him in hospital temporarily. I was present when his clothes were restored to him and in his jacket pocket, the nine of diamonds—'

'Ah,' Macfie interrupted. 'That's significant.'

Faro shook his head. 'Webb claims that he doesn't gamble and denied all knowledge of how it got there. However, he was unable to produce any convincing alibi for the time of the murder of Doris Page and as far as Gosse is concerned, he is ready to arrest him on suspicion.'

Macfie nodded. 'A prime – and so far, the only – suspect, who claimed to be attacked; although his injuries were quite superficial, this seems the perfect alibi. However, it is not unknown in police records, where malefactors have used self-inflicted injuries to substantiate an alibi. Please continue.'

'The latest alarm was when Ida Watts, a maid at Lumbleigh Green, failed to put in an appearance.'

Macfie refilled their coffee, and inviting Faro to another bannock smiled wryly. 'A procedure all too frequent, I'm afraid.'

'That was to be the general assumption except that her mother arrived at the house in a great panic. Her daughter was devoted, never let her parents down and this had been her birthday party. Convinced that there was something amiss, Mrs Laurie went to the police office and reported the girl as a missing person.'

'Very laudable,' Macfie put in. 'So what had happened to her?'

'We were soon to find out, sir. A suicide was reported to us, off North Bridge, and it turned out to be the missing Ida. At least, suicide was presumed – medical evidence was that she had been strangled first and then thrown off the bridge.'

'Strangulation – like the woman in Fleshers Close,' said Macfie. 'Does this indicate that we have a serial killer on the loose?'

'Perhaps so, as you suggested at our last meeting. That would seem to be the general opinion, but in Ida's case there is more to come.'

'Proceed.'

'My friend Lizzie, who as you know is Mrs Lumbleigh's personal maid, told me that Ida, who had never confided in her before, was very excited that Friday. Said she was eloping, that she might be pregnant by her secret lover, a wealthy young man who had promised to marry her.'

'A valid reason for this wealthy young lover wishing to dispose of her. That is not unknown either.'

'Except in this case, the post-mortem produced no evidence of pregnancy. And in common with Doris Page and the attack on Jock Webb, the nine of diamonds in her reticule was found by the constable.'

A clock struck the hour and Faro was aware that his friend had a train to catch. 'There is a little more, sir.'

Macfie smiled. 'Plenty of time, lad. There are always other trains.'

'Ida was Catholic and the young priest who conducted her funeral service was very emotional. I decided to talk to him as I had been told that she was at confession shortly before her death. I wanted to know the name of this secret lover, but if the priest knew it, he took refuge in the sacred ritual of the confessional.'

Faro shook his head. 'He was adamant and could not be persuaded. That he might be protecting a killer seeking other victims was of no avail.' He paused. 'And now the latest, which you may have read in the newspapers. The priest has gone missing, and fearing some disaster while about his parochial duties, a search has been underway on Arthur's Seat.'

Again he paused. 'I am certain there is a link with Ida's murder. Is he a victim? Is he already dead because Ida told him her lover's name?'

Macfie thought for a moment. 'The other alternative is doubtful as we discussed earlier. But I put it to you anyway. Could this young priest have been her lover and feared exposure?'

'I have thought of that too, but the playing card does not fit in.'

'Unless the priest is a madman who killed both women,' Macfie put in grimly.

'Having met him, sir, I can't believe that.'

Macfie smiled wryly. 'Mad priests have also been known. Think of Rasputin. But I take your point.' He sighed. 'It's the presence of this playing card that is the most baffling ingredient. Who and why?'

'There is one final incident, sir. Mrs Mavis Rayne has been attacked outside her house in York Square.'

Macfie beamed. 'Mavis Rayne, the notorious perfumer. Well, well, I could tell you many tales about her famous establishment. But please continue.'

'She believed that rape was intended. Her screams and struggles attracted a constable who blew his whistle and raced to the spot.'

'Saving her virtue, no doubt,' said Macfie who, Faro suspected, was enjoying this piece of local drama.

'The constable duly reported the attack. Gosse

sent me to interview her. She couldn't see her attacker's face clearly since he was behind her, an arm about her neck, but she said he was tall and strong and she had learnt about dealing with prospective rapists in her time.'

Macfie chortled. 'I am sure she was speaking the truth about that.'

'The constable who came to her rescue, not to be deterred, dashed off in pursuit and picked up her reticule which had been dropped, presuming it to be the reason for the attack. Mrs Rayne explained that it was new, the contents were intact, nothing stolen. Except there was one addition to its contents.'

'Ah,' said Macfie. 'That card again?'

'Yes, it wasn't hers, she doesn't play cards and she threw it in the fire. When I asked for more details, she said it was either hearts or diamonds—'

He hadn't got to the point of it yet, the visit to Webb yesterday. There was still so much to say as Macfie sighed and consulted his timepiece. 'I really have to go, lad. Care to walk me to the railway station?'

A final word to the housekeeper and they set off over South Bridge and down towards Waverley Station.

Walking on the pavement, avoiding other

passers-by with the noise of carriages and horses clattering alongside over the cobbled road, made carrying on a conversation almost impossible. From under the North Bridge, the hiss of steam rose from waiting trains.

Macfie said: 'Come and see me when I get back. I hope you make some progress. You know what is missing from all this and what you must find.' Without waiting for Faro's reply he repeated emphatically: 'A motive, lad. Every murder must have a motive and so far that is missing. Find it and it will lead you to your killer.'

Down the Waverley steps and Macfie bought his ticket. The train was leaving in three minutes. Faro followed him on to the platform where he got into a carriage, pulled down the window.

'You might begin by having a closer look at Lumbleigh Green. And good luck!'

As the train gathered steam and began to move off, Macfie leant out to wave to Faro standing on the platform. This fine young man, who was so like Sandy, his own lad. They would have been the same age, and Sandy had wanted to be a policeman. He closed the window and sighed. Jeremy Faro had become increasingly important in his life, taking over the role of the son he had lost.

* * *

In the Central Office, the inspector's chair was empty. Faro sighed with relief, for once escaping the sergeant's taunts at his inability to solve two murders and produce a killer like a rabbit out of the magician's hat.

At the reception desk, the constable shook his head. DS Gosse had mentioned that he was away 'down East Lothian way' and would not be back until late afternoon. Reassured that he was free of Gosse's imminent arrival, Faro took the opportunity to sit down, take out his notebook and, recalling the precise details of his recent conversation with Macfie, he picked up the pen and wrote:

Suspects.
1. Jock Webb (according to Gosse).

Faro frowned. He knew the sergeant's methods and his reputation by now, determined that the most obvious and most accessible from his point of view was also the most likely.

1. Jock Webb, ex-boxer, elderly but in good condition, 'tall and strong' could fit the killer's description. His alibis might be conveniently verified by his lady friend

Annie with whom he is living at the moment.

2. Paul Lumbleigh. A medical student who would know how to strangle the two women victims.

A more likely suspect, not passed on to his sergeant for obvious reasons regarding his claim to remote kinship. If Gosse dashed off with a warrant, this might have disastrous consequences, not only for those intimately concerned but also for Lizzie whose future hung on a thread after the furore caused by what Archie Lumbleigh termed her 'interference' in connection with Ida's murder.

Had the actress Doris Page been accosted by Paul Lumbeigh outside the theatre, and in an unexpected struggle to keep her silent he had strangled her, thrown her out of the carriage in the insalubrious, notorious area of Fleshers Close in the High Street? A neighbour had heard a carriage in the early hours.

Paul fitted Ida's description of her handsome, wealthy young lover, as well as the tall, strong, cloaked man, Jock Webb's attacker and Mavis Rayne's potential rapist in York Square.

Faro put down his pen with an exasperated sigh. All this he realised was purely circumstantial, unless Paul's presence at all places at the times of the murders and attacks could be verified.

The main question remained. Why and what was the motive common to all these incidents and what was the significance of the playing card, the nine of diamonds?

Regarding Doris Page, drunk and attempting to stop the woman's screams, the verdict could well be accidental murder, or manslaughter, but no such excuse could be used by Ida's secret lover, or as the reason for the priest's disappearance.

Faro was now almost certain that Fr Burren had been abducted and murdered. If and when his dead body was found, the motive was almost certainly that Ida had given him the name of her secret love in confession.

Except for the playing card the attacks on Webb and Mrs Rayne, and the murders of Doris Page and Ida Watts, could be unrelated.

He thought again about Mavis Rayne. And if circumstantial evidence pointed in the direction of Paul Lumbleigh, what was his reason for lurking about a basement entrance in York Square that particular evening? True, the perfumer's establishment was also a high-class brothel but why spring out and attack the madam? Did she know something to his discredit, or something that concerned the two murders – or had he mistaken her for someone else?

In fact, did Paul have a motive – or was he just insane?

And that would account for the nine of diamonds, the curse of Scotland left by the killer. Was this another link with Paul? Not only was he in disgrace with his stepfather who had to pay his gambling debts, but he had also shown by popular demand (from Vince) at Lizzie's birthday party several of his tricks, including the notorious 'pick any card' which so baffled onlookers but the secret of which, as Vince demonstrated to his mother later, was that all the cards were of the same denomination.

Later, when Faro went to bed, he felt too wide awake to fall asleep, but just as he was dropping off at last there came to him a picture of Mrs Biggs and his jacket drying over the fire, of Mavis Rayne and her poodle's wet wool. The missing priest. Heavy rain – his rescue by Clara's carriage – Jock Webb's cape . . .

He had it – the answer! He sat up.

But too late, he had to let it go; this fleeting shadow of a nightmare was too far-fetched to have any credibility.

CHAPTER THIRTY

'Laurie – Laurie, wake up! For heaven's sake – please!'

Lizzie sat up, confused, wondering if this was a dream. Dawn streaked the sky and Clara stood over her, trembling.

'What is it, madam, what is wrong?'

Clara sat down on the bed and put her hands over her face. 'Oh dear God, Laurie. He is here! Here!' she sobbed.

'Who, madam, who are you talking about?'

'My stepfather, Bodvale.' Clara sat up. 'He came to my bedroom, just minutes ago.'

Lizzie got out of bed, calmly threw a shawl over her mistress's shoulders, shivering in her thin nightgown. She had dealt with this situation before . . .

'Come along, madam. You'll catch cold, let me get you back to bed. You've had another of your horrible nightmares—'

'Nightmare! This was no nightmare, Laurie. This was real. He tried to make me go with him. When I said no, he said he would . . . would kill me . . .' The rest was inarticulate as she sobbed. 'Please help me, Laurie.'

Lizzie looked at her, shivering, clearly terrified. What could she do? She put an arm around her shoulders. 'Let's go to your room, madam. I'll make you a cup of tea.'

She ushered Clara back to her bedroom, eased her into her bed and prepared to go down into the kitchen.

'No, no, don't leave me,' Clara cried. 'He might come back.' She stared across at the window. 'He could be lurking about outside.' She took Lizzie's arm. 'Promise me you won't leave me – promise.'

Lizzie was prepared to humour her, convinced that this had been yet another of her mistress's nightmares. She sat down, taking her cold hand in hers. The usual procedure was to stay with her until she fell asleep again.

'Close your eyes, madam,' she said gently. 'You're quite safe—'

'Safe!' Clara almost shrieked. 'I thought I was safe. That was my dream for the past few years. Now I know I will never be safe. I will never be safe again.'

'Madam, believe me, it was all just a horrible dream.'

Clara sat up in bed, rolled up the sleeves of her nightgown. 'Dream, was it? If you don't believe me, look at the marks on my arms – and my throat too.'

And there in the lamplight there were indeed red blotches; bruises on both her arms were clearly visible.

'I was fast asleep. Suddenly I was awake, someone had turned up the lamp. I thought it was my husband paying me a rare midnight visit. Then I heard Bodvale's voice in my ear, calling my name.

'"Clara, Clara." Horrified, I opened my eyes, I saw his shadow. He called me his little beauty and said he had waited a long time for this moment. He tried to kiss me, I struggled and he got hold of my arms. "I've come to take you away, you're coming with me where you belong." I started to scream and that was when he took me by the throat, said one yell and he would finish me off. Like he once told me, if he couldn't have me, no one else would. He said he'd been patient, tracking me down – he'd waited. Now the waiting was over.

'He said, "Prepare yourself, you're coming with me. Not tonight, I have things to do first, scores to settle, then we'll be together for always, for the rest of our lives, just as I've always dreamt about. If you won't come with me, then I'll kill you too." I think I must have fainted. I opened my eyes but he was still bending over me. Then he said to me, "I mean you no harm, my dearest girl, as long as you wait and do as I tell you . . . Here, drink this." And he gave me a glass of water. I drank it. I think I fainted again for when I opened my eyes, just before I came to you, he had gone.'

Lizzie said: 'Why didn't you go to the master?'

'Oh, Lizzie, you know perfectly well why I couldn't do that,' she cried. 'He knows nothing of my past. Only you know,' she added reproachfully. 'You're the only one I could trust.' She paused, then wailed, 'But what shall I do? He must be lurking about, waiting. Outside somewhere.'

Still unconvinced despite those bruises, which in a nightmare Lizzie believed could have been self-inflicted, she had some questions that needed answers.

'How did he get into the house, madam?'

'Oh, how do I know? He was just . . . there.'

Lizzie persisted. 'But how did he know which

348

was your bedroom – or that you had a separate one from the master?' she added as delicately as she could.

Clara shook her head. 'I don't know – I don't know anything, only that he was standing by my bed.'

Lizzie thought for a moment, reconstructing the scene in her mind. How could he get across the garden and into the house without the dogs barking? The master liked to think of them as guard dogs and they made a terrific din when disturbed.

Clara took her hand and whispered, 'Who can help me, Laurie, who can I turn to?'

If it was true and the intruder was real and not the figment of a nightmare, then, to Lizzie, there was only one person or persons who could help, who could protect Clara. The police, but in particular one DC Faro. But Clara had said: 'Tell no one.'

If the intruder was real, had her mistress been drugged so that he could make his getaway? One sip of the water was enough to confirm that the bitter taste was laudanum.

She kept this sinister information to herself, but seeing Clara still distraught throughout the day and with Archie away on business, when she was usually given permission to see Faro, she had a better idea.

First of all, she had to tell Clara what she intended.

'You need someone to help you, madam, isn't that so?'

'Oh yes, anyone, Laurie. Anyone who can get me out of this horror. I am absolutely desperate.'

'There is one person, someone we both know, who we can trust, who is the soul of discretion.'

Clara stared at her, bewildered. 'Who, Laurie, who? I don't understand. Someone we both know?' She shook her head.

'Yes, madam. DC Faro.' Lizzie smiled, trying to keep the pride out of her voice.

'Your policeman friend, Laurie? No, my dear, that will not do at all,' Clara said firmly. 'The police must be kept out of this. For reasons you already know, if they are involved then it will all come out. My past,' she shuddered. 'All that I have concealed from my husband. Once he knows, then he will show me the door; my safe and secure future, my marriage will all be at an end.'

Lizzie put a hand on her arm. 'Please don't distress yourself, madam, we are not talking about the police. You can tell Jeremy Faro. Explain what happened. I am sure when he knows the truth he will be persuaded not to inform official sources. He will keep a promise too, that I have made—'

'And are about to break,' said Clara reproachfully.

'Then I beseech you, for your own sake, madam, to release me from that promise.'

Clara sat motionless, silent, thinking, then she sighed. 'Very well, Laurie, if you are sure there is no other way. I have no option.' And clasping her hand, 'I do trust you, dear Laurie,' and stifling a sob, 'you are all I have to trust.' She sat up and said firmly, 'When can you arrange this?'

'With your permission, I will bring him when he comes to meet me outside the gate tonight.'

Faro was somewhat taken aback when Lizzie hurried towards him. She was not wearing outdoor attire and seizing his arm said: 'Come with me.' Bewildered he allowed her to lead him through the kitchen door where a surprised Mrs Brown looked up from her household accounts and demanded:

'And where do you two think you're going?'

Heading for the door into the main hall, Lizzie said: 'We have an appointment with the mistress. We are expected.'

They heard Betty giggle as the outraged housekeeper sprang forward. 'This is most irregular. Wait! I must announce you first. The mistress is in her room – she has given orders that she is not to be disturbed.'

But she was too late; even as she undid her apron they were gone, their footsteps echoing down the stairs.

At the top of the staircase Lizzie whispered: 'The mistress thought it was safer to talk in her bedroom, less chance of being overheard, or listened to downstairs.'

Faro put a delaying hand on her arm. 'Wait a minute, Lizzie. What is all this about?'

'Madam thought she was having a nightmare last night, came and woke me up. That has happened before. But this was no dream, it seems we had an intruder, a man who threatened her—'

Faro was taken by surprise. Was this a further attack by the killer on Clara Lumbleigh? 'This is a police matter, Lizzie,' he said sternly. 'She should have called the beat constable immediately and his escape might have been prevented—'

'No, Jeremy, no. She has her own reasons for not wanting the police involved. She will tell you herself . . .'

Faro's protests were ignored as Lizzie hurried him along the corridor and tapped on the door.

CHAPTER THIRTY-ONE

Clara looked relieved to see Faro with Lizzie and as she invited them to take a seat, Faro said: 'Lizzie has told me very briefly that your life was threatened by an intruder and that you need police protection, madam—' As Faro was about to repeat what he had said to Lizzie, Clara interrupted.

'Not police protection, Constable. There are circumstances that require discretion.' She paused, looked at him, sighed and shook her head.

Still mystified, Faro said: 'Perhaps you would be so good—'

Clara straightened her shoulders and said: 'I will begin at the beginning, Constable. As a child I had a vile stepfather who abused me. My mother died and I was at his mercy, a virtual prisoner. Then, in my teenage years, he was sent to prison for some criminal activity. I escaped from his clutches but had to make my own way in the world. My means of survival would not be entirely suitable for my husband to hear. I had changed my name and my identity, but I was not the innocent young woman Mr Lumbleigh thought he was leading to the altar.' She paused, sighed deeply. 'I say no more, Constable. I leave that to your imagination. Should he learn the truth, I fear that our marriage will be at an end.'

Resisting the temptation to take out his notebook, Faro nodded sympathetically. 'And last night? This intruder?'

'I recognised him as my vile stepfather. He had tracked me down and come, he said, to claim me.' And she proceeded to outline what he had said in much the same words as she had to Lizzie, and ended by saying: 'I will never forget his words. They will be engraved on my heart for ever.'

Faro's mind had been working quickly as he listened and there were many practical questions for which he needed answers.

'You had no problems recognising him again?'

She shook her head. 'Only by his voice. It was dark, and although he kept well out of the lamplight's range, he had turned it up when he entered the room. I could see only his eyes when he wakened me. The rest of his face was hidden, by some sort of mask, but those eyes . . .' She shuddered. 'They have haunted my whole life.'

There were the usual queries about a break-in to be noted. Again Faro regretted that he could hardly produce his notebook but at least he could rely on his remarkable memory for retaining precise details.

'How did he get in unobserved?'

Clara shuddered. 'I have no idea. A door left unlocked or a window open? There are trees close to the house, he could have climbed one and slid along a ledge, if he is agile enough. But I doubt that, Mrs Brown is most reliable, she checks all windows before retiring each night, and in my husband's absence, the front and back doors as well.'

'I see. But how did he approach the house in the first place? He must have approached through the gardens. What about the dogs, were they not alerted to an intruder's presence?'

'If they barked, then no one heard them and they did not scare him off.'

That was odd. Boy was one of the two dogs who were not house pets but kept in the kennels at the stable for Brown to put out at night to guard the grounds.

'I take it that nothing was stolen, the intruder took nothing?'

'Of course not,' said Clara. 'It was not his intention to steal.'

Faro sat back and considered the evidence so far. The fact that the dogs did not bark suggested that the intruder was a familiar sight, that he had got into the house and found his way upstairs in the dark unaided into Clara's room. That he had kept his face covered also suggested that not only was the intruder Jabez Bodvale (as borne out by Clara's confident recognition of his voice) but that he was someone known to the inhabitants of Lumbleigh Green.

His own suspicions, which had seemed so impossible, were beginning to make sense. He asked: 'Why was your stepfather in prison?'

'He was leading a murder gang long sought by the police.'

'You mentioned that he escaped.'

'Yes, there was a fire, perhaps he even started it, and in the confusion he escaped. When he lived with us he never talked about his business activities. Even at that age I suspected it was something illegal, like smuggling. My mother told me that his father had once lost a fortune on the turn of a card. That was why he was so bitter about everything, he had lost his birthright, she said. But he always seemed to have plenty of money.'

Faro eye's gleamed. Was this a link with the playing card at last?

He said: 'He told you to prepare yourself to leave but first he had a score to settle – were those his exact words?'

Clara shivered. 'They were.'

Faro thought for a moment, wondering how to phrase the question delicately. 'May I ask you, concerned as you are regarding your own past, have you any notion of anything that was, well, discreditable in your husband's past?'

Clara looked startled, then uncomfortable. 'I once came across an envelope with some newspaper clippings in his desk drawer – I was looking for a pen,' she lied, flinching at this disclosure of her curiosity. 'I think it was about his partner's suicide, claiming to have been ruined by him.'

'Did you happen to notice this partner's name?'

Faro could have found this out for himself later, but time was running out fast. Any minute now and they would be confronted by Bodvale. That shadow at the back of his mind had moved forward, taken shape. The motive, the essential presence of a carriage at these incidents, Webb and his Inverness cape, the smell of wet wool . . .

Clara was shaking her head, 'There was no opportunity – I heard my husband approaching. I fled.'

'Mrs Lumbleigh, could I ask you to go and get that envelope again?'

Clara looked confused and embarrassed. He thought she was about to refuse and put his hand on hers. 'It is very important, believe me. I wouldn't ask you to do this but your life may depend on it.'

Clara sighed. 'I was ashamed of what I had done. It seemed so despicable. I've been waiting for an opportunity to put it back. So awful if I was caught in the act. Spying on my husband, he'd never forgive me—'

Faro interrupted hastily. 'You mean you still have it?'

Clara hung her head. 'Yes.'

'Please, Mrs Lumbleigh, we must see it.'

He thought she was about to refuse, but with a shrug Clara unlocked her writing desk, and silently handed the envelope to him with a grimace as if the action burnt her fingers.

'You mean that you haven't read it?' Faro asked amazed.

She shook her head. 'No, I no longer wished to pry into his past. I prefer to go on thinking of him as he is today, so good and kind.'

She did not add that she had been overcome by a bad conscience concerning matters in her own past which did not bear scrutiny. 'I don't want to know the contents,' she said miserably.

Faro scanned the cuttings quickly. 'I think you should. The name of the partner who committed suicide was Bodvale. Arthur Bodvale.'

Clara sat back, her hand to her mouth. 'Arthur Bodvale,' she repeated. 'Jabez's father?'

Faro realised that this revelation gave the answer to many of the questions he had been wrestling with, not least providing the motive that Macfie had told him to look for: revenge, the most enduring and most cruel of all motives.

But this was no time to linger . . . Faro was now certain of the killer's identity. Ten years can change a man's physical appearance but he wondered if Bodvale's face had been scarred during the prison fire, facial hair a perfect disguise for a coachman muffled up to the eyes, an anonymous creature in a house where servants were expected to melt into the woodwork when the master – or mistress – appeared.

Lizzie stood, a bewildered observer to this extraordinary scene and, aware of the danger, her thoughts were for her boy.

Where was Vince? He should be home from school and he would be here soon. Mist and rain, as well as the police search on the hill for the missing priest, had put an end to their target shooting. Paul had decided he'd introduce Vince to billiards and Lizzie remembered that it was today he was to come straight from school, sit in the library and wait for Paul.

Lizzie decided that Vince was outgrowing his boyhood too fast when he had produced the small pistol Paul had given him for doing so well in their target shooting.

At her cry of alarm, Vince said, 'Don't be silly, Ma, it isn't loaded.' It made him feel like a policeman, although the beat constable only carried a truncheon. He was sure that DC Faro knew all about guns, and imagined that detectives carried arms when faced with dangerous criminals.

Lizzie was not wholly convinced. As for Faro he suspected that Ida's death had upset Paul and with good reason. At their last meeting the week before she died, Ida had hinted to him that she might be pregnant. Horrified, Paul had recoiled at the idea and what it implied, although he knew that it was most unlikely. As a medical student who enjoyed women's sexual favours he was well acquainted with all methods of contraception. Had he been guilty of her condition, suicide would have been deplorable and he was almost relieved that her death was murder.

Having slept with her a few times, she was seeing him in the role of her future husband, but his matrimonial intentions lay far beyond a more than willing servant with ambitions above her humble station in life.

Meanwhile in Clara's room they were running out of time.

'Prepare yourself to leave immediately.' Bodvale's words meant to Faro that careful plans of escape had been already made for imminent flight after the fatal score was settled. The grim revenge that had been corroding Bodvale's heart for many years.

For his plan to succeed, timing was crucial. Bodvale could not risk Clara regaining her courage to tell Archie.

Faro knew he had to be planning to return this evening and no doubt Bodvale was keeping the house, the comings and goings of everyone within, under close observation, ready to seize the right moment, which meant that he had to have an accomplice.

Faro realised that Clara had no idea of what was about to happen. Had Archie been at home, warning him would be fatal. His reaction to a policeman lurking upstairs in his wife's bedroom would be nothing short of disastrous.

There was only one grimly dangerous answer.

Archie Lumbleigh, potential victim, had to be bait in a trap set for Bodvale.

Downstairs they heard Betty leave, Mrs Brown telling her not to be late in the morning. What was the housekeeper's role in Bodvale's plan?

Light footsteps on the stairs and Vince, all smiles in this grim-faced gathering, looked in to see his mother. Startled by her more than usually anxious embrace, he was persuaded to wait there for the moment until Paul arrived. Unaware of the tensions all around him, or what Faro was doing here, he talked calmly to Lizzie about progress on the school football field.

A sound on the gravel drive. Faro ran to the window.

The carriage had arrived. The coachman stepped down, Archie and Paul emerged. The weather was so bad that Paul had requested he be picked up leaving Surgeons' Hall en route home, a request which fitted admirably into Bodvale's plan.

'Instead of sitting here, Lizzie and I could have been safe, miles away,' Clara, now thoroughly terrified, whispered reproachfully.

Faro shook his head. 'No time for that.' Trying to calm her without putting it into words, he knew the only way to capture Bodvale was to have not only Archie but Clara too as bait in the trap he had set.

Downstairs, the two men, discarding cloaks, had gone into the dining room, Mrs Brown at their heels with a tray of pre-dinner drinks.

Vince said: 'I'll go now. Paul will be waiting—'

'Wait!' Faro and Lizzie held out restraining hands. For what was in store, Faro wanted the boy out of the way, out of danger. 'Vince, can you do something for me – can you take an urgent message to the beat constable?'

'PC Craig, you mean?' Vince was mystified but guessed that there was something urgent going on that the grown-ups hadn't told him about. A surprise perhaps as Faro added:

'Without being seen, Vince.'

That gave the boy an idea. He went to the window. 'Open this, please.' Faro did so.

Vince leant out. 'There's a ledge and see, that tree! I've always wanted to climb it.'

'Oh no,' Lizzie groaned and ignoring her protests Faro scribbled the message while Vince looked on delighted.

'Is it very important?'

Handing it to him Faro said: 'Very important. Our lives, your mother and Mrs Lumbleigh, all of us depend on it.'

Vince was already astride the window sill.

'Off you go, and take care.'

'Oh, I will. This is super – just like one of those adventure stories in the boys' annual,' he grinned happily.

Lizzie was scared, reproachful even, as at Faro's side she watched Vince edge along and then swing himself on to the overhanging tree branch. The carriage had moved out of range. There was no sign of the coachman. Vince's exit had been just in time.

Footsteps on the stairs. Their waiting was over.

CHAPTER THIRTY-TWO

The door opened and Bodvale entered. Apart from his usual cloak, bonnet and muffler, gone too were the whiskers and moustache.

He was now clean-shaven; Faro realised this transformation was to aid his escape.

Clara's cry, her sharp intake of breath, identified the man she knew and feared. In one hand a revolver, with the other he touched his face ruefully, looked across at her and said:

'Come closer and you will see the scars left by the fire, a painful blessing.' And rubbing his chin, 'What better disguise for my purpose than a fashionable beard and moustache?' Pausing he said to her: 'You broke your promise to me, my own true love. You never looked the coachman in the eye. Oh, I know about that, the master's rules were to avoid eye contact with the servants, just like the Queen at Balmoral.' He laughed harshly. 'All to the good, couldn't have been better for me.'

He looked round. 'And I see you have company.' The gun upraised, he motioned them towards the door. 'The rest of the company are downstairs, so if you'd care to join them, we need delay no longer.'

And looking at Faro, he smiled mockingly. 'You have been a thorn in my flesh for too long, Constable, so you might as well consider yourself deserving of what is in store for the rest of this family.' Sounding almost genial he said: 'I'm surprised we have not had a confrontation earlier, considering your reputation.'

Faro signalled the women to stay put and well aware of the diabolical criminal he was dealing with he said calmly: 'No time like the present, and before we follow you I'm sure you would like to take this chance of enlightening us about what you have in store – and why?'

Bodvale needed no second bidding. Scowling at Faro, he said: 'All right, I'll tell you all – you might as well take this to the grave with you. Archie Lumbleigh ruined my father, cheated him out of his fortune on the turn of a card.' He added slowly, 'And he murdered him. Suicide, they said, but I knew better. It was as if he held the gun at my father's head when he pulled the trigger that left us penniless, my mother dying and me forced to leave university and take a menial, ill-paid job labouring. I swore then I would avenge his death—'

Pausing he looked at Clara, smiled. 'But when I tracked him down to Edinburgh I never expected to find that my own true love was his wife. Another excellent reason to hate him, if I hadn't enough cause already.' He shrugged. 'Oh, it was easy to become his coachman. One or two excellent references, good forgeries I admit, and Lumbleigh was so impressed at the titles of my previous employers he never had the temerity to enquire further and check them. He needed a discreet coachman for some of his activities, and the same sort of carriage as half the well-off residents, one that nobody would recognise or look at twice.

'As for Paul, I soon knew there was bad blood between them; I guessed from servants' talk that he hated him as much as I did. Revenge for his mother's death in an insane asylum, so that Archie could marry the love of my life, fitted perfectly into what I had planned.'

Suddenly impatient, he waved the gun and shouted: 'That's enough – downstairs all of you. We mustn't keep them waiting.' And putting an arm around Clara, 'We haven't much time, my own true love. I hope you did as I told you,' he added sternly.

Trembling, terrified, warned earlier by Faro that she must pretend to go along with him, she managed a nod of agreement.

He looked at Faro then at Lizzie with pity. 'Afraid your presence has made it inevitable that you are included in what is to come. Such a shame my lady will have to do without her maid.'

He moved so that Lizzie was in front of him, the gun to her head. Faro instinctively stepped forward and as Clara cried out in protest, Bodvale said: 'Don't be afraid. Your ordeal will soon be over. Tomorrow at this hour we will be safe, in another country, and I will be your lady's maid. I'll brush your lovely hair every night just as I did when you were a wee girl. Remember the old days?' he added softly.

Lizzie stumbled on the stairs and he gave her an angry glance. 'Do that again and you're dead, miss.'

The dining-room door was open, Mrs Brown waiting for them, just inside, grim and silent. Looking at her expressionless face, Faro would have given much to read her thoughts. Bodvale's ally, she had helped him to this evil hour, but seeing the expression on her face as she watched him reunited with his true love he wondered what was to be her reward.

In two armchairs facing each other across the fireside, sprawled motionless, were Archie and Paul.

Clara gave a little cry.

Bodvale seized her arm. 'Not yet. You can save that for later.' Faro looked at the two glasses on the tray and guessed that once again Mrs Brown's assistance had been indispensable. They had been drugged.

'A pretty scene, eh?' Bodvale chuckled. 'So peaceful, do admire it in the little time you have left to you.'

'You will never get away with it, you know,' Faro said sharply.

Bodvale smiled. 'A pity you won't be around to know whether I did or not, Constable. But having come this far, I will have to take that chance. Just look at the two of them; surely it is obvious what I have in mind. The perfect crime. Paul, who hated his stepfather, shoots him and then' – he glanced round, grinning as he studied the faces of Lizzie and Faro – 'unfortunately two people who heard the shot and tried to intervene also became his victims.'

Faro heard Lizzie's sharp intake of breath. Bodvale had released her and she ran to Faro's side.

He looked at them both and sighed. 'Yes, they had to go. He was quite insane, having already killed twice, so he shoots himself. He will be found with a gun in his hand. Archie's wife, my own true love . . .' Pausing he looked at her. 'She will be the only survivor, but by the time the bodies are found we will have vanished. A train to London and a ship out of the country.'

Faro said: 'I wouldn't bank on it. The police will track you both down and Clara will also be implicated in the murders, an accessory.'

Bodvale regarded him, still smiling. 'I am sure she will be set free, but,' he shrugged, 'I don't really care. I would rather she went to the gallows with me. If I can't have her, I took an oath long ago that no other man would.'

'First you have to kill four people in this room. How many bullets are there in that gun? You will never get away with it,' Faro repeated.

'Oh yes, we will. We will.'

'No, you won't.' This from Mrs Brown who had been the silent observer of the scene. She came forward.

They turned and looked at her. 'I have stuck by you all these years, Jabez, while you plotted your ultimate revenge.' And staring at Clara, her eyes full of loathing, she added: 'This is not how we planned it.'

And this was no longer the efficient obedient housekeeper but a very different woman. What they were witnessing was a wife about to be abandoned. Dowdy, plain, middle-aged, she was no match for the beautiful, elegant Clara.

And Faro felt almost a shaft of pity as she went on: 'Do you think I am going to sit back and watch quietly while you take her . . .' She jabbed a finger towards Clara. Her voice raised. 'And leave me – without a thought for my future. Not only a deserted wife but as an accessory to your murders.'

Bodvale did not even look at her, but said coldly: 'You can make your own arrangements. You have served your purpose and, incidentally, we were never married. That was a fraud too, that ceremony, I needed a partner for my plan to succeed.'

It was too much for the housekeeper. The plain woman had become a screaming virago as she launched herself at him, clawing at his face. The attack took him by surprise, and trying to fight her off, he dropped the gun.

It slid across the floor, Faro in pursuit seized it and as Bodvale struggled to be free, there was another sound – hammering on the front door.

Lizzie rushed to it and let in Gosse followed by a batch of policemen, behind them Vince, who she took in her arms with a cry of relief.

Gosse took in the scene and without waiting for any explanations, watching the constables disentangle the struggling couple, he arrested Bodvale for the murder of Doris Page and Ida Watts.

Handcuffs were produced and as they were leading him away, Faro went forward: 'Wait a moment. Where is Fr Burren? What have you done with him?'

Bodvale turned and stared at him, scowling. 'Never heard of him.'

'The Catholic priest!'

'Still never heard of him.'

Was that the truth or was the priest lying dead?

Gosse pointed to the housekeeper. 'Take the woman too, for questioning,' and to Faro he added grudgingly, 'Well done.' Explanations would come later while he thought of a means to divert praise for this captured murderer to his own ends.

CHAPTER THIRTY-THREE

The full story came out at Bodvale's trial when the abandoned Matilda Brown turned Queen's evidence. The plan was always to kill Archie Lumbleigh and throw suspicion on Paul.

He believed that his plan for the perfect murder was infallible when the housekeeper told him that Paul blamed his stepfather for his mother's death, and his hatred included Clara, despite all her attempts to be a kind, understanding stepmother. Bodvale began to make his plans accordingly. A first murder to lead the police on a false trail and incriminate Paul.

He got his chance, provided by Paul himself. In his role of the discreet coachman, no questions asked, he regularly drove Paul, usually drunk, and usually unsuccessful, to pick up one of the dancers after the evening performance at the Vaudeville.

One of those attempts had been frustrated by a passing policeman, namely, DC Faro. For Bodvale's cruel purpose any of the girls would have served equally well; it just happened to be Doris Page who was not too choosy about being picked up by strange men, young or old, as long as they were prepared to spend money on her.

She had been disappointed to find the waiting carriage empty, but Brown leant down, handed her a sovereign and said: 'The master wishes for your company, I am to take you to him. You will find a bottle of champagne inside.' The rest was easy. He drove around for a while, then in the Queen's Park he strangled her and deposited her body in Fleshers Close.

Would one murder be enough to incriminate Paul? He thought not. He needed another victim and preferably nearer Lumbleigh Green. Then he learnt that Paul had been sleeping with the maid Ida and the sharp-eyed housekeeper, seeing evidence of morning sickness which hinted at pregnancy, had laughed: 'And she'll think he'll marry her, more fool her.' Bodvale rubbed his hands with glee. This created a perfect situation for the next murder.

'The young master wishes you to meet him on the North Bridge at ten this evening. He has tickets for a train journey.' Ida's eyes had gleamed. An elopement, of course! Mrs Brown had continued: 'Do not bring any luggage' (not that Ida had much in that nature apart from her uniform) 'he will provide you with a wardrobe.'

That was enough. Brown strangled her in the carriage and dropped her body off the North Bridge, in keeping with the suicide tradition of many unfortunate pregnant girls. It suited his plan to further incriminate Paul in her death, since the housekeeper suspected that he was Ida's lover. Unfortunately the post-mortem discovery that this was not so in Ida's case led to suspicions that she had been murdered.

As for Jock Webb, Bodvale had lost a considerable amount of money betting on a sure fight in Glasgow. A long time ago, but he had never forgiven him. A chance encounter in a local pub with the ex-boxer boasting about his early successes in the ring aroused bitter memories and Bodvale's ire. His murder would help satisfy what was a growing taste for killing. That final moment when his victim's life expired, the feeling of power over the whole universe. But he hadn't bargained for the still-strong ex-boxer.

As for Mavis Rayne. He drove Archie there regularly and decided that the murder of his hated enemy's mistress fitted neatly into his revenge plan. However, Mavis had grappled with many men in her time as a madam and his attempts to strangle her were frustrated by the approach of a policeman.

As for the playing card – the nine of diamonds left at the scene of each crime. That too was the final touch, Bodvale's vanity, the idea that this would add a touch of the macabre. The nine of diamonds, which his mother called 'the curse of Scotland', she believed was the card Lumbleigh played when cheating Arthur Bodvale of his fortune, causing his suicide and the subsequent ruin of their lives.

There was one missing factor. He still denied that he had murdered the young priest. Mrs Brown too shook her head over this. And suddenly the mystery was solved.

Fr Burren staggered into the rectory he had left two weeks ago. He was dishevelled, his head bandaged, his arm in a sling. Two weeks ago after seeing the verger he had walked towards Musselburgh where he believed there were men, vagrants, waiting to be shown the light and be converted. He had been knocked down, perhaps by one of them, and pushed into the hedgerow.

An elderly spinster, something of a recluse and just a little this side of madness, turned out to be the Good Samaritan. Passing by in her pony carriage, she had spotted this young man. He was unconscious, bleeding and she thought about to die. So she took him home. Shabbily dressed in ordinary clothes, without the customary dog collar, she had no idea he was a priest. It did not take more than a day or two for her to fall in love with this handsome stranger, like someone from a fairy tale. She had rescued him and decided that until he came to himself again, finders were also keepers.

She had no idea that he was in a coma and might die without treatment. Miraculously he had survived with her care and two weeks later, just after Bodvale's arrest, he had sat up, genuflected and said the Lord's Prayer. She was shocked. He did not know where he was or what happened; utterly confused he wished only to return to his church and his people. He would pray for her, with that she had to be content, and he refused to give the police her name or address.

In the Central Office, Gosse basked in the success of two murders solved while striving vainly to divert Chief Inspector McIvor's approval for his detective constable's invaluable contribution. Meanwhile Faro was enjoying a congratulatory dram with Macfie on his forthcoming marriage to Lizzie Laurie, an announcement further reminding Gosse of his dismal failure to put an end to Faro's hopes in that direction.

'You did well, lad,' said Macfie. 'You were on to it, from the beginning – that hunch about the scarlet dress.'

'I can't claim success about finding out who she was, though. When I came back from Glasgow with that information, her husband had been in touch with Gosse.'

He paused and Macfie said: 'But by then the first threads were already falling into place.'

Faro nodded. 'And who would have ever imagined that we would have Edinburgh's abominable weather to thank? All those constant drenchings, the smell of wet tweed drying and Brown's Inverness cape, a cast off by Mr Lumbleigh and its significance that day when I was given a lift in the driving rain to Jock Webb's house. But most of all, we owe a debt to Mrs Rayne.'

'Mrs Rayne?' queried Macfie.

'Yes, indeed, the perfumer's extraordinary sense of smell was an invaluable clue. Her description of her attacker, stinking like a wet dog, the woolly smell of her pet poodle. Then there was this constant smell of drying outer-garments, threads here and there touching what seemed an impossible solution. Until Mrs Lumbleigh's stepfather's visit. Then it became clear when I asked myself, how did Bodvale get into the house, through locked gates in the dark, past the guard dogs and find his way upstairs to her bedroom?

'There was only one answer. The killer had to be someone familiar with the house and he must have had an accomplice. The truth could only be that the coachman Brown must also be Mrs Lumbleigh's villainous stepfather. A callous, ruthless killer and worst of all, the motive for the murders of those two innocent women was merely part of his long-planned revenge on Archie Lumbleigh by also incriminating Paul.'

Leaving Macfie, Faro promised to bring Lizzie to meet him when they got back from honeymoon in Orkney. He guessed that his mother would be delighted to see him settled down at last although he wasn't sure how she would react to meeting Vince, whose courage had saved several lives that terrible night of Bodvale's arrest.

By the time the newlyweds were moving into their first home, order had been restored in Lumbleigh Green with the installation of another coachman and housekeeper, their references carefully checked by Clara, whose marriage had not, as she had imagined, been shattered by her early life with Bodvale.

Indeed, once Archie knew the truth, he realised that they were both lucky to be alive, with ample reason to forget the past, including Mavis Rayne, and forge ahead to a new life. But Laurie had not been forgotten. As Mrs Faro she was firmly established as Clara's devoted lady's maid and companion, an enduring friendship between two women with much in common.

There remained only one scene to remember before the curtain fell on this grim tale of murder and revenge.

As Bodvale was being led away, the noise and confusion had stirred Archie from his drugged slumbers. He sat up and shrilly demanded:

'What are all these policemen doing in my dining room? I did not give permission for them to enter.' And to the still-struggling housekeeper: 'And where is my supper?' Trying vainly to focus his eyes on the coachman, firmly held between two constables, he said: 'I am rather tired, Brown. I won't be needing the carriage after all.' This for his once-weekly visit to York Square.

Paul was also being shaken by Vince who,

fearing the worst, had rushed to his friend's side. Paul tried to sit up; dazed, he shook his head violently as if to banish a more than usually disagreeable hangover.

Looking at Vince, he managed a sheepish grin. 'Sorry, lad, kept you waiting. I must have rather overindulged. No billiards tonight, think I'll have an early night.' Rubbing his eyes, he stood up, swayed and was neatly held by Faro and Vince.

They had smiled wryly at each other. The bond that was to last a lifetime was forged.

ALSO BY ALANNA KNIGHT
The *Rose McQuinn* Series. . .

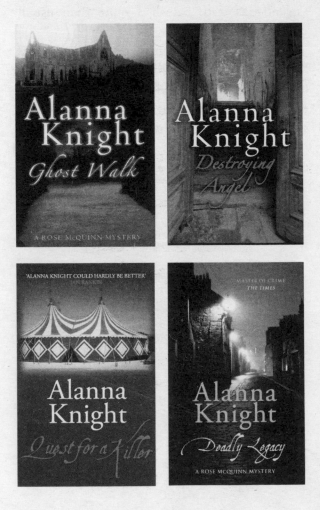

To discover more great books and to
place an order visit our website at
www.allisonandbusby.com

Don't forget to sign up to our free newsletter at
www. allisonandbusby.com/newsletter
for latest releases, events and exclusive offers

 Allison & Busby Books
 @AllisonandBusby

You can also call us on
020 7580 1080
for orders, queries
and reading recommendations